Always on my Mind

D1444636

SAMANTHA CHASE

PRAISE FOR SAMANTHA CHASE

"If you can't get enough of stories that get inside your heart and soul and stay there long after you've read the last page, then Samantha Chase is for you!"

-NY *Times & USA Today Bestselling Author* **Melanie Shawn**

"A fun, flirty, sweet romance filled with romance and character growth and a perfect happily ever after."

-NY *Times & USA Today Bestselling Author* **Carly Phillips**

"Samantha Chase writes my kind of happily ever after!"

-NY *Times & USA Today Bestselling Author* **Erin Nicholas**

"The openness between the lovers is refreshing, and their interactions are a balanced blend of sweet and spice. The planets may not have aligned, but the elements of this winning romance are definitely in sync."

- ***Publishers Weekly, STARRED review***

"A true romantic delight, *A Sky Full of Stars* is one of the top gems of romance this year."

- ***Night Owl Reviews, TOP PICK***

"Great writing, a winsome ensemble, and the perfect blend of heart and sass."

ONE

Coming back to Magnolia Sound was never part of the plan.

But then again, Parker Bishop rarely had one.

Unfortunately, right now she desperately needed one.

Driving aimlessly around her small hometown, she wondered how she was going to get herself out of her current crisis. Sure, she could pick up the phone and there were countless friends and relatives who would offer to help her out, but...if the last eight days were anything to go by, it was only a matter of time before she would need assistance again.

Tears stung her eyes–which she loathed because she never cried–and decided to pull over for a few minutes and attempt to pull herself together.

"I hate this," she murmured as she parked her car. This was the first time in her entire life that had her feeling like a complete failure and the one person in the whole world that she could normally turn to...well...that was no longer a viable option.

Resting her head back against the driver's seat, Parker

closed her eyes and it was as if she were back in Florida that awful day so many months ago...

"I'm getting married!"

"Um...what?" She was certain she'd misunderstood what her best friend–her rock, her everything–Tyler was saying. "What are you talking about?"

He smiled so brilliantly and everything in her melted a little–just like it did every time he smiled at her. His words, however, devastated her.

"Maybe I'm being a little premature," he went on. "I mean...I haven't officially asked Kaitlyn yet, but I'm doing it tomorrow night." Then he reached into his pocket and pulled out the box to show her the gorgeous ring he planned to propose with.

Her heart was beating erratically and her stomach clenched hard as he held out the box to her like she always imagined he'd do for her one day.

But he wasn't.

Ever.

"Tyler," she began, her voice shaking. "Don't you think it's too soon? You've only been dating for a few months! How well do you even know this girl?"

And that's when things went from bad to worse.

"Does she know you're allergic to apples or that you hate all the new superhero movies? Is she aware of your Harry Potter obsession? How she'll never get you on a roller coaster? Or...or...how you only eat M&M's in even numbers of the same color? And the fact that you wet the bed until you were nine?"

His eyes went wide before he carefully put the ring back in his pocket. Then his expression softened before he reached out and took her hand in his.

"Parks...you know she'll never know me the way you do. You and I have been best friends since the second grade."

"But..." Taking a steadying breath, Parker decided to lay it all out on the line. She'd harbored this secret for years and maybe if Tyler knew exactly how she felt, he'd realize proposing to Kaitlyn was a mistake. "Pick me."

"What?!"

She nodded vigorously. "Me. Marry me. We would be amazing together! Hell, we already are! I always thought you and I would be the perfect couple, and if you'd just give me a chance..."

"Parker..." He paused and gave her a smile that was full of pity.

"Just...I love you, Ty. I've always loved you, and if you'd just give us a chance..."

"You are my best friend and I love you, just...not like that. I'm in love with Kaitlyn. I'm happy and I'd hoped you'd be happy for me." He squeezed her hand, seemingly at a loss for words. They sat in awkward silence for what seemed like forever before he finally said, "C'mon, I'll treat us to sundaes down on the pier. I know how much you like that."

And just like that, she'd realized she was getting a consolation prize.

She'd lost him and there wasn't anything she could do about it except try to move on.

Only...moving on didn't go quite as smoothly as she'd hoped.

Kaitlyn had, of course, said yes to Tyler's proposal and they wanted to get married right away. Parker had started packing immediately because she didn't want to be there for the big day, but...Tyler convinced her to stay–saying he couldn't imagine getting married without her. And because she was a glutton for punishment, she stayed and watched him marry someone else.

And left for home the very next day.

Leaving Florida wasn't a big deal. Parker had been house-sitting for months and working odd jobs, so it wasn't like she had any big commitments.

But figuring out where to go hadn't been easy and she was beginning to notice a pattern.

Okay, she didn't notice it, per se, but when she told Tyler her plans, he didn't hesitate for a second to share that observation with her.

Apparently, Parker was a runner.

At eighteen, she ran from the only place she'd ever known and swore she'd never look back. It had always been her dream to travel, but because Tyler knew her so well, he pointed out how that was only an excuse. She ran from her family–both immediate and extended–because she never had the same ambition they all do and always felt like a slacker comparatively. She also ran from any real responsibility. The steady stream of house-sitting, dog walking, and a dozen other little jobs that sustained her without any heavy commitment. She traveled thanks to her inheritance from Pops, but rather than enriching her life, it simply gave her the excuse to keep avoiding being an adult.

It would have been impossible to argue with him because he was completely correct. What he didn't realize, and what she couldn't tell him, was that he had been the only constant in her life. Tyler Burke–the person who she both clung to and took for granted–was the only person who ever kept her grounded. He was the one person who truly understood her and never passed judgment on her.

Until now.

That final conversation went downhill after he called

her out on the way she was handling this whole situation. And, to add insult to injury, he told her he'd never had romantic feelings for her and he felt that what she was claiming to feel for him wasn't real. His final words to her before he walked out of her life had hurt more than she ever imagined.

"I've been nothing but a crutch for you, Parker. It's time for you to grow up and move on."

Back in Magnolia, however, it was like she was back in school and never left.

Once she had decided to sever all ties with her life in Florida, it just seemed logical to go home and figure things out. For years she'd been flitting in and out of town, visiting her family on her own terms, but when she showed up unannounced, it didn't take long to realize how much everyone's lives had moved on without her.

Tears rolled down her cheeks and she didn't bother to wipe them away. Right now, she was essentially homeless. She'd lasted all of two days with her parents and, for once, it wasn't her mother who made her want to leave. Her parents were doing major renovations on the house and leaving on a month-long cruise, so staying there wasn't an option.

"Really, Parker, if you only bothered to call once in a while, you wouldn't be in this situation," her mother had harped.

Oddly, it was almost comforting to get that bit of disapproval.

Then, she stayed with her brother Mason and his wife, and that lasted another two days before she was asked to leave. It wasn't his fault. Apparently, Parker was a bit too much of a distraction for her young nephews and her poor sister-in-law was pregnant again and feeling way too overwhelmed.

"I still say I could have been a great help if they'd just let me spoil the boys for a little while," she whispered sadly. "We all would have calmed down eventually."

The last stop was staying with her sister Peyton and her fiancé, Ryder.

Just thinking about the two of them gave her a massive headache.

Two overachievers who were hell-bent on fixing her. Every minute of the four days she spent with them had been filled with them giving her suggestions and helpful hints for getting her life in order. It was like living with two over-caffeinated motivational speakers in her face from dawn till dusk!

Exhausting

As soon as Peyton left for the cafe, Parker pretty much packed her bags, tossed them in her car, and took off.

And was driving around aimlessly since.

Now she was tired, hungry, homeless, and her head was pounding. Forcing herself to straighten and look around, she realized she was in the library parking lot. Her cousin Sam's wife worked there and maybe she could help.

Pushing the car door open with a heavy sigh, she murmured, "Even though I'm probably beyond helping."

Yeah, she wasn't feeling particularly good about herself, but the next option was leaving town and, honestly, Parker had no idea where she would even go.

Which was a first for her.

Stepping inside the Magnolia Public library, she took a moment to get her bearings. It had been years since she'd been here and yet it somehow managed to still look exactly the same.

"Just like everything else in this town," she said quietly with a sigh.

"Parker! Oh my goodness! I heard you were back!" Shelby Westlake–her cousin's wife–came walking over with a big smile before giving her an even bigger hug. When she pulled back, she was still smiling. "Sam and I were just talking about you last night! How long are you in town for?"

This was her opening.

"Actually, I think I'm going to be sticking around for a while..."

"Really? That's wonderful! Are you staying with your folks?"

Shaking her head, Parker quickly shared the tale of the cruise and renovations.

"Well, that's too bad. So...are you over with Mason and Scarlett?"

"Um...I was, but...Scarlett's pregnant again and I think I added a little too much chaos for her."

Now Shelby started to look as uncomfortable as Parker was feeling. "I guess that means you're over with Peyton and Ryder. I know they have a ton of space and..."

Parker held up her hand. "I'm going to stop you there. I was staying there, but they were both a little...um...overbearing? I think that's the word. They saw me as a project and...I don't know...it was all just a little too much. They were totally smothering me with ideas and opportunities and trying to push me into things I'm not ready for. I moved out this morning."

"Then where are you staying?"

The nervous laugh was out before she could stop it. "That's the million-dollar question, right? I'm sort of trying to figure that out."

For a moment, Shelby didn't say a word. Then she took Parker by the hand and led her to a table back in the far corner of the library. It wasn't until a box of tissues was put down in front of her that she realized she was crying.

Mortified, she wiped her tears.

Taking a seat beside her, Shelby gave her a moment to compose herself before saying anything. "You can crash on our sofa if you need to. Our place is a little crammed right now, and you'll probably step on your share of toys, but you are always welcome to stay until you figure things out."

"Thanks, Shelby," she said softly.

"Maybe it's not my place, but...you know Peyton and Ryder were just trying to help, right? I mean...they both have a ton of connections, and I know Ryder owns a lot of properties around town. Maybe you can rent one of them?"

"We talked about it, but none of them are vacant right now. The place Peyton used to rent was what I really wanted, and I thought she was holding on to that lease, but...she didn't."

"Why would she hold on to it?"

Shrugging, Parker realized how ridiculous it would have been for her sister to do that. It was her own selfish dream.

They sat in silence for several minutes before Shelby asked, "So what brings you to the library?"

A small snort was her first response. "I honestly had no idea where I was pulling into. I've been driving around all morning and just sort of zoned out. Then I started to cry and knew I needed to get off the road and...here I am."

"Oh, Parker...I'm so sorry."

"Thanks."

"Do you have any plans? A job or...anything?"

That made her chuckle a little. "You and I haven't spent a whole lot of time together, have we?" It wasn't really a question.

"Maybe not, but I do know you're the free spirit in the

family. I'm sure coming back here wasn't an easy decision for you."

"It wasn't, but...I'm here and I need to make the best of it." Then she laughed again. "Once I get this whole homeless thing figured out, I'm sure everything else will fall into place."

"You're never going to be homeless in Magnolia, Parker. Trust me. There will never be a shortage of relatives willing to take you in. And I told you, you are more than welcome to stay with us."

"And I appreciate it. It's just..." Her words trailed off as she watched a guy walk across the library to a large bulletin board. Who knew those were still a thing? He looked vaguely familiar, but considering what a small town Magnolia was, she figured they either went to school together or were neighbors or something. "Um...what's that?" she asked, pointing to the board.

"Oh, that's our community bulletin board. People come in and post flyers about local events or for jobs and services they either offer or are looking for." Pausing, she let out a small gasp. "You know, it's also a great place to either find a place to rent or a roommate! I'll bet if you looked, you might find something for yourself!"

It wasn't the worst idea...

"I don't know..."

"Shelby?" someone called out.

"Excuse me for a minute. I should have told them at the desk that I was taking a break. I'll be right back."

Parker nodded but her gaze stayed on the board. "No worries."

It wasn't until Shelby was out of sight that Parker let her words sink in. Maybe finding a roommate wasn't the worst thing in the world. After all, it would mean cheaper rent.

She could try to find a house-sitting situation, but houses here on the coast tended to rent out year-round so it wasn't really a viable option.

The guy at the board was still standing there and she couldn't figure out if he was searching for something specific or getting ready to post something for himself. It looked like he had a sheet of paper in his hand but he was gripping it tightly rather than pinning it up. He kept looking around and that's when Parker got a better of a look at him— chocolate brown hair, stubbled jaw, glasses, khakis, a thick sweater, and loafers...he had the whole hot nerd look going on and it was totally working for him.

I swear I know this guy...

It was tempting to get up and just talk to him, but...she certainly wasn't looking or feeling her best so she simply slouched down in her chair and figured she'd pass the time checking out a hot guy and forgetting about her own miserable life for a while.

* * *

"YARD SALES, BAKE SALES, TUTORING SERVICES..." Ethan Harlow read some of the flyers on the Magnolia Sound Library's bulletin board and wondered if he was making a huge mistake. There was a part of him that still questioned whether he actually needed to do this, but... he was practical—overly practical.

Okay, he was straight-up uptight about finances and putting up a flyer looking for a roommate was quite possibly the only thing that was going to keep him sane.

With a quiet sigh, he looked at the ads for homes and apartments for rent and wondered if anyone even looked at these things. Was he being a little too old-fashioned by putting a flyer on a community board instead of posting something online? Maybe. His reasoning was that by doing things this way, he'd possibly be spared from dealing with any freaks or weirdos.

"God...I think I'm turning into my grandfather..."

It wasn't the first time Ethan had that thought about himself and he was fairly certain it wouldn't be the last.

Staring down at the flyer in his hand, all those doubts in his mind grew louder and louder. Would he even be able to handle having a stranger live with him? Up until a couple of days ago, this wasn't even an issue. His co-worker Jeff was going to rent a room from him and everything was all set.

And then it wasn't.

Jeff had a girlfriend and, at the last minute, she asked Jeff to move in with her. There was no way Ethan was going to compete with that, so...here he was, standing in the middle of the library and trying not to freak out about tacking up a piece of paper to a bulletin board.

Maybe I really don't have to do this...

Yeah, it had been something he'd agonized over before buying his first place. When his father passed away six months ago, he'd left Ethan enough money for a down payment on a house. His job as a professor at the local community college didn't offer him a great income–yet–but that final gift from his dad allowed him to achieve his dream of owning his own home. On paper, he knew he could cover his mortgage and all his other bills, but there was something to be said for having a bit of a safety net.

That's where the roommate idea came in.

Wanted: One roommate. Mature. Professional. No pets.

If only he could be absolutely sure he would be compatible with said roommate...

"Okay, this is getting me nowhere. For all I know, no

one will even see this flyer or be interested." And with a fortifying breath, Ethan pinned the flyer to the board and took a giant step back.

And banged right into the head librarian, Shelby Westlake.

"Oh!" she cried as Ethan steadied her. "Oh, Ethan, I'm so sorry. I guess I wasn't watching where I was going."

His ears felt like they were on fire and he didn't make direct eye contact with her. "No, it was all my fault. Are you okay?"

"I'm fine," she told him and when he glanced up, he saw her smiling. "I don't think either of us was paying much attention." She looked over at the bulletin board. "Any chance you're offering tutoring services?"

"Um...what?"

"The board. I thought maybe you were putting up a flyer for tutoring services. I get a lot of requests from parents looking for science tutors. You always come to mind, but then I forget to mention it whenever you come in."

Tutoring was another way to make a little extra money– and then he wouldn't need a roommate–but...

"Hey, Shel, do you happen to have a phone charger? I think I left mine at Peyton's."

"Of course. It's in my purse back in the break room. Hang tight and I'll go get it." Shelby went to walk away but stopped. "Ethan Harlow, this is my cousin Parker Bishop. Parker, this is Ethan Harlow. He's a science professor up at the community college." And with a smile, she walked away.

"Ethan Harlow?" Parker repeated slowly before her eyes went wide. "Oh my goodness! We went to school together! You were our valedictorian, right?"

Nodding, he took a small step back. "That was me."

"Wow, and you're a professor now! That's pretty exciting!"

He and Parker weren't friends back in high school, but he always remembered her being the girl with the big personality who was always smiling. It seemed that hadn't changed.

"I don't know if I'd call it exciting, but I enjoy it," he said quietly, mindful of them being in the middle of the library.

"Well, good for you! So how have you been?"

For a moment, he wasn't sure how to respond. Was she seriously asking how he'd been for the last ten years? Was there a simple way to answer that kind of question? Or was she referring to how he was right now? Because if she was, he'd have to say he was feeling a little stressed out and not particularly comfortable making small talk.

"Uh...Ethan?" she prompted.

Straightening, his hands slid into his trouser pockets. "Um...good. I've been good. And you?"

Her smile faltered a little. "Honestly? I've been better. You're kind of catching me on a pretty crappy day. Just a few minutes ago Shelby was pushing a box of tissues at me and probably wishing I'd gone anywhere else in Magnolia except here." She let out a small laugh that Ethan recognized because he tended to laugh like that too.

She was nervous and uncomfortable.

"I'm sorry," he told her, and he meant it.

"Thanks." She glanced around, presumably for Shelby, before looking at him again. "So, what brings you to the library today? Are you offering tutoring services?"

"Why does everyone keep asking me that?"

This time her laugh was more relaxed. "Well...I can't speak for everyone, but I figured maybe that's why you were here by the bulletin board. You know, putting up a flyer and all that." Parker turned her attention to the board before walking up to it and...

She grabbed his flyer.

Crap.

Taking a tentative step forward, he tried to play things cool. Clearing his throat, he moved a little closer to her. "So, um...yeah. That's my flyer. I'm looking for a roommate and figured I'd start by advertising here." Gently, Ethan tried to take the flyer from her hand but she wasn't letting go.

"You're renting a room out?" she asked, her eyes never leaving his neatly-typed flyer.

"Yes. My friend and co-worker, Jeff..." He paused. "Do you remember Jeff Waltham? He graduated with us."

"Um...no?" she replied slowly.

"Anyway, he was going to rent it but he decided to move in with his girlfriend instead."

She nodded. "Can't blame him there, right?"

"I guess," he murmured.

Suddenly, she turned to face him, giving Ethan a paper cut in the process. Hissing, he took a step back.

"Oh no! I'm sorry!" she said, resting her hand on his arm and leading him to a table in the corner.

What is happening right now?

As soon as they were seated, Parker grabbed her over-sized purse and dug around until she noticed the box of tissues on the table and offered him one. "I can't believe I did that, Ethan. I didn't even think it was possible to give another person a paper cut that way!"

It would be ridiculous to explain all the ways it was completely possible, so instead, he opted to focus on wiping away the tiny amount of blood. He realized that was also ridiculous. There wasn't any need for a tissue and by accepting one it kind of made him look like a complete wuss.

"How big is the room you're renting?" she asked, interrupting his thoughts.

"Do you know someone who's looking to rent the space?"

She nodded. "Yeah. Me."

All Ethan could do was stare. There was no way Parker Bishop was asking to move in with him.

She's not looking to move in with you specifically, he reminded himself.

"Don't you have a bunch of family here in town?" he blurted out before realizing how rude he was being. "Sorry. I mean...why do you need to rent a room?"

Parker let out a long breath as she slouched down in her chair. Ethan didn't think she was going to say much, but then she launched into a very long and rambling story about how she used to be a house-sitter in Florida, her best friend getting married, coming home and something about a cruise, home renovations, being too fun of an aunt, and overbearing siblings. By the time she was done, she was a little breathless and looking at him with the biggest, most hopeful eyes he'd ever seen.

"So, what do you say, Ethan? Can I rent the room?"

"No!" He hadn't realized how loud he'd spoken until he heard several people shushing him. When he looked at Parker, however, she didn't look the least bit put off. "No," he said a little more softly. "I'm looking to rent the room to another guy and...you know...that's not you."

"The ad doesn't say you're only going to rent to a guy."

"Yes, well...I guess I didn't think I'd have to clarify that," he reasoned. "But now that it's out there, I just think it would be better if the person who rented from me was...male."

She nodded but he had a feeling the conversation wasn't over.

"I'd be a really great roommate," she said after a moment, and Ethan knew it would be rude to point out how she'd lived in the homes of three families in the last week who might disagree with her.

"I'm sure you would," he countered, "but...I'd really prefer if it were another guy renting the room."

"So you keep saying." The way she kept staring at him and the way she straightened in her seat and crossed her arms just screamed challenge.

And Ethan wasn't sure he was up for it.

"I bake some amazing chocolate chip cookies," she told him conversationally. "And I always make more than enough to share."

"That's nice."

Her eyes narrowed slightly. "I love cleaning, too. One of my favorite things to do is vacuum. Weird, right?" she added with a laugh. "What can I say? I just love making sure my house is neat and clean."

"It's a very admirable trait."

"Oh, come on, Ethan!" she hissed, leaning toward him. "Are you seriously not going to rent me the room because I'm not a guy?"

"Well..."

"Because that's discrimination! And shame on you for being like that." She shook her finger at him and he was seriously beginning to feel chastised. "I thought you were one of the good guys and yet...look at you. Just look at yourself! You're forcing me to live on the street. And for what, huh? Because I don't have a penis?"

He looked around frantically and prayed no one else was hearing this conversation. "Parker, please. We're in the middle of the library," he whispered. "And I'm not discriminating. It's my home and I should be able to pick whoever it is I want to live with me. I'm not going to be guilted into it with promises of cookies and a clean floor."

Right there, Ethan was fairly certain he'd won. He'd been polite but firm, putting his foot down and proving that he wasn't a pushover. Crossing his arms over his chest, he mimicked her earlier pose, but it immediately felt wrong. And considering her bottom lip was trembling, he thought maybe he'd gone too far.

"Parker, I..."

"It's okay, Ethan. Really." She wiped at her eye before quickly looking away. "I shouldn't have pushed you or tried to manipulate you like that. You'd think after everything I've been through in the last few weeks that I'd know better, right?" Softly, she cleared her throat and stood, a small smile on her face. "It was nice to see you and...here." She handed him his flyer back. "I hope you find a great roommate." And with a slight wave, she turned and walked away.

For a full five minutes, he sat there and thought about what had just transpired. The promise of cookies and cleaning was definitely a little manipulative. But were the tears her Plan B? And if so, was he going to fall for them?

Twisting around, he spotted Shelby hugging Parker.

Comforting her.

Not my problem...

Staring down at his flyer, he took this entire situation as a sign that having a roommate just wasn't meant to be. He wasn't cut out for this sort of thing and one way or another, he'd find a way to be comfortable with his finances. He could make his own coffee at home and make his own lunch a couple of days a week. None of it was a big deal.

Slowly, he made his way across the room and did his best not to look over at Parker again. Unfortunately, he happened to catch a bit of her conversation with Shelby.

"I wish we had a spare room," Shelby was saying. "I feel bad it's going to be the couch, but I promise to keep the kids and the dog away from you while you're sleeping."

Closing his eyes, Ethan had a vivid picture of Parker curled up under the blankets on a too-small sofa and a group of small children and a large dog jumping up and down on it and on her. He had a feeling she'd go with the flow and make it seem like she was having fun, but...could anyone truly enjoy that?

Before he could second-guess himself, he closed the distance between them and handed the flyer to Parker. "If you're interested, the room is yours. You can move in immediately."

Then he had his arms full of Parker Bishop and he had no idea what to do.

"You won't regret this, Ethan! I promise!" Then she kissed him on the cheek before stepping back. "Can I follow you home right now?" The smile she gave him was downright impish.

She was going to disrupt his nice, orderly world. He just knew it.

TWO

There were probably dozens of questions Parker should have asked before simply inviting herself to move into Ethan's house, but she'd been so excited about not living with or staying with family that she'd thrown caution to the wind.

As per usual.

Now, as she pulled up to a rather small Cape Cod, she began to wonder if maybe this was the one time she should have thought things through.

For starters, even though she remembered Ethan from school, that was a long time ago and they were basically strangers. And from what she'd observed so far, he was still a fairly quiet and reserved guy. He drove a hybrid Toyota Corolla which was a completely practical vehicle. He worked as a professor, was a little uptight about living with a member of the opposite sex, and his home was small and somewhat basic. Nothing about Ethan Harlow screamed fun or easy-going and she had a feeling they were going to be butting heads.

A lot.

"Too late now..."

Parker climbed from her car–a sporty red Jeep Wrangler–and tried to hide her amusement when she spotted Ethan looking at her with apprehension. She had a feeling he was hoping she'd changed her mind but...nope. As much as she appreciated Shelby's offer to let her crash on her couch, having a space to call her own–albeit a small space– was way more appealing. As much as she loved being around people, she also enjoyed her privacy and having a space of her own where she could unwind at the end of the day.

Walking over to him, she did her best to give him an endearing smile. "Cute house! How long have you lived here?"

Ethan hitched his satchel up over his shoulder and straightened his wire-rimmed glasses before responding. "I moved in six weeks ago. I'm not even done unpacking yet, so...don't hold it against me." He walked up to the tiny front porch and unlocked the door before stepping aside so Parker could go in first.

Stepping inside, she froze. "Um..."

Ethan moved around her and walked in. "Like I said, I haven't finished unpacking yet and there were a few improvements I'm working on, so..."

Parker was fairly certain her jaw was on the floor because this wasn't just a matter of a few boxes being left to unpack. There were boxes everywhere. And drop cloths draped over random pieces of furniture, along with an array of ladders and tools scattered around. "What kind of improvements were you planning on?" Carefully, she moved farther into the space. The front door opened directly into the living room and beyond it was the eat-in kitchen. There appeared to be one bedroom off the living room as well and Parker assumed the other was down the hallway she saw off the kitchen.

Not the greatest floor plan...

"I was planning on painting," Ethan explained. "When Jeff was going to move in, he said he'd paint with me, but obviously that didn't work out and I just haven't gotten around to doing it yet. I was thinking maybe this weekend would work."

"Ooh...fun! I love painting! At least...I think I do. The last time I painted a room was about five years ago. A friend had moved into a new place and had a painting party." With a soft gasp, she walked over and playfully touched his arm. "Maybe we can do that! You know, you invite a bunch of friends over and we can order pizza and get it all done. What do you say?"

The look of sheer panic on his face pretty much answered that question.

"Or...you and I can tackle it ourselves," she cheerfully corrected. "Either way, we can totally get this done." Glancing around, her curiosity got the better of her. "So which room is mine?"

He hesitated for just a moment and Parker could still sense that he wasn't fully comfortable with this situation just yet. "Um...upstairs. There's a bedroom and a full bathroom up there so you'll have some privacy."

It made sense and without waiting for him, she made her way over to the staircase and practically ran up. There was no door. You simply stepped into the bedroom space. It wasn't ideal but it also wasn't a deal breaker. The walls were painted a hideous orange color that she knew she would most definitely be painting over before she did anything else. Moving around, she noticed there was no furniture in the room and realized that was a serious flaw in her plan.

"Well...crap." All the years of house-sitting meant there'd never been a reason for her to own any furniture. And whenever she came back to Magnolia to visit, she stayed with other people. "Why couldn't Peyton just hold onto that damn bungalow for me?"

"Everything okay?" Ethan asked as he came to the top of the stairs. "I know it's not much, but hopefully your furniture will fit."

"Funny story," she began, the nervous laugh out before she could stop it. "I don't have any furniture. Yet."

He stared at her as if she'd lost her mind. "How is that even possible, Parker?"

"I already explained that to you!" she snapped defensively. "I've been house-sitting! I never needed furniture of my own!"

Ethan looked around the room before focusing on her again, and his silence spoke volumes.

"Look, my cousin Mallory owns a décor shop in town so...I'll just go there and order some stuff. Or I can probably order some pieces online if she doesn't have what I'm looking for. It's not a big deal."

"You'll be sleeping on the floor..."

"So?" she snapped again, hating how foolish she felt. "It's not like anyone's asking you to do it! I've slept on plenty of floors and I can handle it for a few nights!"

Pinching the bridge of his nose, Ethan seemed to be trying really hard to hold on to his patience with her.

Sadly, she got that reaction from people more often than not.

"This is one of the reasons I was looking for a specific roommate," he finally said after a long moment. "I don't want to dread having conversations with you because you're easily defensive."

"I wouldn't say I'm easily defensive..."

"Parker, all I did was comment on how you'd be sleeping on the floor and you nearly bit my head off."

He had a point, but that didn't mean it was going to apply to every conversation. "It's been an emotional couple of weeks, Ethan. Cut me some slack, okay? I swear once I'm in and settled, you won't have to walk on eggshells with me. I promise."

"I don't know," he said warily. "Maybe this just isn't a good fit. Shelby said you could crash at her place, didn't she?"

It was crazy how easily she was crying these days, but after losing Tyler and being tossed around from house to house and now having someone who was basically a stranger already giving up on her just made her crumble. Before she knew it, she was sitting on the floor with her face in her hands and bawling like a baby.

In the distance, she heard Ethan groan. "This isn't going to work," he said with a hint of firmness. "Maybe you're used to manipulating people by crying, but I'm not going to be swayed and I find it insulting that you're even trying." He let out a long breath. "I think you should go."

Out of the corner of her eye, she saw him head back down the stairs and she clumsily got to her feet to go after him. "You think I'm crying to get my way?" she shouted as she ran down the stairs.

"You admitted to doing it earlier back at the library," he countered.

Swiping away the tears, she went and crowded him until they were toe to toe. "Yeah, I might have tried that earlier, but that wasn't what was happening right now. It suddenly hit me how...how no one wants me!" Flinging her arms out in exasperation, she moved away from him. "Do you have any idea what that's like? To know that no one–not even the people who claim to love you–actually wants you around?"

"Um..."

"And then to have a total stranger trying to shove me out the door was just the last straw for me and I...I hit my limit!"

"I wouldn't say we were total strangers..."

She growled with frustration. "I get it, Ethan! I get it! I'm an emotional mess right now and I'm a lot to handle. I swear this isn't who I am normally." Her shoulders sagged as she faced him. "The thing is, I really need this. I need a place to stay. A place where I can regroup and get my shit together. Please. Please just give me a chance. You won't regret it. I promise."

She loathed begging and hated how she was pretty much at rock-bottom here, but hopefully he'd take pity on her and give her a roof over her head until she truly figured out how to reclaim her life.

It was possible she was being overly dramatic, but it was crazy just how overwhelmed she felt right now. It seemed like all the things that had gone on for the last two weeks had finally caught up with her. If Ethan truly forced her to leave, she knew she'd go, but beyond that, she had no idea where she'd actually land. Sure, there was Sam and Shelby's, but it would be another temporary spot for a couple of nights and she was just so damn tired.

If she had a bed, she had no doubt that she'd sleep for a week.

Ethan looked at his watch and sighed. "I have a class in an hour and I need to go." Then he looked at her. "Don't make me regret this, Parker. I know we have a lot to talk about and you don't even know how much the rent is..."

"It was on the flyer," she said, careful not to get her

hopes up. "I can give you two months' rent right now and sign whatever you need me to sign."

"Damn. I don't have any kind of lease ready. I didn't think I'd have any takers this soon."

That made her smile because she had a feeling Ethan was always prepared. "How about this—let me give you the rent money so you can go to class. While you're gone, I'll make arrangements for some furniture and maybe..." Pausing, she glanced around. "Maybe I'll get this place organized a bit more."

"You don't need to do that. I'm more than capable of getting the rest of my stuff unpacked and put away." The statement didn't come out overly confident, but he seemed resigned to their arrangement. Walking into the kitchen, Ethan pulled an envelope out of one of the drawers before walking back to the living room and handing it to her. "Here."

"What's this?"

"The keys." Then he shrugged. "This way you can go into town and maybe see your cousin and then you can come back in without having to wait for me."

Her smile refused to be subdued but she didn't attempt to hug him again. "Thank you, Ethan. You have no idea how much this means to me."

All he did was nod before turning and walking out the front door.

Parker walked over to the front window and watched as he drove away. As soon as his car was out of sight, she let out the loudest, most excited scream she could muster while doing a little dance. After several minutes, she calmed herself down and collapsed on the covered sofa and took in her new surroundings.

It wasn't like this was anything new; she'd been living in

other people's homes for years. This was the first time, however, that she had the opportunity to make at least part of the space her own and put her own stamp on it.

And boy did this place need a stamp.

A fresh coat of paint was a necessity all around. Getting to her feet, Parker couldn't help but walk around and truly check out the house.

Including Ethan's bedroom.

The door was open so she didn't feel like she was really snooping.

Even though...she kind of was.

The walls were painted a pale gray, the trim was bright white, and the bedding was navy blue. Everything looked new and clean and it didn't take long for her to realize this was the one room he actually did work on.

"Good for him," she said as she walked to his en suite and checked it out. It all looked newly renovated as well– new tiled shower, new vanity, and if she had to guess, she'd say the tile floor was heated. That's when she realized she never got the chance to look at her own bathroom and headed up the stairs.

And wished she hadn't.

This bathroom–though spacious–was definitely not newly renovated. It was old and dated and she wasn't sure if a coat of paint would even help.

"That just means I'll have to get creative with my décor," she assured herself as excitement started to take over. The last time she had free rein to decorate, she'd been sixteen and her mother had finally agreed to let her change her room from bubble gum pink to something a little more grown up.

Running down the stairs, she grabbed her purse and pulled out her phone and immediately raced back up the stairs to take some pictures. Hopefully once Mallory saw what kind of space Parker was working with, she'd have some ideas about what kind of furniture she should get.

Twenty minutes later, she was back in her car and heading into town.

And unlike her earlier cruise around Magnolia, this time she was full of hope.

* * *

"CLASS DISMISSED."

For several minutes, Ethan watched his students walk out of the massive classroom and, as usual, not one of them made eye contact with him or even said goodbye. It shouldn't bother him, but...it did. Several members of the faculty commented on how friendly their students were and how sometimes they had to force them to leave after class, even though they were having great conversations.

Ethan had never experienced anything even remotely close to that.

Then again, he knew his strengths and weaknesses and that he was an almost painful introvert. Striking up conversations with people was not his strong suit and for the most part, he was okay with it. But for some reason, today it stung.

And if he had to hazard a guess, he'd say it had something to do with his new roommate.

What the hell was I thinking?

That question had been playing on a continuous loop in his head ever since he walked out of his house earlier.

It had been years since he'd thought about Parker Bishop. Sure, they'd gone to school together, but they certainly didn't hang out in the same circles and they'd never been friends. Hell, he wasn't even sure if they'd ever spoken two words to each other. His memory of her was the girl who was always laughing and smiling and seemed to be friends with everyone.

Except him.

For the most part, Ethan was okay with who he was and his ridiculously small circle of friends. It was comfortable for him. Still, after spending so many years being the socially awkward outcast, he thought he'd started to outgrow it. College had been good for him—mainly because he met people who were a lot more like him than any of his high school classmates had been.

Then he'd foolishly returned to Magnolia Sound because his father's health was failing and simply took the job at the community college for the sake of convenience. Unfortunately, a lot of his students were like his old high school nemeses and it was more than a little intimidating for him. It seemed absurd to still feel insecure at this point in his life and career, but apparently some things simply took longer to outgrow. What he would give to have the confidence of someone like Parker—to be able to step into any situation and feel like you had the upper hand simply because you had tenacity.

Once the hall had emptied, Ethan packed up his satchel and headed out to his office. He shared it with two other professors, but at this time of day he knew he'd have it to himself. There were papers to grade and lesson plans to work on, but as soon as he sat down, the only thing he was able to think about was Parker.

Maybe...maybe having her as a roommate wouldn't be such a terrible thing. Perhaps she could help him figure out how to be more comfortable in front of his class or how to just relax enough to engage with them even a little bit.

It wasn't his worst idea.

He just had no clue how he'd broach the subject with her without coming off like a total loser.

For more than an hour, he tried to focus on his work, but eventually gave up. It had been four hours since he'd left home and he knew there were plenty of things for him to do there to keep him busy. Having a roommate gave him that little push he needed to motivate him to get some of the renovation projects done. As much as he appreciated Parker's willingness to help with the painting, he had a feeling it would be better for him to do it himself. She could focus on the upstairs and the space that would be hers, but he felt responsible for all the other common areas. While home decorating wasn't exactly his thing, he wasn't trying to win any awards with it either. As long as the walls had a fresh coat of paint and his furniture wasn't too worn, he'd be happy.

When he pulled into his driveway a little later, Parker's car was there and he took a minute to compose himself. If Jeff had moved in, Ethan knew he'd be able to come home each day without having to engage in conversation until he was ready. He had a feeling Parker would be chatty from the moment he walked through the door.

"This is definitely out of my comfort zone," he muttered, but forced himself to face the challenge.

But when he walked into the house, Parker was nowhere in sight. The sound of music playing told him she was upstairs, and he warred with himself for several minutes whether he should go up and say hello.

He put his satchel down in his bedroom and kicked off his shoes and basically puttered around for several minutes before curiosity got the better of him. Walking up the stairs, he found her singing softly to a song he'd never heard before while she painted over the orange walls. She'd chosen a shade of aquamarine and moved around with no real method to her painting–something that made him cringe slightly–but half the room was already covered, so perhaps it wasn't such a bad thing. It wasn't until she needed to refresh the paint on her roller that she spotted him.

"Oh, hey! How was class?" she asked with a big smile before lowering the music.

"It was fine," he replied. "I can't believe you accomplished so much already."

Looking at him over her shoulder as she began rolling out the paint, she smiled again. "Well, the orange was a little loud for me and I knew if I had a color I liked on the walls that it would make it easier for me to decorate and furnish up here."

That made sense. "Did you go to your cousin's shop?"

"I did! Mallory was a great help but a lot of what she had was a little out of my budget. I did buy a few small things that will get delivered this weekend." She shrugged. "So I ordered a mattress online and it should be here in a few days too. I don't mind living out of my suitcases for a bit. I did pick up a couple of pillows and a comforter set so I can camp out up here."

The thought of her sleeping on the floor definitely bothered him. "Why don't you at least sleep on the couch?" he suggested. "I was planning on working on the living room tonight so hopefully it won't be too cluttered for you and at least you'll be a little more comfortable." Then he remembered her conversation with Shelby. "Plus, no kids or dogs will be jumping around on or near you, so..."

She laughed.

A genuine, lyrical laugh.

"Ah, so you heard that part of my conversation, huh?"

Then she laughed again. "Don't get me wrong, I am beyond grateful that she and Sam were willing to let me crash with them, but considering my own brother asked me to leave because he claimed I got my nephews too riled up, I'm pretty sure my cousin would have felt the same way. And no one wants to continually be asked to vacate the premises, right?"

The fact that he'd essentially asked her to do that very thing earlier had him awash with guilt. There wasn't anything he could say that wouldn't make him sound trite, so he simply nodded.

"But yeah, I will gladly take you up on the sofa thing if you're sure you're okay with it."

"I wouldn't have offered if I wasn't," he told her.

"Well...why don't you go and do your thing while I finish up here?" She paused while reaching up to paint above one of the windows. "I was thinking of ordering a pizza for dinner if you'd like to share."

That...was something he hadn't considered either. Not that he thought they were going to be eating together every night, but he supposed it was bound to happen. "Uh...sure. That would be great. Thanks."

The music started up again and he figured that was his cue to head down and begin tackling the boxes that were scattered all over the living room. Most of them were filled with books for his home office–and were mostly just for show–but it seemed silly to keep putting off unpacking them.

So for the next hour, he moved what felt like hundreds of books into the third bedroom, which he'd turned into his office. The bookcases were assembled several weeks ago, but now that the books were on them, the room was finally starting to feel like a space he could work in. It was the only room in the house that he didn't need to paint. Three of the four walls were covered in shiplap and the fourth wall was painted in a dark hunter green. Maybe at some point he'd change that, but it worked for now.

Out in the living room, he cut down all the boxes he'd emptied and took them out to the recycling pail. When he came back inside, he couldn't help but smile because the room looked bigger already.

"Wow, look at that!" Parker said as she came down the stairs. "You made some great progress! Good for you!"

Just as he remembered, she was the girl who was always smiling.

Okay, not always. It seemed like he genuinely caught her on a bad day with all the crying earlier, but the woman walking toward him definitely reminded him of the girl he went to school with.

"I know there's still a lot more to do, but I feel like I made a pretty decent dent in it," he commented as he looked around with pride. "I think if I move the tools to one designated spot and fold up the drop cloths until I'm ready, this room will almost look livable."

"As soon as you do, I am definitely running the vacuum. And then we'll dust off the rest of the furniture and it will start to feel a little homey. Won't that be nice?"

All Ethan could do was nod.

They worked together for another hour before Parker collapsed on the couch and pulled out her phone. "Any preferences for pizza toppings?" she asked around a yawn.

"I'm good with whatever you're getting. I'm just glad I don't have to cook."

"Me too. I don't think I could even heat up a can of soup right now," she joked before turning her attention to placing their dinner order. When she hung up, she told him it would be thirty minutes before it was delivered and was about to say something else when her phone rang. "Oh no..."

"What's the matter?"

"It's my sister. I'm guessing she just got home and found my note." With a weary sigh, she answered. "Hey, Peyton..."

Then she got up and went upstairs.

It was obvious she needed privacy, but considering there wasn't a door at the top of the stairs–and Parker wasn't the quietest talker–he was able to hear a lot of the conversation.

Her side of it, at least.

"I wasn't looking for you to fix me!" she yelled before pausing. "Well, maybe you and Ryder should get hobbies!" Another pause. "I needed a few days to get settled, Peyton! I didn't need the two of you trying to force me into doing things I had no interest in!"

Part of him felt like he should find something to do so he wasn't listening, but...it was a small house and he had a feeling unless he went outside, he was going to hear her.

"Why can't you just be supportive, huh? Couldn't you tell that I was devastated? That my heart was broken? When you left Ryder that time, didn't I feed you ice cream and just let you take the time you needed until you were okay?" Pause. "Oh, please, I withheld one stinking bowl of ice cream!"

Were they seriously arguing over ice cream? Was that normal? And what did it have to do with Parker needing a place to stay? As an only child, he never quite understood the sibling dynamic, but even this seemed odd to him.

"No one was asking you to coddle me!" she went on, louder than a moment ago. "All I'm saying is that it wouldn't have killed you to let me breathe for a damn week before you both started trying to micromanage me!"

Now he felt like a voyeur and decided to go and dust the furniture like Parker had suggested.

Only...he didn't.

If anything, he was now at the foot of the stairs and leaning heavily into them to hear even more of her conversation.

"I know you love me and only want what's best, but right now, that was giving me a little time. I've lost my best friend, my home, my job..." She paused before growling with frustration. "I know I need a job! That's not what I'm saying..." There was a long silence and he figured her sister was pleading her case and Ethan wished he could hear what she was saying.

One minute.

Two.

Three.

Obviously the sister is just as chatty as Parker...

"You know what? This is getting us nowhere. I think we need to just...take a break right now." He heard her sigh. "I'm fine. I have a place to stay and everything's good. Let's touch base next week, okay?"

At that point, Ethan did finally move away and went into his office and pretended to be busy. If Parker came down and saw him hovering on the stairs, she'd never trust him. And right now, he felt like she needed someone in her corner. Listening to the one-sided conversation told him more about her than he would have imagined. She needed a friend–a person who wasn't going to try to tell her what to do–and he knew he could be that person.

There was a soft knock on his office door and he turned

and saw her standing there looking defeated. "Everything okay?"

A mirthless laugh was her first response. "Sorry about that. I know I was pretty loud..."

"You were fine." Leaning against his desk, he studied her. "Want to talk about it?"

"Not really."

All he could do was nod.

After a long moment, she seemed to pull herself together. "How about we go and finish cleaning the living room? Maybe by the time we're done, the pizza will be here and we can watch some TV while we eat?"

"That sounds like a plan."

"Do you have cable or any streaming services?" she asked as they walked down the hall.

"I have all of the streaming services," he told her. "No cable, though. I don't find it necessary."

This time she was the one to nod and after that they worked together to get his living room looking like an actual place people could sit and relax rather than a storeroom for tools and boxes. When the doorbell rang with their dinner, they were both more than ready to collapse on the couch and eat.

"You find something for us to watch, and I'll grab drinks, plates, and napkins," Ethan said as he made his way to the kitchen. Within minutes, they were side by side and helping themselves to a couple of slices. It wasn't until he looked up at the TV that he realized he'd possibly made a mistake. "Um...what are we watching?"

"*The Bachelor*. Why? Don't you watch reality TV?"

"I do, just not...this." Now wasn't the time to get into his position on how these reality shows weren't exactly real, so he decided to keep that to himself.

"Oh, uh...okay. What do you normally watch?"

"I'm a big fan of *Doctor Who* and I enjoy catching the latest documentaries on National Geographic." Even as he said the words, he could tell how bored she was. Maybe it wouldn't kill him to watch something else once in a while. "But...it's your first night in the house, so...if this is what you want to watch, we'll watch it."

Her eyes went wide. "Really?"

He nodded. "Yes. Really."

Her smile was big and bright. "Thanks, Ethan. I know it's silly, but...I needed this. Thank you."

So, for the first time in his life, Ethan Harlow sat through several episodes of *The Bachelor*. It was ridiculous and he had to bite his tongue several dozen times to keep from pointing out how unrealistic the scenarios were, but by the end of episode three, Parker looked completely relaxed and happy. And after everything he'd witnessed about her today, he realized just how much she needed this.

As crazy as it sounded.

But what was even crazier was that somehow...so did he.

THREE

It took a week, but her room was finally done. She'd painted, hung some pictures, found cute curtains to match her new comforter set, and the last of the furniture she'd ordered had been delivered today. Tonight, she'd get to sleep in an actual bed and it was funny how much she was looking forward to it.

Ethan probably was too because every morning he got up and walked past her on the couch and shook his head. Sure, most of the time he thought she was still sleeping, but she saw it. They were definitely a little like that old movie *The Odd Couple*–although, she wasn't sloppy and he wasn't compulsively neat. However, she was way more laid back than him. Ethan seemed very rigid in just about every aspect of his life. He had a schedule–a routine–that he adhered to and did not like to sway from it.

And she was making him sway quite a bit.

Besides their TV likes and dislikes, Parker tended to... live all over the house. When he was home, she liked talking to him. It took a few days for her to realize he preferred a quieter approach to his return home and now she knew to give him an hour before engaging in conversations. They had painted the living room and kitchen over the weekend and all the boxes were finally unpacked as well. They hung pictures and curtains and blinds and other than the seriously outdated kitchen cabinets, the place looked pretty darn good. And now, so did her room.

Downstairs, she heard him coming through the door and wanted to call down for him to come up and see the finished product, but...she refrained. Instead, she fluffed pillows and smiled at her new TV that her cousin Austin hung for her. She'd thought about asking her brother, but she was still a little hurt about him kicking her out.

Although...maybe she had been just a little much for them to handle. She did give her nephews cookies when they weren't allowed to have them, and then there was the dance party when they were supposed to be in bed. But in her defense, she didn't get to see them very often and she was loving being the fun aunt. She just didn't realize how disruptive it was to Scarlett and Mason's schedule or rules. So maybe she'd cut him some slack and give him a call sometime this week.

Maybe.

And then there was her sister. This was the longest they'd ever gone without talking to each other. They were always texting and it felt weird not to be sharing this whole part of her life with her.

But then again...she'd kept a lot of her feelings to herself where Tyler was concerned and look where it had gotten her. Maybe if she'd shared some of it with Peyton, Parker wouldn't have spiraled so far.

Groaning, she flopped down on her new bed and willed herself to think of something–anything–else. Confessing her feelings...ugh. She would give everything she had to go back in time and take that moment back. It wouldn't change what was most important–Tyler was never going to be in love with her and he was always going to marry someone else.

The strange thing was...looking back...it was hard to say if she was truly *in* love with him or just loved him like a friend. She knew she loved him, but...as he'd pointed out to her that day, maybe she wasn't in love. Part of her was seriously leaning to just loving him as a friend, a person, because...well...she couldn't quite put her finger on it. But now that she was so far removed from the situation and had time to truly come to grips with it all, things didn't feel quite so intense. Maybe she harbored those feelings for him because he was truly everything to her.

As a buddy.

A confidant.

Never as a lover.

Hell, there'd never been a time when either of them had even flirted with each other or fooled around. They'd snuggled together while watching TV, and hugged each other a lot, but...there was nothing romantic about any of it.

"So why did I have to go and open my big mouth?" she whispered with a sigh.

Because I'm impulsive and stubborn and stupid...

Yeah. Parker was certain that anyone who knew her would use those exact adjectives to describe her. They fit and they were the reason she was living in a rented room with no friends or family around.

"They're probably all wishing I'd never come home." Tears stung her eyes but she refused to cry again. Things had been good the last several days. Working on the house and her room kept her busy and made her happy. She'd kept a low profile around town because there were so many extended family members around Magnolia—practically one on every corner—and she just needed to settle in before seeing any of them.

Well, other than Mallory and Austin, but they were the only exceptions.

Tomorrow she'd start reaching out and reconnecting and go on the big apology tour with her siblings.

"I should probably stop and see Mrs. Henderson first and get as much cake as possible to help me beg for forgiveness." It was pretty much a proven fact that no one could stay mad at you if you showed up with a pink box from Henderson's Bakery, and considering how much groveling she needed to do, she was going to need all the help she could get.

Her mind wandered to what kind of cake she was going to get when she heard...

"Parker? You up there?"

Ah...so Ethan was going to be the one to break the silence first tonight, she thought, and it made her smile.

"Yup! Come see what I did today!"

His sigh was loud enough that she heard it, but she didn't hold it against him. After all, she'd been touching pretty much everything in his home and turning his quiet and boring world a little sideways so he was entitled to a little sighing.

"What did you...?" He paused at the top of the stairs and took it all in. "Hey, the rest of your furniture came."

Nodding, she jumped off the bed. "It did, and if I do say so myself, it all fits really well." After painting the room aqua, she opted for white furniture and white window treatments to brighten things up. She'd hung a heavier, room-darkening type of curtain at the top of the stairs that was currently tied back so it would offer her a little privacy if she needed it. She also now had low bookcases, a dresser, a bedside table, and pretty crystal lamp. The room was very feminine and she loved it.

"Is that a...bean bag chair?"

Grinning, Parker walked over to what was possibly her favorite piece of furniture. "Sort of. It has all the makings of one, but it has more of a structured back and arms so it's really a chair."

"Made out of beans," he reasoned.

She shrugged before sitting down on it. "I don't care what it's made out of because it's so comfortable."

He didn't look the least bit convinced.

"Oh, and go check out the bathroom!" she told him as she stood up. "I know we didn't talk about doing any work in there, but..."

"What in the world, Parker? How did you manage this?"

Sidling up beside him in the doorway, she looked at the slightly remodeled space. "Like I said, I know we didn't talk about it, but when my cousin Austin came by to hang the TV, I was telling him how much the bathroom kind of bummed me out and he offered to freshen some things up."

Actually, he'd offered to change out the faucet on the sink and then ended up changing out the vanity, installed some new hardware, a new mirror, and a new light fixture.

"This had to have cost you a fortune," Ethan said solemnly. "I really wish you would have talked to me about this. It wasn't in my budget to do this."

Parker waved him off. "Ethan, please. This was my idea and I don't expect you to pay for it. Besides, Austin's in the construction field and used his contractor discount." Then she shrugged. "I didn't go overboard on anything, but you have to admit that it looks great, right?"

"Parker..."

"What?" she asked wearily. "It's not costing you anything and I just helped put value into this investment of yours, so why not just say thank you and move on?"

Then she waited for him to come back at her with some sort of logical argument, but...it never came. Instead, he looked at her and smiled. "You're right. This looks great and I appreciate it, so...thank you."

Looping her arm through his, she gave him her most endearing smile. "See? That wasn't so hard, right?" And before he could say her name with exasperation again, she quickly changed the subject. "I was going to order some celebratory Chinese takeout for dinner. Care to join me?" It was sort of becoming a thing with to eat dinner together. Ethan had worked late two nights, but other than that, they ate together. And Parker had to admit, it was nice not eating alone.

"I wish I could, but...I've got a date," he said, not making eye contact with her.

Slowly, she put a little space between them. "Oh, well... good for you! I won't keep you. I'm sure you've got things to do to get ready."

"That's actually what I wanted to talk to you about."

It wasn't what she was expecting him to say and it definitely piqued her interest. Walking back over to her comfy chair, she sat down. "Okay. What's up?"

Looking wildly uncomfortable, Ethan slowly roamed around her room for a bit before saying anything. "So, um... this is a first date and other than dinner, I'm not sure what else there is to do. I thought maybe you might have some suggestions."

Wow. Dating advice. That was...unexpected.

Parker hadn't had a steady boyfriend in a long time–and

not because of the whole Tyler situation–but because she had a group of friends who always did everything together. So thinking about what to do on a first date wasn't exactly her strong point either. Although...she supposed she could simply draw on what she would like to do on a first date, couldn't she?

"Well, I guess it depends on your date. Tell me a little about her."

Ethan's cheeks flushed slightly and he fidgeted with his glasses. "Um...she's also a professor. She teaches British Literature and has a master's degree. She enjoys foreign films, but I don't think there's anywhere here in Magnolia to see one, and she's allergic to shellfish."

It was hard to envision this woman being even a little fun, so all her thoughts of doing dinner and playing putt-putt golf went right out the window. "What does she do for fun?"

"Like I said, she enjoys foreign films." He paused. "Would it be awkward to invite her back here to watch one?" Another pause. "Actually, she mentioned going back to her place and doing that so...maybe I'm overthinking this?"

"Maybe?" she said slowly. "Going back to her place isn't that big of a deal, but it's your first date and..."

"And what?"

"I don't know, Ethan. I would never ask a guy back to my place on the first date. And if I did, it would only be about sex."

His eyes went wide and if anything, his whole face turned red.

Parker immediately jumped up and tried to put his mind at ease. "I'm sure that's not what your date is doing. I mean...unless that's what you want her to do. Do British Lit professors do that sort of thing? Aren't they a little primmer and reserved?" Then she let out an awkward laugh. "Although, how would I know, huh? I barely passed any of my lit classes in high school and couldn't handle college, so for all I know, this woman could be completely cool and flirty!"

If anything, he looked even more appalled.

"Unless...she's not and that's totally okay too!" she rambled on, hating herself more and more by the second. "So, um...maybe dinner and a movie? You know, a regular one that's not at anyone's house?"

"I...I think I'll just go and get ready. Um...thanks." And he turned and quickly went down the stairs.

"Ugh, what is wrong with me?" Parker wondered out loud, sitting back down. Granted, she didn't have the most exciting dating history, but she'd never just flat out blathered on so awkwardly in her entire life!

Still, she was a little envious of his night out. Maybe it was time for her to start reconnecting with old friends and maybe getting herself a date or two. It could be exactly what she needed to get back into the swing of things and make her feel a little more at home now that she was... well...home.

So, besides visiting her siblings and making things right, now she was adding reaching out to friends too. It was all so easy and yet complicated at the same time. There were going to be so many questions about what brought her back to Magnolia and, of course, everyone who knew her knew she and Ty were always inseparable so she was going to have to talk about that whole debacle without going too deep into detail.

"I'm already exhausted and changing my mind." That didn't stop her mind from wandering to all the potential scenarios and what she'd say and what she'd do and where she'd want a date to take her the first time they went out. At some point, she heard the front door open and close and then the sound of Ethan's car driving away. It took a little longer for her to find the will to get off the bed and go and order her dinner. There was the option of going and picking it up and maybe running into someone she knew and striking up a conversation, but ultimately, she opted to stay in and be a hermit for a little longer.

And considering how her last conversation just went, it was probably for the best.

* * *

IT WAS A NIGHTMARE.

The entire night had been one awkward encounter after another and Ethan was beginning to think he was jinxed.

After Parker's bizarre and rambling advice, he thought he'd be fine. Once he arrived at Michael's Italian Restaurant and Sarah, his date, showed up, things got progressively worse.

Apparently Sarah was allergic to more than just shellfish and there was a moment when he thought she was going to have to use her EpiPen. Then, he knocked over her glass of wine—luckily it wasn't red—and she claimed she needed to go home to change.

And that's when she suggested they go back to her place together so she could slip into something more comfortable.

As in...her bed.

So yeah, Parker kind of hit the nail on the head with that one and once that thought took hold, Ethan couldn't seem to stop thinking about Parker.

That was not a good sign considering he was out on a date with another woman.

Fortunately, Sarah hadn't pushed when Ethan claimed that they should just call it a night, but he felt like a total loser returning home so early. So, he drove around town, got himself some ice cream and sat on the pier for a little while, people-watching and doing a little reflection.

Well, it wasn't really reflection as much as it was thinking about Parker some more.

He'd learned a lot about her this last week. For starters, she sort of just went with the flow. She'd essentially moved into his house with a couple of suitcases full of clothes, a minimal amount of personal items, and zero furniture. She'd slept on his couch and didn't seem to have a problem living like a kind of laid-back nomad.

But there was a whole other side to her that she tried to hide.

The insecure and anxious side.

He'd seen glimpses of it that very first day in the library and then when she was on the phone with her sister. As the week went on, however, he found that when she let her guard down, she wasn't as confident as she liked to project to the world.

And he liked that side a lot more. It made her much more relatable and human. For the life of him, he couldn't understand how she could be two extreme personalities or why she would want to be. What made her feel the need to be the outgoing, always-smiling woman if she had so many internal struggles? He didn't know her well enough to ask, but he was dying to know. He believed in being who you are one hundred percent of the time and thought everyone felt the same, but...clearly he was wrong.

Tonight he'd hoped that she could help him—maybe give

him some advice on how to be a little more confident out on his date–but she'd almost been as nervous as he was, which...didn't fit.

"So she's a little complex," he commented to no one in particular. But those complexities were drawing him to her and confusing him. Honestly, he'd hoped she could teach him how to come out of his shell, as if some of her confidence could rub off on him.

Now he wasn't so sure.

All he knew was he spent way too much time thinking about Parker and he didn't think it was a good thing.

Or appropriate.

Either way, he didn't want to have to avoid going home to his own house, so he finished his ice cream and made his way back to his car. It wasn't particularly late, but he'd been gone long enough that hopefully Parker wouldn't comment on it.

Twenty minutes later, he opened the door and found Parker curled up on the sofa wrapped up in one of her fuzzy blankets. Most of the lights were off and she was watching yet another season of *The Bachelor*. Rather than say anything, he took off his jacket and sat down and watched the remainder of the episode with her.

Why can't I be as smooth and confident as these guys? They say all kinds of cheesy things and it's endearing. I say stuff like that and people look at me like I'm crazy...

When the episode ended, Parker sat up straight and turned on one of the lamps before facing him. "So? How was your date?"

The groan was out before he could stop it, and then he slouched down and told her about everything that happened. Turning his head toward her, he ended with, "You were right."

Her eyes went wide. "What? Really? So British Lit professors can be a little sexually aggressive! Who knew?"

"Apparently, you," he replied. "How did you know that without ever meeting her?"

"I think it's just a girl thing. Every female I've ever known—myself included—only invites a guy back to her place on the first date if the end goal is sex." Then she grinned at him. "Look at you, Ethan Harlow! Getting all the lady professors chasing after you!"

Oh Lord...

"Definitely not *all* the lady professors," he corrected. "Just this one and...I didn't go home with her."

Parker blinked at him as if she didn't understand what he was saying. "But...I don't get it. Why wouldn't you go home with her?"

It felt like the room had gotten hotter. "I don't know. It's just...you got in my head and it all felt wrong. I mean... Sarah's a perfectly nice woman, but I just don't feel that way about her."

And just like that, Parker's expression changed—she went a little pale and somber on him.

"Parker? Are you okay?"

She didn't respond right away; she simply crawled off the sofa and rolled her blanket up into a ball. It was then that he saw she was in a pair of flannel pajama pants that looked to be about two sizes too big for her, an oversized sweatshirt, and fuzzy socks. Her long, dark hair was up in a messy bun and yet she looked...pretty. Attractive. Sexy.

Uh oh...

That was a brand-new observation and Ethan mimicked her move and quickly scrambled off the couch. "So, um... you don't have to shut off the TV on my account," he told her. "I think I'm going to go and grade some papers so..."

"No. No, it's okay. I think I'll finish watching TV up in my room. I forgot that I have one up there now so I don't have to hog yours." She let out a nervous laugh. "I'll bet you'll be glad to go back to watching your science documentaries instead of my reality dating shows."

"They're not as bad as I thought they'd be," he admitted.

And then, thankfully, Parker seemed to relax. "Oh, well...then I guess I should give one of your shows a try, huh? Maybe I'll learn something." Then she shook her head. "Although, I doubt it." After a brief pause, she turned and murmured, "Good night."

"Why do you do that?" he asked, causing her to stop in her tracks.

"Do what?"

"Put yourself down like that. I don't get it."

For a minute he didn't think she was going to reply, but the answer she finally gave was definitely an attempt at deflection.

"That's just me goofing around. No biggie."

Ethan knew there had to be more to it than that. These little digs at herself added on top of the other things he'd noticed about her and he was beginning to think that no one knew the real Parker Bishop.

Including herself.

Taking a tentative step toward her, he couldn't help but push a little. "Parker, you're an intelligent woman. I don't get why you don't see that."

She wouldn't look directly at him and he knew somewhere in the back of her mind she was trying to escape gracefully. It would probably be best to let her just go upstairs and drop the subject, but...he couldn't.

"From everything you've told me, you've been living

your best life up until recently. And I get that you're recovering from a lot of disappointment, but that doesn't have anything to do with who you are as a person. Don't you know that?"

The eye roll was almost expected, but her response wasn't.

"You don't know anything about me, Ethan. Back in school, I was flunking everything. It took a team of tutors and I'm sure a little bribery from my parents for me to actually graduate. I'm not smart by any stretch of the imagination. I left Magnolia Sound as soon as I could because I couldn't stand to be surrounded by overachieving siblings and cousins. There is all this pressure to live up to the great Coleman name–that was my great-grandfather and he was one of the founders here–and it's a lot to have to deal with. I don't want to put my stamp on this town; probably couldn't even if I wanted to because I'm not smart enough." With a sigh, she took a step toward the staircase. "I had to learn to use charm and humor to get by." She let out a mirthless laugh. "It's a great distraction when you don't want anyone to realize how dumb you are. So...yeah. That's me. Now you know the kind of person you're really living with," she added quietly before turning and walking up the stairs.

Leaving Ethan completely speechless.

Part of him wanted to go after her and talk about all of this, but...he had no idea what to say.

Or if this revelation made any difference in how he felt about her.

It didn't.

He knew instantly that it didn't change anything. All it did was help him understand her a little more.

He just wished he were the kind of guy who could have said something right then in the moment to make her feel better. Knowing what to say was never his strong suit, and normally he was okay with it. But seeing the sadness on Parker's face and seeing the look of utter defeat in her eyes just gutted him.

It was shocking to realize she struggled with her own insecurities just like he did, but maybe this whole roommate thing could be beneficial to both of them. Perhaps they could help each other out. Earlier he had genuinely wanted her help and input on his date with Sarah, but the more he thought about it, Ethan knew he could use Parker's help in a lot of aspects of his life and maybe, just maybe, she could use his help as well.

Tonight wasn't the night to bring it up, but he made a mental note to bring it up the next time the two of them sat down to dinner together.

FOUR

"So basically what I'm saying is...I'm sorry. I behaved like a brat and I know you were only trying to help me." Her words were met with total silence and that was unusual whenever she was surrounded by her family. They were all at Peyton and Ryder's house–the one on the beach that they finally moved into–and having dinner. Once she'd reached out to her sister and said she wanted to get together with everyone, things fell into place immediately.

As in a matter of hours.

Right now, she was addressing her sister and her fiancé, but her brother and sister-in-law were right there at the dinner table with them. "Somebody say something. Please."

Peyton spoke first. "Of course we forgive you, Parks. I just hate that you felt the need to run away rather than just talking to us."

It was on the tip of her tongue to argue that she *had* talked to them about how much they were smothering her, but she figured if she wanted everything to go back to normal, she'd keep it to herself. Instead, she said...

"You're right. I should have spoken up. I was just overwhelmed with everything and I guess it was selfish of me to come crashing back into everyone's lives and expect you to know what I needed."

It was amazing no one was calling bullshit on her.

"Parker," her brother began, "you are always welcome to come crashing into our lives. We're family and we love you. It's just...we all have lives too, and it's not easy for us to be able to read your mind. I mean...Scarlett and I have kids and jobs and our lives are hectic enough. When you showed up, we were happy to see you but..."

"I know, I know. I should have respected your rules and not tried to make everyone change for me," she said solemnly. "I'm sorry for that."

"You don't have to be sorry," Scarlett told her. "I'm partly to blame because I'm hormonal and everything seems to upset me lately. The kids loved having you there and I was a big downer who took all the fun away. If you ever want to babysit..."

That made Parker laugh. "Anytime. You just give me a call, and I'll do my best to be there."

Reaching over, Scarlett squeezed her hand. "We love you, kiddo. And if you still need a place to stay..."

"No, but thanks. I'm renting a place and I'm all settled in. It was fun getting to decorate and buy furniture that I know is going to be mine. I haven't done that since high school."

"Where's this place?" Ryder, her sister's fiancé, asked.

"Oh, it's on the edge of town–closer to the Laurel town limits, on the Sound side. It's two blocks in from the water. Super cute."

"And you're renting the whole house?"

"Well...no. I'm renting a room." Then she paused. "I mean, it's more of a roommate situation with someone I went to school with, but I have the whole upstairs all to myself. The rest of the house is a common area. So far it's working out great."

"Oh, someone from school?" Peyton asked. "Who is it?"

"Um..."

"Please don't tell me it's one of your flaky friends," Mason chimed in. "I've seen Lauren and Tina around town and they are still as immature as they were back when you all used to hang out together in high school."

Just thinking about her old friends made her laugh. "No. It's not anyone I was close to. You've never met them."

"Them?" Peyton asked.

Crap. She hadn't considered how everyone would react when she mentioned her roommate was a guy.

Too late to back out now.

"His name is Ethan Harlow," she said confidently. "He was the valedictorian of our class and now he's a professor at the community college."

"Professor of what?" Mason asked.

"Science. Physical science, I believe." She shrugged. "We haven't talked a whole lot about his job."

"And what about you?" Ryder asked. "Where are you working?"

"Um..." Dammit. It was the same interrogation she got back when she was staying with him and Peyton all over again.

Stay calm. Don't freak out. They're only asking because they care...

"I haven't really started looking. I saw Mallory last week and she mentioned maybe giving me some part-time work at the shop, so there's that."

"And you know you can come work at the café," Peyton

added. "It's not glamorous, but the tips are great. Have you thought about what it is you want to do?"

Ugh...this again.

"Still no," she said with a forced smile. "I've been dealing with a lot and now that I'm settled with a place to live, I can start thinking about it."

Everyone nodded except Ryder, and Parker knew it was only a matter of time before he started...

"How can you not know what you want to do with your life?" he asked, sooner than she expected.

Sighing, Parker reached for a bottle of wine and poured herself a half a glass. When she glanced up, everyone seemed to be looking at her with a crazy amount of anticipation.

"Fine. You want to know how?" she asked the group at large. "Because of all of you." First, she faced her brother. "You've always been the golden child. Everything you did was perfection. My whole life I had to listen to Mom and Dad say how amazing you are, how talented, how perfect. Do you have any idea how hard that is to deal with?"

"Uh..." Mason looked around but didn't seem to have a response.

Then she faced her sister. "And you. You've known since you got your first Easy-Bake Oven that you wanted to own a restaurant. You've been focused on that dream since we were little and then you did everything humanly possible to make it happen. Both of you were great students and were big cheerleaders for living here in Magnolia Sound and following in Pops' footsteps." She let out a long breath. "I was never going to live up to those expectations. I was never going to be smart enough or focused enough to do anything great, so...I put my focus on traveling."

"Oh, Parker...sweetie," Peyton began with a small

frown. "Why didn't you ever say anything? For a long time you talked about opening your own spa. Was there any truth to that or were you just saying that to pacify all of us?"

"I don't know. I guess there was a time when it sounded like a good idea, but..." she looked helplessly at her family. "There's a part of me that doesn't want to add anything to Magnolia. I love it the way it is. I love driving down Main Street and seeing all the things Pops built." She glanced at her soon-to-be brother-in-law and frowned. "I get that you're all about making improvements and bringing in new businesses and that's fine, but it's not for me. I don't want to contribute to that."

"Okay, we can all respect that, Parks," Mason said, "but at some point you're going to have to do something. You can't just keep flitting around crashing at people's houses or working a variety of part-time jobs."

"Why not?" And seriously, she was curious. "I mean, where is it written that I have to choose a career and do it for the rest of my life? Why can't I work at different things if that's what feeds my soul?"

No one had a response.

"So is this just a pit stop for you?" Peyton asked quietly. "Are you going to just kill time here in Magnolia until...until you're over this whole Tyler thing and then you're going to pack up and move again?"

All she could do was shrug. "I honestly don't know. Coming home seemed like a good idea at the time," she admitted. "But if my being here means you're all going to be passing judgment on me and making me feel bad about my life, then maybe this isn't where I'm supposed to be."

There. She'd said it.

"No one is trying to make you feel bad," Scarlett immediately assured her. "But you do have a point. It's not written anywhere that you have to have one single career. For years I worked in my dad's garage, did social media marketing, and built custom dog houses." She let out a small laugh. "None of those things went together, but by doing them all, I was happy. So if working a couple of odd jobs makes you happy, then I say you do you, Parker. Don't let anyone tell you how to live."

Sure it all sounded great when Scarlett said it, but would Mason and Peyton feel the same way and lay off? Would Ryder? And...most importantly...would her parents?

As if reading her mind, Peyton said, "You know Mom's going to chime in on all of this when she gets back, right? You have at least another three weeks before you have to deal with that, but...you know that's her thing. She disapproves and she's vocal about it."

"She is getting better," Scarlett countered. "I think we can all agree that Georgia is mellowing." Then she looked at Parker. "But you're her baby and she never gets to hover over you, so you might have to deal with a few lectures once they get back from the cruise."

"Great. Something to look forward to."

Peyton stood and began clearing the dinner dishes. "So, tell us about Ethan. How did you end up as his roommate?"

Luckily there wasn't anything accusatory in that question, so Parker felt like she could relax a bit.

"I ran into him at the library," she said. "I was there chatting with Shelby and Ethan walked in to put up a flyer advertising for a roommate. We started talking and it seemed like the perfect solution. He wasn't really a stranger, Shelby spoke highly of him, so...it all just fell into place."

"Yeah, but...isn't it weird?" Scarlett asked as she got up to help Peyton. "Were you friends with him in high school?"

"Oh, God no. Ethan was a total brainiac. He intimidated the hell out of me. I guess I knew more of him than actually knowing him personally, if that makes sense. He was always quiet and a little shy and seemed to keep to himself."

"The super smart ones usually do," Mason commented, leaning back in his chair. "Is he still quiet and shy?"

"Definitely. Like I said, he's a professor at the community college and it seems like that's all he does and he has practically no social life. He had a date last night and he was a nervous wreck getting ready for it. I almost felt bad for him." She stood and picked up her plate, bringing it over to the kitchen sink. "Which reminds me, anyone know of any decent single guys? I don't think I'd mind going out on a date."

There was a collective groan around the room and she took the hint.

"Fine. Don't fix me up with anyone," she murmured. "I just figured I'd ask."

"Are you sure you're ready to date?" Peyton asked. "It seems to me that you were pretty devastated when you left Florida."

"That had nothing to do with dating. Tyler and I were never romantic, but we were always together. I missed that relationship—the friendship. I realize now that maybe I...you know...misread my own feelings."

"Well that sucks," Scarlett said before coming over and hugging her. "Do you think you'll ever reach out to him and make things right?"

"Who knows? I'm still pretty mortified that I behaved the way I did. Ty was my best friend for so long and I was the one who screwed things up. He's happy now and no one deserves it more than him. I'd feel horrible if I made things worse again, so maybe..."

"Never say never," her sister said as she wiped down the granite counters. "There may come a day when you'll be ready to talk to him. In the meantime, maybe reconnect with your friends here."

"And maybe don't pick another guy as your best friend," Mason said with a hint of amusement. "If anything, you should spend some time reconnecting with your female friends and stay away from the male population for a while."

"Mason," Scarlett warned lightly. "She's not a child. Plus, she's got a guy roommate. She can't exactly stay away from him if they're living in the same house."

He groaned. "Don't remind me. I already feel like I need to go over there and threaten him just in case."

"Oh, stop," Parker told him. "Ethan would never hit on someone like me. Trust me. And I'm too old for you to be going around threatening guys."

"You're never too old for that," he said confidently. "You're my little sister and if any guy messes with you, I will be the one to go and set him straight. I don't care if he's sweet or shy or super smart. If he messes with my sister, he'll have to deal with me."

Rolling her eyes, Parker walked over to the kitchen island where all the boxes of cake she'd gotten from Henderson's Bakery were sitting and carried them over to the table.

Dessert was the perfect distraction, plus...the conversation was over. A guy like Ethan would never be inappropriate with her.

Ever.

And that reality hit her harder than she expected.

Which is why she ended up eating three cupcakes for dessert.

* * *

ETHAN PRIDED himself on always being organized and prepared, especially in the classroom. Unfortunately, he was completely out of sorts today and somehow managed to leave home without his laptop. It was so unlike him and had him more than a little frazzled. But then again, ever since Parker moved in, he'd been a little off balance.

After her big revelation three nights ago, he'd hardly seen her. If he had to take a guess, he'd say she was avoiding him and if that was the case, he hated it.

And felt a little guilty.

The last thing he wanted was for Parker to be uncomfortable where she was living. It had seemed like she was finally starting to relax and now she wasn't. He hoped he was wrong about her avoiding him because right now, he desperately needed her help. Picking up his phone, he typed a quick text to her.

Ethan: Hey. Are you by any chance at the house?
Parker: I am. What's up?

Ethan: Forgot my laptop. Do you think you could possibly bring it to me? I know it's a lot to ask…

Parker: Um…I guess so. I don't have anywhere to be until two. You'll just need to give very specific directions on where I can find you. I've never been to your campus

Relief washed over him as he sent her instructions on

where to park, which building he was in, and which classroom.

Ethan: Thank you, Parker. Tonight dinner is on me

Parker: See you soon!

It would easily be a half hour before she arrived and his class started in ten minutes so he'd have to come up with a way to stall before getting on with his lesson for the day. It still galled him that he was unprepared, but how hard could it be to pass the time? Science was his passion. Surely he could talk about it without any visual aids for twenty minutes. They were currently working on astronomy, so perhaps he could talk about the different planetariums they could utilize or even what kind of telescopes they could invest in for recreational usage. This was one of his favorite personal hobbies, so it shouldn't be too big of a challenge to share his knowledge.

Only...it was.

Without the use of the projector and PowerPoint presentations, Ethan was forced to actually face his students and talk to them.

Make eye contact with them.

And that's where he saw just how bored they all looked.

Clearing his throat, he did his best to just keep plugging along. "The uh...the great thing about going to the planetarium is that they offer so many um...different shows and programs." Reaching for his water, he took a long drink. With another quick clearing of his throat, he continued. "One of the more fascinating shows to see is the one that focuses on the current night sky. It's...it's especially helpful when you go during the time of a meteor shower." He shrugged. "It's just a suggestion."

More blank stares.

Great.

A quick glance at the clock showed that–with luck– Parker should arrive any minute.

Any...minute.

If anything, the clock seemed to slow down and Ethan had to stifle a groan while he droned on about all the different programs and shows people could see at the planetarium.

He knew the instant Parker entered the building. The sound of the exterior door slamming was followed by the sound of someone running, and he'd worked in this particular building long enough to know that sort of thing never happened during classes.

Finally, she stopped in the doorway and held up his laptop before walking in as if she owned the place. "Sorry I took so long," she whispered.

Or...attempted to whisper.

"I passed the building twice so..." She gave him an apologetic smile before turning and facing his students. "Mind if I sit in and watch you teach?"

"Um..."

His classroom was like a mini lecture hall and had several levels. Before he could stop her. Parker walked up to the third tier and took a seat.

Now he had even more reason to be uncomfortable.

Instead of obsessing over it, Ethan set up his laptop and got his scheduled presentation up and going. The remainder of the class was spent *not* looking at Parker, and by the time he was handing out the homework assignment and students were leaving, he felt a little more in control. Once all his students left, he looked up and saw Parker walking toward him.

"Wow," she said with a hint of amusement. "So was this your typical type of class?"

"You mean other than missing my laptop and having nothing to teach? Um...yeah."

"Ethan...you really need to work on...relaxing."

Slipping his laptop into his satchel, he stared at her. "What do you mean?"

"I mean you're obviously uncomfortable being in front of your class! You don't look at them, you don't engage with them...to be honest, you're a little robotic."

"Robotic?"

She nodded. "Yup. Definitely robotic."

"Don't you think that's a little insulting?" he questioned. "Today was obviously an off day! I'd forgotten my computer–something I never do, by the way–and you show up and judge my teaching style based on the one hour you watched me?"

Parker didn't look the least bit put out. She leaned on his podium with a sympathetic smile. "Ethan, I think I'm getting to know you fairly well. I already know you're not someone who enjoys speaking to large groups. But seeing you here today pretty much confirmed it. You need to be able to make eye contact with people without looking like it's painful."

He wanted to argue that it certainly was painful, but kept that to himself.

"I've been teaching for several years, Parker, and no one's complained."

"Not that you know of..."

The sigh was out before he could stop it.

"Ethan, you barely make eye contact with me and I live with you!"

"It's not that easy, Parker!" he yelled, his voice echoing around the lecture hall. "Maybe it's easy for someone like you, but I've never been comfortable with it! And you know what? I think there comes a time when you just have to accept who you are!"

"But you don't have to be like that," she challenged softly. "Here. Try this." The next thing he knew, Parker was standing toe to toe with him and firmly cupping his face in her hands. He felt himself stiffen and she gave him a sympathetic smile. "First of all, relax."

Easy for her to say.

"Now, I want you to look me in the eyes, Ethan. Don't try to look away. Just focus on my eyes."

This was the closest he'd ever been with her and also the most uncomfortable. What he forced himself to do was take in the details of her face–how her eyes were the color of whiskey with hints of amber in them. Her lashes were long, and she had a patch of freckles under her left eye. Her gaze was steady and Ethan had to fight the urge to close his eyes and savor how soft her hands were against his jaw and how she smelled like jasmine–which was incredibly intoxicating.

"Don't fidget," she whispered. "You're doing great. Just focus on me."

As if he could possibly focus on anything else. Right now he was practically on sensory overload and wasn't sure how much longer he could stay like this without doing something stupid, like pulling away and having a full-blown panic attack.

Or kissing her.

Because right now–having her this close–it was all he wanted to do. He wanted to see if her lips were as soft as they looked and to touch her face and skim his fingers along her jaw and throat and find out if her pulse would race as wildly as his was.

But more than anything, Ethan was dying to know if Parker Bishop was even remotely attracted to him the way he was attracted to her.

I'm treading into dangerous territory...

It would be one thing if they'd run into each other somewhere and had the chance to hang out together or go out for coffee and get reacquainted–but they were living together, roommates. Kissing Parker had the potential to make things even more awkward at home and considering how awkward they already were, did he really want to make things worse?

Yes.

He didn't even need to think about it. The answer was a loud and resounding yes.

"Parker," he murmured, leaning ever so slightly closer to her. "I can't...I mean...I need..."

Her expression instantly changed–like she understood what he was trying to say even though he was barely making sense. She licked her lips and Ethan wasn't sure if it was intentional or not, but he hoped it was.

"What are you thinking right now, Ethan?" her question was barely a whisper, and he swore she moved closer. Her breasts were gently resting against his chest–only just touching him–and yet it was more erotic than anything had been for him in a really long time.

"I'm thinking that..." Swallowing hard, he forced himself to say what he wanted. "I think I really want to kiss you."

Her eyes went wide for the barest of moments before her hands moved from his jaw and slowly raked up into his hair. "Then I think you should."

Surprise shook him for several seconds before he realized he was wasting precious time. Then he reached up and did exactly as he imagined a minute ago–he cupped her face before caressing her jaw. Her skin was softer than he imagined and when she licked her lips a second time, Ethan couldn't help but close the distance between them and gently pressed his lips to hers.

It was chaste as far as kisses went, but he was too unsure of himself and what they were doing to take things too far too fast.

Parker clearly wasn't on the same page because she moved in until she was pressed up against him from head to toe, ran her tongue along his lips and deepened the kiss to a whole other level. Fortunately he caught up fast and before he knew it, they were nearly devouring each other in the middle of his classroom. One hand snaked up into her long dark hair and fisted there as if to keep her close, but her arms banded around him as if he were a flight risk too.

Ethan couldn't remember ever feeling this kind of heat and need before. Kissing and sex were always very satisfying, but kissing Parker was like sampling an extremely decadent dessert–the kind that you can't get enough of but want to savor all at the same time.

And boy did he want to savor her.

His hands twitched with the need to touch her more. He felt like he couldn't get enough air into his lungs but stopping the kiss wasn't an option either. It was painful in the most arousing ways and all he could think of was how to get them from the lecture hall and back to the house without breaking the mood.

The sound of someone clearing their throat behind them made Ethan freeze. "Excuse me, Professor Harlow, I was wondering if I could talk to you about my geology paper."

Immediately, he stepped away from Parker and noticed the dazed look on her face as she tried to catch her breath. They never broke eye contact as Ethan casually replied, "I'll meet you in my office in ten minutes, Mr. Calloway."

"Yes, sir."

He mentally counted to ten to make sure they were alone. "Parker, I..."

She nodded and took a step back. "Um...yeah. Me too."

Wait...what?

With another lick of her lips–a gesture that was becoming more arousing by the minute–she fidgeted with her hair and glanced nervously around the room. "So, uh...I guess I should go."

Ethan watched and knew she was ready to bolt–would possibly run from the room any second–and he couldn't let her leave that way. "Don't go!" he blurted out, and heard her gasp softly. "Please don't run off."

Another glance around proved she was more than likely estimating the distance between herself and the door. "You have a student waiting and...and I'm sure it doesn't look good for you to be caught kissing me like that."

It would be wrong to point out how his students would probably like him a lot more if word got out about this...

"It's fine," he assured her and then struggled to find something to say. "Are you okay?"

Ugh...lamest thing in the world, dude...

"What? Oh, I'm fine. I just don't want to keep you from your job and..." She looked around and seemed to stop when she spotted the clock on the wall. "And I really do need to go. I'm heading over to Happy Tails to see about doing some volunteering."

"Happy Tails? The animal rescue?"

She nodded. "My cousin Garrett's fiancée...well, her family runs it. I figured while I was in between jobs and all that, I could go and help out."

Which reminded him...

"Can I ask you something?"

She was fidgeting again and inching farther and farther away from him. "I really should go, Ethan."

"I know, but...how are you surviving without a job, Parker? I don't understand it."

The smile she gave him wasn't quite the response he was expecting. "I had a decent amount of money in savings to help me in situations like this. I'm going to be working a couple of shifts a week with my cousin Mallory and then doing the same over at my aunt's B&B." She shrugged. "They'll keep me busy until I figure out what comes next for me."

Ethan slowly walked toward her. "And what does come next?"

Another shrug. "I haven't figured that out yet."

The urge to ask if he had any part in that was strong, but...he didn't. After all, it was only one kiss.

One freaking magnificent kiss that ended way too soon.

Parker took advantage of his silence to make it to the doorway. "I'll see you at home, Ethan." And with her usual smile and a wave, she was gone.

Leaving him standing all alone and wondering just what was going to happen when he saw her later.

And wasn't sure if he should look forward to it or dread it.

FIVE

Working with the puppies had been a wonderful distraction, but sadly, Parker couldn't stay and play with them all night. Eventually she had to leave and go home.

Home.

It had been a long time since somewhere felt that way to her, but the house she was sharing with Ethan was certainly starting to feel like it. It was possible it was because she was allowed to put her own stamp on the place, but she had a feeling it was more than that.

It was him.

Ethan.

The shy and quiet nerdy guy who should not kiss like a damn dream and make her want to do it all again.

It was utterly reckless to kiss him at all–especially in the middle of his classroom–but when he admitted that he wanted to, she was helpless to say no. For so long, she figured guys like him would take one look at her–or maybe talk to her for five minutes–and lose interest. But Ethan's interest seemed to be growing and it was more than a little confusing.

And exciting.

Getting involved with him would cause some serious complications for them. After all, they lived together and if things didn't work out, she'd be out of a place to live.

Again.

So...reluctantly...Parker firmly told herself that there would be no more kissing.

With Ethan.

"Ugh...I seriously should have made some calls and gone out with friends. Maybe one of them could have fixed me up with someone."

It was easy to blame her pitiful dating life on why she was so enthusiastic about kissing Ethan. After all, it had been months–easily more than six–since she'd gone out on a proper date. When everything went down with her crazy profession of love for Tyler, Parker had pretty much become a social recluse. So maybe she was just a little starved for affection.

Liar.

"Or...maybe I should just start being honest with myself and stop making everything so damn complicated."

After the dinner with her siblings, she'd been doing a lot of self-reflection and all the ways she was making her life more difficult. It had become habit for her to take on a fake persona and let everyone think she was this happy-go-lucky girl who didn't have a care in the world. The truth, however, was she was someone who felt like she never fit in with her own family. It was her own issue–she knew that–but having two overachieving siblings, successful parents, and a whole slew of cousins who were doing great things just left Parker feeling...

Inferior.

Honestly, she was getting better about the whole thing

and was coming to realize that everyone had their own issues and insecurities. All of her cousins had shared their personal struggles with her and even though her brother seemed to go through life relatively unscathed, her sister hadn't.

Something Parker only found out about somewhat recently.

Still, the bottom line was that she was someone who still lacked direction and motivation.

Well, maybe not motivation. There was a part of her that dreamed of world domination in something.

She just had no idea what.

Liar, liar.

Okay, fine. The spa thing had been real and part of her still wanted to make it happen, but it terrified her to take that leap. What if she failed? What if it were a total flop and then she'd be the only one in the entire Coleman-Bishop-Westbrook clan to fall flat?

And honestly, that was her biggest issue, the one thing holding her back more than anything else—the fear of failing.

So rather than even trying, Parker had decided to just sort of float through life simply being...there.

Nothing gained, nothing lost. Merely existing.

It wasn't nearly as satisfying as it once was.

Once she'd traveled to the places she wanted to thanks to her inheritance from her great-grandfather, she'd been more than a little lost. It turned out that it wasn't the travel that she wanted as much as it had been the escape. A chance to be away from her family and simply be Parker, not Parker Bishop, the sister of Mason and Peyton, or the daughter of socialites Beau and Georgia, and not the great-granddaughter of the most beloved man in the entire town.

Anonymity was actually quite nice.

But now those days were over because of her own big mouth and lack of impulse control. Now she was back in the place she'd run from and doing her best to blend, but so far it wasn't really working for her.

If she were finally being honest with herself, then she needed to acknowledge a teeny-tiny secret that she'd never told anyone.

Hell, she'd never even said the words out loud.

Way back when...all the way back in high school, she had a bit of a crush on a certain super-smart boy in school but refused to even talk to him because she was afraid he'd realize what a loser she was.

"All these years later and I should have stuck with that plan," she murmured as she pulled into the driveway. Back then, her insecurities had been almost too much for her. She had her circle of friends and an even bigger circle of acquaintances, and she'd developed a version of herself that she let them all see. But because Ethan was so damn smart—something everyone in Magnolia High knew—Parker just knew he'd see right through her. So she'd look away if he ever looked in her direction and she did her best to steer clear of him.

"Again, I should have done that in the library."

Ethan wasn't home yet, thankfully, and Parker knew she was going to have to come up with something to say when he did show up. There was no way she could keep avoiding him at home like she'd been doing for days—not after what happened today.

Then she remembered he was taking care of dinner for them and knew with great certainty that she couldn't avoid him.

Unless he forgot that he'd promised her dinner.

Immediately she pushed the thought aside because he was a man of his word and never forgot anything.

"Dammit."

Although...he did forget his laptop this morning, so maybe...

She never got to finish the thought because while she'd been sitting in her car obsessing over the state of her life, Ethan had arrived at home. He pulled up beside her and when she turned her head to look at him, he gave her a small smile.

And just like that, a million butterflies took flight in her belly.

I am in so much trouble...

Knowing she couldn't sit in the car any longer, Parker let out a long breath as she pushed open the door and climbed out at the same time Ethan did. He held up two grocery bags with a boyish grin. "I felt like grilling tonight. I hope that's okay."

Grilling? He had a grill?

That's when she realized she'd never even looked at the backyard. Hell, she'd never even opened the back door! "That sounds great! But I would have been fine with pizza or something. You didn't have to go to any trouble on my account."

They walked up the front steps and Parker was the one to unlock and open the door. Inside, they walked to the kitchen and she was curious what he planned on making.

"We've had pizza several times as well as a lot of takeout and I realized I hadn't used my grill since I moved in, so..." He shrugged. "It seemed like a good excuse to finally use it."

"I didn't know you had one," she told him as she walked straight to the back door and opened it. As soon as she stepped outside, she froze. "Oh my goodness..."

Ethan stepped out beside her. "What? What's the matter?"

"I had no idea...I mean...I never imagined the yard was like this!" It was a multi-level deck with two different seating areas with heat lamps, a state-of-the-art grill, a hot tub, and a decorative privacy wall. Then there were stairs that led down to the yard where there was another seating area around a firepit in the middle of a beautifully land-scaped yard. "This is amazing!"

He nodded. "I can't even take credit for it. It was like this when I bought it. Believe it or not, I haven't come out here much either. When Jeff was going to move in, I figured we'd use the space more, but once I got settled, there always seemed like there was too much to do." Turning his head, he smiled at her again. "Tonight seemed like a good night to break it in."

Parker moved away and casually walked all around the deck and touched one of the tables and ran her hand over the cover of the hot tub. "So what are we having?"

"I picked up a couple of steaks, a bag of salad mix, some vegetables, and two potatoes. Nothing fancy. As you've probably already figured out by now, I'm no gourmet. I can cook the basics."

It was true. Besides all their takeout, she had seen him make pasta, soup, grilled cheese, and tacos.

"Me too," she admitted. "Peyton got the cooking gene and she keeps trying to get me to create dishes with her, but...it never works. I'm comfortable with breakfast foods and putting together a fairly easy meal. I've never come close to starving so I guess I'm doing okay."

He laughed softly. "Me too."

That's when she noticed he'd moved a little closer.

They could play this little cat-and-mouse thing for a

little longer or Parker could put it all out there and hopefully they'd be able to move on and enjoy their dinner without any lingering tension.

"So...I guess we need to talk about...you know...what happened earlier," she said, hoping she sounded casual.

Ethan took another step closer. "Okay."

Damn. She'd hoped he'd be the one to expand on the subject.

Parker moved over to one of the sitting areas and sat down, taking a minute to collect her thoughts. "Here's the thing, Ethan. It was a great kiss and I have to admit you completely took me off guard."

He walked over and sat beside her. "But...?"

"But...it shouldn't have happened." She stared down at her hands so she wouldn't have to look at him, which was ironic since she'd been the one talking about the importance of making eye contact earlier. "We're roommates and we barely know each other. This just...it isn't..."

God, how she hated it when she couldn't form a coherent sentence!

"I'm going to stop you there," Ethan said mildly. "I get what you're saying and...I agree. It was wrong of me to say what I said and even worse that I acted on it." He paused for a moment. "I crossed a line and I'm truly sorry. I'd hate it if I made things awkward for you." Then he let out a soft laugh. "For us."

Parker knew she should have been relieved, but...his little admission put her back in her original mindset.

She was okay to kiss, but not the kind of girl a smart guy like him would get involved with.

It hurt more than she thought it would.

With a soft sigh, she nodded. "I get it." When Ethan

didn't respond, Parker forced herself to look up and found him studying her thoughtfully. "What?"

"That's what I'd like to know."

"Um...what do you mean?"

Now it was his turn to sigh. "Parker, I honestly thought we were on the same page, but as soon as I agreed with you, your whole demeanor changed. Did I say something wrong?"

Yes.

"No," she lied. "I guess I don't know what I want."

His gray eyes stared at her intently, and Parker couldn't help but notice just how handsome he truly was. Dark hair, stubbled jaw...she practically had to sit on her own hands to keep from reaching out and cupping his face again and kissing him again.

He seemed to consider her again for a long moment before saying, "Yeah. Me too."

It was cryptic, but part of her felt like maybe he felt what she did—the attraction was there, but the timing was wrong.

So in typical Parker fashion, she decided to make the best of a bad situation. "C'mon," she said as she stood. "Let's crank the grill up and get started on dinner."

The smile he gave her was part relief and part something she couldn't quite put her finger on. All she knew was when he smiled, it made her feel good.

Really good.

Too good.

Yup. I'm definitely in trouble.

*   *   *

"MY STUDENTS HATE ME."

"What?!"

He nodded as he cut the last piece of his steak in two. "It's true. I bore them to death and they hate me."

"I think you're maybe exaggerating just a bit, Ethan. Students don't hate the boring teachers. They hate the mean ones. And I know I only sat in for an hour of your class, but I didn't see anyone ready to shoot daggers at you."

"You don't get it." He took a bite of his steak and tried to figure out how to explain how he felt. "Science has always been my passion. I loved it ever since I was a little boy. When I talk about it to friends, even if they're not big on the topic, I can at least get them to engage. I can't seem to do that with my students. Any of my students. I've been teaching now for several years and it's not getting any better."

Parker took a sip of her wine and he knew she was probably trying to come up with something diplomatic to say.

He hated when people did that.

What he wanted was someone to tell him the truth–to give him criticism and critique and tell him how to fix the damn problem.

"Maybe I'm just not meant to be a teacher," he said when the silence became too much. "Maybe I should go into research or go and work for the planetarium or something. Or maybe I could..."

"Oh my God! Or maybe you could figure out how to unclench when you're standing behind the podium!" she said with exasperation.

Ethan was pretty sure his eyes were bugging out and his jaw was hanging open because her response was way more than he expected. "Um..."

"Seriously, Ethan," she interrupted. "I said it after class today and I meant it. You are so uncomfortable up there and tense and you need to find a way to change that. How did you do when you were back in school and had to do a report in front of the class?"

The snort of derision was out before he could stop it. "Pretty much the same as what you saw today."

"Okay, then we need to work on getting you to relax. You're very tense and monotone when you're up there..."

"I'm monotone too?" Now he muttered a curse. "See? This is why they hate me!"

"Again, no one said hate," she reminded him. "But they are more than likely bored."

"Great."

"We can fix this! Trust me. I know what I'm talking about." Parker stood and walked over to the freezer and pulled out a gallon of ice cream. "I think better when there's dessert."

There was literally nothing he could say to that so he waited for her to explain.

"Here's a little something else you don't know about me." She pulled a bowl down from the cabinet and then grabbed a spoon and seemed to stay in motion as she described her theory. "Back in school, I was a lousy student. We already covered this. But I still had to get through all the classes so I could graduate. And you know what senior year was like—there were tons of presentations we had to do and all those crazy mock interviews that were supposed to prepare us for college and all that crap."

Nodding, he groaned because he remembered it all too well.

"Well, I was terrified that I was going to fail and hated doing any kind of report because I never felt confident in what I'd written. So you know what I did to get through it all?"

"If you tell me you pictured everyone in their underwear, I'm going tell you it doesn't work. Been there, done that, never helped." Taking a sip of his wine, Ethan waited for her to confirm.

"Um...no. That wasn't what I was going to say."

"Oh."

"But...I know what you mean. I had a lot of people tell me that too and I thought it was weird and a little creepy when I was only seventeen!" Laughing, she made two bowls of ice cream before sitting down and handing him one. "No, I made myself treat it all like a conversation at a party. I wasn't *teaching* anyone anything; I was sharing–like telling a story. I would imagine we were all at some fabulous party and I was telling everyone about this awesome...whatever it was the report was about. I found the more charismatic and dazzling I appeared, the less the teachers focused on the actual content."

"That's...not great," he commented. "I mean for the teachers."

"Oh, I know. And looking back, I can totally see that, but at the time I was so freaking relieved to get it over with and not get an F that I didn't care what tactic the teachers used to grade me. Hell, I think most of them just took pity on me, but at the end of the day, I didn't overly embarrass myself, I didn't fail, and no one thought I was an idiot, so..."

"No one thought that about you, Parker," he assured her. "Ever."

"You don't know that."

"I do."

"Ethan..."

"Parker..." he mimicked her tone, making her laugh.

"I'm serious. You didn't know me back then!" She

laughed again. "And you really don't know me now. So you can't..."

Planting one hand firmly on the kitchen table, he did what she tried to teach him to do earlier. He looked her in the eye as he said, "Back in high school, my only real friends were the teachers. I spent a lot of time in the teachers' lounge and there was a lot of conversations about the students. Honestly, I think some of them didn't even notice I was there and so they didn't monitor what they discussed. A lot of them talked about which students they liked, who they didn't, and sometimes it was a lot of responsibility for me to have that kind of knowledge about my classmates."

"Yikes. That's a little unprofessional too."

Nodding, he took another sip of wine. "But here's the thing, Parker, any time your name came up, it was only to say positive things. No one thought poorly of you. You were the girl everyone liked."

She grinned. "All part of the act."

This time he shook his head. "No. I don't think it was all an act. I think part of it was a defense mechanism to make sure no one knew you were struggling. The rest was all you. The real you. Academics aside, you're an amazing person. A good person. And from everything I've learned about you since you moved in, you seem to be doing just fine with your life."

"Well...I don't know about fine..."

"You hit a bump in the road, Parker. We all do at some point. Yours was just a little more personal."

Her expression grew a little sad before she slowly dipped her spoon into her ice cream and took a taste. "You want to know something weird?"

He reached for his own dessert. "Sure."

"Don't get me wrong, I hate how things ended for me

and Ty. I really do. But what I hate more is that...I don't think I meant what I said to him."

She had shared the whole sordid story with him so there was no point in asking for specifics. He knew exactly what she was referring to.

"I always loved Tyler as a friend. A best friend. I think I mistook those feelings for something more. And when he said he was going to propose to Kaitlyn, I panicked." She took another spoonful of ice cream. "I wish I could go back in time and take it all back, but...I can't." Then she shook her spoon at him. "This is the story of my life–I'm mouthy and impulsive and normally it works for me, but this time it didn't. And now I have to live with the outcome."

"Now can I tell you something weird?"

Her eyes lit up. "Of course!"

"Tyler's not going to hold this against you. Most guys wouldn't. We're not programmed that way. Right now he's settling in to married life and becoming a version of himself without you. That's got to be hard for him. But somewhere down the road, your paths will cross again and you'll possibly be able to look back on all this and laugh."

She was already shaking her head. "I don't think so."

"Trust me. And for all you know, Kaitlyn might have something to do with all of this."

Now she frowned. "What do you mean?"

"I mean...there's a good chance she wasn't so thrilled that her boyfriend-slash-fiancé-slash now-husband had such a beautiful friend. She probably felt a little threatened by you. There's a very real possibility that Tyler would have been the one to end your friendship simply to please his wife. Have you thought of that?"

"No..." she replied slowly, as if this were truly brand new information.

"Of course, I can't know any of this for sure, but it's plausible. Friendships drift apart all the time. And for all the years the two of you were friends, Tyler had to know you had this impulsive side. From everything you shared with me about that whole situation, it didn't sound like he took you too seriously. I mean...he sort of gave you a pat on the head and bought you ice cream."

"Damn. You're right!"

Nodding, he took another spoonful of ice cream. "Like I said, I can't possibly know any of this for sure, but it's always helpful to look at the situation from all sides and even have someone who's not directly involved give a little input so...there's mine."

They finished their dessert in silence and he could tell she was deep in thought. Maybe he should just leave her be so she could think things through, but he had a feeling a distraction might be more helpful.

"How do you think I can change my teaching style? Like how difficult would it be?" he asked and watched as she startled slightly. "Do you really think it's possible? Can I salvage this semester or is it a lost cause?"

"I don't think anything's a lost cause, Ethan. We just have to find the right approach for you."

"And how do we do that?"

That simple question seemed to stump her for a minute.

"Oh! I've got it!" she said excitedly, jumping to her feet. "We're going to set up the living room like your classroom and you're going to teach me!"

"Parker...come on. There's a huge difference between teaching one person and teaching forty."

But she wasn't listening. She was already in the living room moving things around. "Baby steps! We start with it here in the living room and just me. Then we maybe invite a couple of friends over and you do a lesson with us." In the blink of an eye, she was back in the kitchen and grabbing two of the chairs.

Curiosity got the better of him and after a final spoonful of ice cream, Ethan followed her. "You know we just got this room looking like a real living room, right?"

"Hush. It's all for a good cause." Then she stopped in her tracks. "Or we can use your office? You know, really start small. Just the two of us in there and then move on to bigger spaces." After a brief pause, she nodded. "Yeah, that's a much better plan. You put these chairs back in the kitchen and I'll fix everything else while you get yourself set up."

It was a little like standing in the middle of a tiny tornado. She never stopped moving.

"Go!" she told him. "You've got five minutes before class starts!"

"What am I even teaching?"

That made her stop again. "Was today the first lesson on astronomy?"

"No, the third."

"Okay, then. Start with lesson one in astronomy. It sounded kind of cool from the little I heard today." Then she gave him a playful shove and sent him on his way.

The entire thing seemed ridiculous to him, but maybe something would come out of it that would make him a better teacher. Back when he was in college, there's been a guest lecturer–an astrophysicist named Owen Shaughnessy–that came and spoke at several of the classes he was attending at the time. Ethan still remembered how much he enjoyed those lectures, mainly because Dr. Shaughnessy reminded him of himself. He was soft-spoken and seemed a little uncomfortable talking in front of a classful of students, but it was clear he was passionate about what he was teaching.

That was who he wanted to emulate, but he was clearly failing at it.

Rather than obsess about it, Ethan set up his laptop and tried to figure out how to set up a mock classroom in a ten-by-twelve room.

Him standing on one side of the room and putting a chair on the opposite side for Parker seemed like the only way to go.

"Okay, Professor Harlow, I'm ready!" Parker announced as she waltzed into the room and immediately took her seat. She had her own laptop, a notebook and pen, and a bottle of water.

It was obvious that she knew how to look prepared.

"Okay, so today we are going start our introduction into astronomy," he began quietly, and Parker's hand immediately went up. "Yes?"

"Can you speak up? I didn't hear you."

Was she insane? He was less than five feet away from her. Rather than argue, he repeated the sentence a little louder and her hand went up again. "Yes, Parker?"

"Was that part of the lesson? I wasn't sure if you were talking to me because you were looking at your laptop."

Ethan let out a long breath, looked directly at her, and said in a loud and clear voice, "Today we are going to start our introduction into astronomy." Then he held his breath for a moment and waited for her to respond.

With a smile and a thumbs-up, Parker settled in for the lecture.

"Astronomy is the branch of scientific studies that focuses on celestial objects, space, and the physical universe as a whole," he began and then went into his full presentation. He was surprised that Parker didn't ask any questions and that she seemed to be thoroughly engrossed in what he was teaching.

An hour later, he was done and relaxed a little.

"Tomorrow we'll break down our solar system and how each planet contributes to our universe." After closing his laptop, Ethan leaned against his desk. "Any questions? Comments? Critiques?" And then he braced himself.

Parker's expression was thoughtful for a moment before she straightened in her seat. "First of all, I thought that was all really interesting."

"Really?"

Nodding, she explained. "I'll admit I didn't understand some of it, but I figured that was to be expected. Anyone taking your class probably knows more about science than I do. Plus, the last time I took a science class was over ten years ago, so..."

Crossing his arms, he nodded.

"I think the presentation was...okay," she said cautiously. "But it's a little dry. Do you ever ask questions in the middle of it or do you just speak all the way through like you just did?"

"Um...all the way through." And it was the first real clue he had to what was possibly lacking in his teaching.

"I would recommend opening the dialogue between you and your students. Give them a chance to participate. Maybe start with a question at the very beginning–something that introduces the topic–and then ask some questions while you're discussing something rather than waiting until the end. Trust me, the way you're doing things now? By the time you're done, they're probably a little bored and just want to leave and don't want to ask a question about something you talked about forty minutes ago."

"Duly noted." He was about to ask her more when she stood up and collected her things. "Wait...are you leaving?"

"I think this was excellent progress for our first night," she said proudly. "Tomorrow when you get to class, you need to take a breath at several points in your presentation and ask some questions and see how it goes. Then we'll work on something else once you're comfortable with that."

She went to walk past him, but Ethan reached out and gently placed his hand on her arm. "What will we work on next?" Whatever it was, it was already starting to stress him out.

"I'm not sure yet," she told him. "You'll do the next lesson with me—remembering to stop and ask me questions—and we'll pick something then." She paused and smiled up at him. "Just remember that I probably won't be able to answer the kind of stuff your students will, so go easy on me."

"Parker, I really wish you weren't so hard on yourself. A lot of people wouldn't be able to answer science questions, not just you."

That seemed to please her. "You're sweet to say so. Thank you." She went up on her toes and leaned in to kiss him on the cheek, but as soon as her lips were on his skin, everything went from casual and friendly, to...not so casual.

Ethan turned his head until they were nose-to-nose and their lips just a breath apart. "Don't thank me, Parker," he said gruffly. "I'm only telling the truth."

She moved the tiniest bit closer. "Do you always tell the truth?" she whispered, and he nodded. "Do you want to kiss me right now?"

"More than anything." And this time he was the one to close the distance between them. This was no tentative or soft kiss. This was the kiss of someone who was desperate and brimming with passion. All afternoon he'd thought about this.

Her.

When she said it was a mistake, he knew she was right, but didn't care. He swore to himself that if ever she wanted to kiss him again, he would–every chance he got.

Like now.

His hands anchored into her hair as his tongue teased at her lips before delving deep into her sweet mouth. She hummed with appreciation and went to touch him when...

CRASH!

Startled, they both broke apart and stepped back. Her laptop, notebook, and bottle of water were all on the floor. They both bent to pick them up and banged their heads together.

"Ow!"

"Ouch!"

Parker straightened while Ethan scooped everything up. The laptop looked to be intact, so that was a relief. But when he handed it to her, he knew right away that the moment was gone.

"I think I'm going to head up to my room," she told him as she scrambled for the door. "Thanks for dinner and...you know...the astronomy lesson. Good night."

And for the second time that day, she was gone.

And once again he was left standing all alone, dazed, mildly confused, and more than a little turned on.

SIX

"We...really...shouldn't...be doing...this."

"I know," Ethan panted as he kissed his way along her jaw.

It had been two weeks since that first kiss and they had been kissing every day since, normally after they did their mock classroom lecture so she could help him.

Who knew she would find his professor mode so damn arousing? Or that she'd enjoy playing school so much?

It was on the tip of Parker's tongue to say that this had to be the last time–that they were friends, roommates. And as such, it was very, *very* wrong for them to keep kissing each other like this all the time.

But as much as she might want to say that to him, she wanted to keep kissing him even more. They were on the couch, tangled up in each other, and the more Ethan kissed her, the more Parker was tempted to throw all caution to the wind and invite him up to her room.

It was farther away than his, but considering he wasn't the one extending the invitation...

"Ethan?" she whispered against his lips.

"Hmm?" His attention instantly went to the shell of her ear, and it was all she could do to keep from squirming deliciously against him.

"We should...I mean...maybe we could..." The sound of her phone ringing totally startled her, and she jumped so hard that her head banged into Ethan's. "Oh my goodness! Sorry! I'm so sorry! But that's Peyton's ringtone and..."

Reluctantly, he rolled off of her and reached for her phone before handing it over to her with a bashful grin. They both rubbed their foreheads. "Talk to your sister. I've got some papers to grade." He righted his glasses before he got up. Parker couldn't help but admire his cute little tush as he walked away.

She took a few moments to catch her breath before answering the phone. "Hey! What's up?"

"Hey, Parks," her sister said cheerily. "How are you doing?"

Parker got comfortable on the sofa, licked her lips and almost groaned at how she could still taste Ethan there a little bit. "Um...I'm good. Things are good. How are you?"

"I'm okay. So what have you been up to? Any news on the job situation?"

If she weren't so relaxed, she would have groaned at the question. "You know exactly what's going on with all of that. I'm working a little with Mallory, I've been volunteering over at Happy Tails, and I've even gone over to Aunt Susannah's and worked a couple of days helping with the housekeeping at the B&B."

Peyton's sigh was soft, but definitely not silent. "You really need to find something a little more...you know. I mean, how are you even surviving right now? You can't possibly be making enough to pay your rent and bills."

It was funny how pretty much everyone thought she

was that much of a scatterbrain. Of course, maybe that was because there was so much of herself that Parker didn't share with anyone.

Not even her sister.

"I'm fine," she said vaguely. "I don't have a lot of expenses and I'm basically frugal, so...it's all good. What's going on with you?"

"Well...I'm kind of freaking out and need you to talk me down from the ledge."

That got her full attention. It was rare for Peyton to freak out–especially since she'd been with Ryder. He seemed to really ground her. "What's going on?"

"I don't even know where to begin."

"Um...at the beginning?"

"Ugh, fine. Okay, so things are moving along at a fast pace with the new restaurant. All the finishing touches are happening and I swear I'm spending way too much time there."

"As you should! This place is your baby!"

"I know, I know." She let out a long breath. "And then there's Ryder's resort."

"Last I heard, everything was moving even faster there." Ryder had talked about it when they all had dinner together a few weeks ago and he seemed incredibly confident that it would all go off without a hitch.

"Construction-wise, everything's great. I swear that man has the Midas touch." She paused. "Except with staffing."

"How is that even possible? I'm sure he pays everyone a great salary!"

"That's what I thought, but he's been through three managers for the day spa and none of them have worked out. He's at the point where he needs to be ordering equip-ment and wants someone to handle it with him–sort of like I first did with the restaurant stuff—but he can't find anyone responsible. It's crazy!"

"I'm sure, but...what does this have to do with you? Why are you freaking out about it?"

"When Ryder's stressed, I get stressed. We're both the kind of people who want to fix a problem as soon as we see one."

Parker couldn't help but laugh because that definitely described the two of them to a T.

"So what are you going to do?"

For a minute, Peyton didn't say anything, and that's when Parker started to get suspicious.

"Whatever it is you're thinking..." she quickly began.

"Just hear me out, Parks! Please!"

Now it was her turn to sigh.

Loudly.

"Fine," she said begrudgingly.

"Okay, there was a time when you had your own plan for a day spa and you had everything all worked out about what you wanted it to look like and all the furniture and equipment you would need. Maybe you could sit down with Ryder and talk him through it so he can move forward for now?"

"Oh." That wasn't what she was expecting. If anything, she figured her sister was going to offer her the job. "So...this is about consulting? That's it?"

"Exactly! He likes picking people's brains and learning about different aspects of all these businesses, so be prepared for him to ask like a million questions!" She let out a giddy laugh. "I'm sure you'll get frustrated with him just like I did, but it's kind of fun plotting out a business like this. Especially with someone else's money!"

"Peyton!" she cried out with a laugh of her own. "I can't believe you just said that!"

"Why? It's true! Trust me. The restaurant I planned with my own budget was nothing compared to what I was able to do with Ryder's help. But this situation with the spa would really just be for fun with you. You don't have to worry about anything other than offering some guidance and suggestions. Will you do it?"

"Sure, but...he's still going to need a manager."

"Definitely, but there will be plenty of time for that. They'll just have to deal with the fact that they don't get to put their personal stamp on the place."

"Yeah, but..."

"I guess down the road whoever he hires can make suggestions or changes if they don't like what you came up with, but at least by getting started like this, Ryder can keep moving forward with his plans."

Then something occurred to her. "I thought this resort was going to be a little more low-key and family friendly. Why put in a spa? Does he really believe the clientele will utilize it?"

"See? These are the kind of great questions you need to discuss with him. I felt the same way, but he believes it will be a great amenity to offer. It's not going to be a luxury kind of spa, but they will offer the basics like manicures, pedicures, and massages because...let's face it...everyone enjoys being pampered."

Parker made a non-committal sound because she didn't know how else to respond.

"So? Will you come for dinner one night and work with Ryder on this?"

"Um...sure. Why not?"

"Great! I really appreciate this and you have no idea

how much better I feel already. Maybe if we put out feelers for managers once the spa is already done, we'll find someone. It's possible the thought of taking on all the responsibility was what was holding them back."

"Maybe..."

"I just need to check both our calendars and figure out a good night to get together, but I'll text you, okay?"

"Sounds good!" They said their goodbyes and Parker tossed her phone on the sofa beside her and couldn't decide if she was excited or offended by the offer.

Honestly, she thought her sister was going to offer her the position of manager. It would have made sense, especially after her whole comment on her current work situation. There was a part of her that was expecting the job offers from her family to start up–especially from Peyton and Ryder. They had been full of suggestions when she stayed with them, but once she moved out, they stopped.

They were simply doing what I asked...

Yeah, she got that and appreciated it, but her sister never let anything go and she had a feeling Ryder was the same way, so...what gives? Didn't they think she was good enough to manage this spa? Even temporarily? So she was good enough to consult but not run it? What kind of crap was that?

Jumping up from her spot on the couch, Parker stormed over to the kitchen and began rummaging through the cabinets to find something to snack on. Whenever she was stressed, she turned to food–preferably cookies, ice cream, or popcorn.

"Hey, what's going on in here?" Ethan asked, walking into the room.

"I'm looking for something to eat," she murmured, slamming another cabinet shut. "Are we seriously out of cookies?

Didn't I bake a huge batch of chocolate chip ones just a few days ago?" She opened and slammed shut another cabinet before Ethan came over and placed his hand over hers, effectively stopping the madness.

"We finished those cookies last night while watching the movie, remember?" he gently reminded her. "I can go to the store and grab some if you really need them. They won't be as good as yours, but I'm sure they'll do in a pinch."

Parker felt all the steam go out of her as she turned to face him. "While I really want to say yes because...you know...cookies, I know I don't really need them. They're simply a coping device or a distraction or...whatever you want to call it."

He gave her a sympathetic look. "I take it your sister upset you somehow?"

Taking a step away from the cabinets, she paced the kitchen and repeated the conversation to him. "I mean...I thought she was going to offer me the job!"

Ethan studied her for a moment, crossing his arms and leaning casually against the kitchen counter. "Do you want the job?"

"Yes! I mean...no! I mean...." The growl of frustration was out before she could stop it. "That's not the point! I just don't understand why she wouldn't offer it to me! If I'm good enough to give advice on how to equip the spa, then why aren't I good enough to run it?"

Saying it out loud that time, it began to hit her just how crazy she sounded.

Without a word, he took her by the hand and led her back over to the couch and waited until they were both sitting before saying anything. "I know we haven't talked about this sort of thing and honestly, it's none of my business."

"But...?"

"But...what are you running from?" he asked.

Um...what?

That was literally the very last thing she thought he'd ask and it seemed to come completely out of the blue with the current topic of conversation.

"What do you mean? I'm not running from anything," she replied as she pulled her hand from his and almost cringed at how defensive she sounded.

"Parker, it seems to me like you're afraid to commit to anything," he said carefully. "You didn't want to commit to getting a degree or going to college. You traveled around for years doing odd jobs, you house-sit so you don't have the responsibility of a place of your own..."

"That's not true! I'm renting here, aren't I?" she countered, and knew it was a weak argument at best.

And the look on Ethan's face confirmed it.

He reached out and caressed her hand. "It's okay to take time to find yourself and figure out what it is that you want to do, but at some point you're going to have to put the effort into figuring it out."

And because she hated being called out like this, she did what she always did.

She lashed out.

"Oh, and what about you?" she challenged. "Did you dream of coming back to Magnolia and being a community college professor? Didn't you want more? Aren't you just settling?" Parker wanted her words to sting–to hurt–but when his expression went completely neutral and he slowly pulled his hand away, she had a feeling she'd really blown it.

"My dream was to teach at a bigger university, but my paralyzing fear of speaking in front of a large group pretty much kept me from even trying," he said quietly. "And then my dad got sick and I wanted to be here with him." After a long breath, he finished, "It was more important for me to be with him for the little time he had left than to chase after anything."

"Ethan, I..."

But he stood up without looking at her. "I've got papers to finish grading. Good night, Parker."

She sat there as unshed tears stung her eyes and when she heard the office door shut, she *knew* she'd blown it.

And had no idea how to fix it.

* * *

IT WASN'T LIKE him to hold a grudge, but three days after his conversation with Parker, he was.

It had been a long time since Ethan had even thought about how much he used to dream about teaching at a large university–someplace like Berkeley or Stanford. The reality was that he lacked the confidence to teach in a large classroom that could sometimes have up to a hundred students in a lecture hall. As it was, his class of thirty was a challenge. Still, once the topic came up, it reminded him of all his shortcomings and it really ticked him off.

Now he was mad at himself as well as Parker.

For her part, he had hardly seen her since. There were no more mock school lectures and certainly no more kissing, and it was crazy how much he missed both of those things.

Especially the kissing.

Those two weeks of foreplay were the sweetest form of torture. They both knew they were playing with fire, but it didn't seem to matter. It had taken everything he had not to scoop her up in his arms and take her to bed.

That would have seriously complicated things.

"Right. Like they're so much better now," he murmured.

Every night it had gotten more and more difficult to pull away and go to his room alone. Part of him wondered if Parker felt the same way, but the way she'd watch him and bite her lip told him she did. Then she'd remind him they were doing the right thing and he always agreed.

They were playing it safe.

And he was sick and tired of it.

He'd played it safe for his entire life–focusing on academics rather than sports because it was safe. He went to a mid-range college because it was safe. He took a teaching job at a local community college rather than even try to apply at a bigger university because it was safe.

Okay, that last one had some extenuating circumstances involved, but still...

Just once he wanted to be reckless–to take a chance and know that it was okay to fail because the real victory was in trying.

At least...he thought it was.

Glancing down at his laptop, he saw it was after ten. Raking his hands through his hair, he yawned. Something had to give. There was no way they could live like this. He knew it had only been a few days, but he was miserable and he was fairly certain that Parker was purposely staying away so she could avoid him.

She was paying to live here and, as such, she shouldn't have to stay away because he was home. One of them was going to have to make the first move and Ethan knew it would have to be him.

Reaching up, he took his glasses off and tossed them on his desk. Off in the distance, he heard the front door close.

She's home.

It was hard not to jump up and spring into action–that simply wasn't who he was–but if he allowed himself to sit and think any more about this, he knew nothing would get resolved.

Slowly he got to his feet and did his best to appear confident as he walked out of the office and...

Walked right into Parker.

"Oh!" she cried as she stumbled back, a pink box from Henderson's Bakery in her hands.

Ethan reached out to steady her. "Sorry! Are you okay?"

She smiled at him–a genuine smile–and held the box out to him. "Here. This is for you."

Taking the box from her hands, he eyed her warily. "Parker, you didn't have to..."

"Yes, I did," she quickly interrupted. "Just like the cookies, I know that getting snarky and lashing out are also defense mechanisms, so I knew I needed to do something to make it up to you. You were genuinely trying to help me and I shouldn't have attacked you like that. I'm sorry."

Could it really be this easy?

Looking down at the box in his hands, he gave it a gentle shake. "And this?"

"Well...I figured if you didn't want to accept my apology right away that I might be able to win you over with something from Henderson's. I don't know anyone who can stay mad when they're eating one of her brownies."

Those were definitely his favorite.

"I remembered you telling me how much you loved them," she went on before nodding toward the kitchen. "Come on. I'll pour us a couple of glasses of milk and you can tell me how your classes have been going." Without waiting for him, Parker turned and walked away. She had a sassy little swing in her hips and her dark hair was pulled back in a ponytail that also swayed as she walked. Her jeans were a little snug and she smelled almost as good as Mrs. Henderson's brownies.

Stop playing it safe...

Ethan followed her into the kitchen and placed the box down on the island. Parker was standing in front of the refrigerator with the door open and was about to reach for the milk when he stopped her.

"We don't have to have milk," she said to him. "I mean... it is the best drink to have with them, but if you want something else..."

"You," he said gruffly, and watched as her dark eyes went a little wide.

"What?" she whispered.

"I don't want brownies and I don't want anything to drink. I want you, Parker." This was the most forward he had ever been in his entire life and yet...it felt good; it felt right.

Powerful.

Stepping in close, he shut the refrigerator door before reaching up and cupping her face. "All day, every day, I think about you. You are always on my mind and these last few days have been damn near brutal."

Parker sighed his name before closing the distance between them. She looked up at him in wonder. "Really?"

He nodded. "Yeah, really."

"I've never...I mean, no one's ever..." She looked away and it didn't seem possible that no man had ever confessed to wanting her. But before he could ask, she explained. "I'm the friend. The buddy," she said with a slight tremble in her voice as she met his gaze once again. "Believe me, I'm not saying that I'm a virgin or anything like that, it's just..." She shrugged. "There was never anyone who looked at me the way you do or who makes me feel all the things you do."

It was beyond crazy how much that pleased him.

"How do I make you feel, Parker?" he murmured, lowering his head to hers.

"Desirable." Her voice was a mere breathless whisper. "No one's ever made me feel that way."

"That's good because that's exactly how you make me feel." The nervous part of him wanted to keep talking–telling her how he felt–because that was the safe route. He could reason and explain and take a more logical approach.

Stop playing it safe...

And for once, he pushed logic and safety aside and took what he wanted.

Ethan claimed her lips without any kind of warning and he was about to pull back and apologize when Parker literally wrapped herself around him. Her arms went around his shoulders as she kissed him back with equal desperation. They clumsily maneuvered away from the refrigerator and over to the island. He lifted her up until she was sitting on the granite and, as soon as she was settled, her legs wrapped around his waist.

All without breaking the kiss.

At that moment, Ethan knew he would never forget this moment–the passion, the promise, and the way she felt in his arms. It was so damn perfect.

Parker Bishop had been wreaking havoc on his thoughts and his overall sanity for weeks. She was bratty and a little socially awkward just like him, and yet she managed to pull it all off and wrapped it up in one utterly enticing package.

And tonight, she was his.

The kiss went on and on and on–much like they had almost every night for the last two weeks–and as much as he was enjoying it, he wanted to move them to his bedroom. With his arms banding around her, Ethan lifted her back up again at the same time Parker boosted herself up. The result was the two of them stumbling backwards until he crashed into the pantry door.

"*Oof...*"

The next thing he knew, Parker was on her feet, the kiss was broken and the two of them were laughing.

"Sorry," she said around a fit of laughter. "So much for my sexy moves, huh?"

"*Your* sexy moves?" he laughed. "I think my ego just took a huge hit! I nearly dropped you!"

That caused them to roll into another fit of laughter and Ethan feared the mood was broken and it was going to be another night full of longing and frustration and being alone in his bed. But just when he had resigned himself to it, Parker reached up and cupped his face and pulled him down for a kiss that was so wet and needy that it bordered on dirty. How she managed to go from laughing to this kind of sexiness was beyond him, but there was no way he was going to question it out loud. All he knew was that he was thankful that they were back on track.

No sooner had the thought crossed his mind, then Parker broke the kiss and took a step back.

"What...?"

Reaching for his hand, she gave him a seductive smile and led them slowly out of the kitchen, and then paused at the foot of the stairs. "Your room or mine?"

He didn't even have to think about it. "Mine."

That seemed to please her as she continued the path to his bedroom. It occurred to him that Parker was the first woman he was taking to bed in his own home.

And how it just felt right, like this was the way it was

supposed to be–that she was the woman he'd been waiting for.

Then he immediately pushed that thought aside because otherwise it would lead him down a rabbit hole about his feelings and if they were making a mistake by crossing this line and what it all meant. And right now, he didn't want to think; he wanted to feel.

He particularly wanted to feel every inch of Parker.

When they stopped next to the bed, they reached for each other in their hungriest kiss yet. Her hands raked through his hair as Ethan boldly reached up and cupped her breasts. She let out a throaty hum of approval and that was all the encouragement he required to continue his exploration.

Her curves had been driving him wild. Parker tended to dress casually and rarely wore anything that overly accentuated her figure, particularly at night when they were watching TV. There were flannel pajama pants, tank tops under hoodies, and so many pairs of fuzzy socks. But now that he was finally getting to feel her, he couldn't wait to peel her clothes off and see the amazing body underneath.

As if reading his mind, Parker pulled back slightly and kicked off her shoes before reaching for the button on her jeans. Ethan's hand immediately grasped her waist and he was torn between helping her or perhaps working on his own jeans.

The sound of her zipper seemed overly loud in the room and he tore his gaze from hers and watched as she shimmied out of her pants and kicked them aside before whipping her top up and over her head.

The sight of her standing breathlessly before him in nothing more than hot pink panties and a black bra practically staggered him. He had no idea where to look or touch first. Her breasts were larger than he imagined and he was helpless but to reach out for them first. The rest of her looked just as soft and sexy as he had fantasized. Whispering her name, Ethan lowered his head and kissed her through the lace of her bra. Parker's head slowly fell back as her hands came up and held him to her.

He had no idea how long they stayed like that, but eventually they moved until they tumbled onto his bed. His glasses were the first thing to go before he reached for the bottom of his shirt and pulled it up and off. Parker's hands were on his fly as she got up onto her knees to help him, and it was an incredibly erotic sight. As soon as his shirt was off, Ethan placed a hand over hers. "I've got this."

Her impish grin was back. "But I want to do it."

His grip tightened on her. "And I wanted to do the same to you but you beat me to it."

Parker crawled up and over him until she was straddling his lap. "I promise to let you do it the next time." She kissed him lightly on his jaw. "And any other time you want."

Now that was something he was going to hold her to.

He released her and let his hand skim up her arm, over her shoulder, up the slender column of her throat, before anchoring into her hair. "You may regret making that promise."

But she shook her head. "Never."

Damn.

And then they were kissing again and together, they got his pants off. Awkwardly, he reached down and got rid of his socks and then they were finally pressed together from head to toe with nothing but his boxers and her bra and panties between them. Ethan tried to calculate how long he'd need to wait before peeling them off of her, but somehow the math started to take over and he had to stop himself.

Right now, Parker was kissing his chest and making sexy little sounds, and that was where his focus needed to be. Her tongue was making him shake with need and if he let her keep going like this, things were going to be over before they ever had a chance to begin.

So, in his boldest move yet, he quickly took control and flipped her over onto her back as he stretched out on top of her. "Now," he murmured.

Her eyes went wide. "Now?"

He nodded as he began to slowly peel her bra strap down over her shoulder. "Yeah. Now. You said I could do this any time I want to." Pausing, Ethan repeated the move on the other strap. "I wanted to do it now because I want to see and touch and kiss all of you, Parker." With another pause, he gave her what he hoped was a heated look. "All of you."

The soft gasp was her only response.

Until she arched her back so he could unhook her bra.

Once he tossed the flimsy garment to the floor, words escaped him. Hell, for a moment he was too in awe of her to even move or breathe.

But then he did.

One soft kiss on her jaw led down to her shoulder and then her breasts. Ethan knew he could spend hours kissing them, but there was so much more of her to explore.

And he had all night to do it.

SEVEN

"Anytime you want to serve me brownies in bed while wearing boxer briefs, I'm just saying that I'm completely on board."

Ethan blushed before crawling back into bed beside her.

Parker thought it was adorably sexy how he responded to her–especially after all the things they'd just done together. It was the sexiest, most passionate night of her entire life and it was wrapping up with brownies!

Could life get any better?

For several minutes, neither spoke as they fed each other pieces of gooey brownies and then shared a glass of milk. When they were done and everything was put on the bedside table, that's when her insecurities set in.

Was she supposed to stay with him all night or go up to her own room? The last thing she wanted to do was assume and then have things get awkward again between them.

"So..." she began and slowly moved away from him, sitting up straighter and kicking one leg out from under the blankets.

"Where are you going?"

"Um..."

As if reading her mind–they were really getting in sync with each other–Ethan reached out and stopped her. "You're not leaving, are you?"

Carefully, she clutched the blankets to her chest before looking at him. "I wasn't sure if you wanted me to. I mean... some people prefer sleeping alone and I don't know if you do, but..."

"Do you?"

"Do I what?"

"Prefer sleeping alone?"

It was a legitimate question and yet it was one she didn't really have an answer to because she'd always slept alone. She'd never spent an entire night with someone else in her bed.

Well...except for her sister. Whenever Parker came back to Magnolia for a visit, they would have sleepovers and stay up all night talking, and it was just easier to share the bed.

But she'd never had the opportunity to with a man.

"Parker?"

Oh, right. He'd asked her a question.

With a small huff, she blurted out everything.

Probably more than she should have.

"Okay, here's the thing," she began. "I honestly don't know if I prefer sleeping alone or not because no one's ever spent the whole night with me. No one's ever asked." She paused when he started to ask the obvious question, but she cut him off. "Obviously I've had sex before, but...either they got up and left or I was asked to leave because they didn't like sleeping with someone. So...yeah."

"Parker, I..."

And for some bizarre reason, she just kept going.

"And there's something else you should know," she went on quickly. "This person that you see? The person that everyone thinks they know? It's not me!"

"Parker, we've been over this..."

"I'm a big fat fraud, Ethan! With my family, I put on this whole outgoing, adventurous kind of persona, but you know what? That is the furthest thing from who I am! I did love traveling and seeing new places, but you know what I would do every night? I'd curl up with a book in my hotel room. Alone! After being 'on' all day, I'd need to go and decompress by myself. So while everyone thought I was flitting around partying all over the place, the truth was...I was seeing the sites and then counting down the minutes until I could be alone."

He studied her for a long moment. "So then...you want to leave?"

"What? No! That's not what I'm saying!"

"Actually, that's exactly what you're saying, and it's okay," he said gently. "The last thing I want is for you to feel pressured to sleep in my bed when you'd rather be upstairs in yours."

Ugh...this wasn't going the way she'd planned.

Twisting in her spot, she faced him head-on. "I guess I'm not very good at explaining myself because...I want to stay here with you. I seriously do. I just...it's important for me that you want me here because of me–the real me and not the woman everyone thinks I am."

Ethan reached out and gently guided her so they were relaxed against the pillows and her head was on his shoulder. "Believe it or not, Parker, I *can* see the real you." He let out a soft laugh before adding, "And not just because you keep trying to explain that side of yourself to me."

"Really?"

He nodded. "There's a part of me that really likes how I'm the one person you're showing that side to."

She hated how Tyler's face flashed in her mind for the barest of moments.

He'd known the real her and look how that went.

"I wish you'd let other people get to know you so you could be comfortable with them and stop the charade," he was saying. "This woman right here in my arms? I think she's far more impressive than the woman you've been presenting to the world. This woman here is amazing and caring and funny and sexy." He placed a soft kiss on top of her head. "But more than anything, this woman deserves to be seen."

As much as his words warmed her, they also made her bristle a bit.

Slowly, Parker ran her hand over his chest. "I appreciate you saying that."

"But...?"

She couldn't help but smile. "But...this all sounds so much like every conversation I've had with my family and I don't..."

Ethan didn't let her finish. "Say no more. I promise I won't mention this again."

Oddly enough, she instantly relaxed. "Thank you. What we have...me and you...I really like it and I don't want this to turn into the kind of relationship where you feel like you have to save me or help me or fix me. Does that make sense?"

He nodded again. "I do. And I want you to know that I get it even though I have really appreciated the way that you've been helping me with my teaching. So...just know that I'd really like us to continue with that little endeavor."

Smiling, she placed a soft kiss on his chest. "You got it." Looking up at him, she admired how tousled and sexy he looked. Bed head looked good on him. "Which brings us back to my earlier question in the kitchen, how have your classes been going this week?"

For the next few minutes, Ethan talked about all the little changes he'd been making in his teaching style and how he was seeing some positive results. She heard it in his voice and saw it on his face how happy he was and it made her really glad that she was able to do that for him.

And then couldn't help but wonder if maybe she was wrong not to ask him for the same kind of help. Coming from Ethan it wouldn't be the same kind of thing as she got from her family. It would be coming from a genuine place with him, whereas with her family, she felt like it was a lot of pressure because she was simply part of the Coleman-slash-Bishop gene pool and she was making them all look bad.

"What book are you currently reading?" he asked, snapping her out of her reverie.

"Um...what?"

"You said you enjoy reading, so I was curious if you were reading anything right now."

"Oh." She had to think for a moment because the question sort of took her by surprise. "It's kind of a women's fiction story but also a romance."

"Yeah, I don't know what that means," he said with a small laugh.

"Okay, so the book is about four lifelong friends who model every Friday night in a bridal fashion show," she explained. "And even though the book primarily deals with their friendship, each of the girls has a romantic subplot—like one is engaged to her elementary school sweetheart and now she's wondering if she's missed out on too much by only being with him. Another has the worst luck with guys to the point that when she meets a great one, she doesn't know what to do. One of the others has been crushing on one of the male models and then finds out he's gay, and the last one is kind of the badass of the group and had a fling with a guy who sort of ghosted her and now wants a second chance."

"Wow. That's...a lot."

"I know, but I'm enjoying that there's so much going on. I'm halfway done and I'm dying to know how everyone's love lives work out!"

"So, is that your genre of choice? Women's fiction?"

Parker shrugged. "I'm a slow reader and so when I find a book that interests me, it takes me a while to get through it. I don't think I have a genre of choice, though. I've also read all the Harry Potter books and all the Narnia ones, The Baby-sitters Club, and I love all the old Agatha Christie books. It all depends on my moods." Shifting, she snuggled a little closer and let their legs tangle together. "What about you? What do you like to read?"

"I tend to read a lot of textbooks for research or science journals. It's not exciting to the average reader, but I enjoy them."

"Nothing wrong with that. You shouldn't read to please other people."

"I agree, but most people I tell that to look at me like I'm weird."

She had an overwhelming urge to hug him, so she did. "I don't think you're weird. I think you're pretty damn awesome."

"You don't have to say that..."

"And I'm not just saying it because we're all tangled up

and naked, Ethan. It's true," she countered as she smiled up at him. "And I kind of like how we can be this quiet and semi-dorky couple together." His expression instantly changed and Parker realized how her words sounded. "I mean..."

His finger on her lips stopped her words. "I kind of like that idea too," he told her. "But...I guess we do need to address the fact that we just changed the dynamics of our living situation."

The sigh was out before she could stop it. "Yeah. I know..."

"Are you regretting it?" One strong hand cupped her cheek, gently forcing her to keep looking at him. Parker could see the uncertainty in his face, hear it in his voice.

"No. No, I don't regret it," she replied confidently. "Do you?"

He shook his head. "Not at all. I just don't know what happens from here. I mean...things could get awkward. What if...?"

She was so tired of the what ifs of life and this time she was the one to place a finger over his lips. "There are no guarantees in life, Ethan. I say for now we just take things slow and see what happens. Can you do that?"

"For you?" he said gruffly, slowly rolling her over until she was stretched out beneath him. "I think I can."

Then he was kissing her and all conversation was officially over.

* * *

"YOUR ASSIGNMENT for the week is to take your telescope out every night and report back to us during the next class what you saw," Ethan said to a stunned group of students. Hands instantly went up.

"Do we need to write up a report on it?" someone asked. "No."

"Will we be doing a presentation?" another asked.

He shook his head. "No."

"Should we document it with photos so we can prove what we saw?"

Ethan grinned up at his class. "All you need to do is go out and quietly observe the night sky. There are no meteor showers or anything particularly exciting going on. I just want you to take some of what we've been talking about and see it for yourself so we can talk about it before we move on to our next subject." He closed his laptop. "Class dismissed."

It was becoming the norm for there to be more chatter and conversation as his students walked out of the class-room and lately most of them had actually paused to talk with him or simply wish him a good day.

And it did amazing things for his self-esteem and overall spirits. It was the first time in his teaching career that Ethan was feeling confident and enjoying what he was doing.

Thanks to Parker.

It had been a week since they'd first slept together and he honestly didn't think his life could get any better. Every day he went home filled with anticipation for the night to come. So much of their lives hadn't really changed–they still ate dinner together and watched TV afterwards–but where they'd usually go to bed in their own separate spaces, they now went together. He was getting a lot less sleep, and yet he'd never felt more alive and energized.

His career was going well, his personal life was going well, and he had the most amazing woman in the world sleeping beside him every night. It would be easy to say things were perfect, but he hated the thought of jinxing anything.

Today he didn't have office hours but he wasn't going straight home. Parker was volunteering at Happy Tails today and then was going to have dinner with her sister tonight to discuss the whole day spa situation. Ethan listened to her talk about it all week and did what he could to encourage her to ask Ryder why he wasn't offering her the management position. She'd waffled back and forth on it and even as of this morning he had no idea what she was going to do. His plan was to stop and see her and wish her luck in whatever she decided.

As he drove up the long driveway to the animal rescue, he wondered if maybe he should have just called or texted instead. It wasn't like they were hiding their relationship, but they also hadn't gone anywhere or hung out with anyone they knew either. Maybe she wouldn't want him randomly showing up and surprising her.

"Too late now," he murmured as he parked his car. There were several buildings plus a house on the property and he realized he had no idea where to even begin to find Parker. For some reason, he just figured there'd be one place and she'd be easy to spot. As he climbed from the car, he shook his head. "I don't think I've ever been more wrong."

A woman who looked to be around his age spotted him and came walking over with a smile. "Hey! Can I help you?"

"Uh...I'm looking for Parker Bishop?" he said hesitantly.

"Oh my goodness! Are you Ethan?"

"Um..."

Her smile grew. "Hi, I'm Emma! My folks own this place and I'm engaged to Parker's cousin, Garrett. Come on! Parker's over in the old barn wrangling up some of the pups!"

"Thanks." He followed her and couldn't help but marvel at how the property was like a kind of dog utopia. There were wide open spaces and it looked like small jungle gyms for them to play on. There were balls all over the place and even now there were about six dogs playfully chasing each other around. "How long have your parents owned this?"

Emma smiled as she kept walking. "It feels like most of my life. We've grown a lot–particularly in the last five years. Parker's mom really did a lot for us in terms of raising awareness and funds. We were able to expand and get more equipment and donations. I love that Parker's here helping out too. It's nice when it becomes a family affair."

Ethan didn't know a lot about Parker's parents, but the little that he did know wasn't great. It seemed odd that her mother would put her time and energy into a place like this.

Chuckling, Emma stopped and faced him. "I can tell by the look on your face that you're a little confused."

"Well...Parker doesn't talk a lot about her parents, but from what she's said, this just doesn't look like it fits."

"Oh, I agree and there are times when I still can't believe it, but..." She paused. "Have you ever met Georgia?"

He shook his head.

"She's a bit like the stereotypical socialite–well-groomed and snooty. But when she comes here and sees all the dogs, she turns into a completely different person. It's really fun to watch." She glanced toward the barn and then back to Ethan. "Between you and me, I think this could be a good thing for Georgia and Parker."

"In what way?"

"It's something they have in common and can bond

over. They haven't been here at the same time yet, but I'm hoping it will happen soon."

"Emma! Garrett's on the phone for you! Did you forget your cell?" someone called out.

She laughed and looked a little embarrassed. "You'll have to excuse me. I think I left my phone in the office. You can find Parker through those double doors right there." And with a small wave, she jogged off toward the house.

There were several people walking around and there were dogs everywhere, but when Ethan entered the barn, he found his girl sitting in the corner with one lone dog. The closer he got, the more he could hear her talking soothingly.

"You're a good boy," she was saying. "Those other dogs just don't know you yet. Give them a couple of days and I bet you'll be best friends." When she spotted him, Parker smiled. "Hey! What are you doing here?"

He knelt down beside her and watched the Shepherd puppy for a moment before slowly reaching out and letting him sniff his hand. "Who's this little guy?"

"This is Ollie. Well...Oliver," she corrected. "He's new here today and hasn't made any friends yet."

"I get that," Ethan replied and grinned when Ollie turned to face him. "It will get better, buddy. I promise."

Parker leaned over and kissed him on the cheek. "I felt so bad for him. He's never been around other dogs and when he didn't join the fray, they all sort of snubbed him." She scratched Ollie's ear. "Poor boy. If I could, I'd take him home."

"Parker..."

But she was already holding up her hand to stop him. "I know, I know. I remember the flyer. No pets."

There was that, but it wasn't what he was about to say.

"Actually, I was going to say it probably wouldn't be the smart thing to do because if you took home every dog you felt sorry for, you'd need a farm just like this."

Giggling, Parker shook her head. "I guess I never thought of it like that." She rested her head on top of Ollie's. "Still...someday I'd really like to have a dog of my own. All this time I've been living in other people's homes and I knew it wasn't possible, but maybe there will come a time when the place will be mine and I can." She shrugged. "Maybe."

It was the first time she ever mentioned a place of her own and Ethan knew it was a good thing, but there was a small part of him that immediately hated the thought of there coming a time when she wasn't living with him.

"So...you never said why you stopped by," Parker said casually.

"Oh, well...as of this morning you still seemed like you were on the fence with what you were going to say to Ryder and Peyton tonight and I wanted to just stop by and say good luck with whatever it is that you do."

Her whole expression softened as she stood up and extended her hand to him. "You are the sweetest man in the whole damn world." And she rewarded him by kissing him senseless. Several minutes later when they were both a little breathless, she grinned up at him. "And when I get home later, I am going to show you just how amazing I think you are."

It was on the tip of his tongue to tell her she didn't need to do that, but...he was just a guy and Parker was an incredibly sexy woman. There was no way he would be able to resist her.

And he didn't want to.

"Thank you," she said after a moment.

"For what?"

"For not pushing me to make a decision. I honestly still don't know what I'm going to say when I get to Peyton's, but I'm kind of known for flying by the seat of my pants, so..."

"You'll know what to do when the time is right. I have faith in you."

She let out a low snort. "At least someone does."

"Parker..."

She silenced him with a kiss.

"What are you going to do for dinner?" she asked after leaving him a little dazed.

"I'm going to go to Michael's and order a pizza. I was going to do a little grocery shopping and use the grill, but yesterday I noticed there were some loose boards on the deck. I was going to do a little research and see how hard it would be to fix. In the meantime, I thought it would be best to not be out there standing on it."

"Ethan, I greatly doubt you were going to fall through the deck," she commented with amusement. "But just in case, why don't I talk to my cousin Mallory's husband, Jake? He owns a construction business. Maybe he can come over and look at it."

"I don't think I need a construction company..."

"Or...maybe we can invite some of my cousins over sometime and then casually mention the deck problem? Two birds, one stone."

"How is it two birds? I didn't know you wanted to invite any of your relatives over." She'd never mentioned it before and he knew she had a rather large extended family...

She shrugged again. "I've been thinking about it, but I didn't want to push since...you know...it's not my house."

He did his best to keep his expression neutral and

mimicked her shrug. "Sure. You pick the date and we'll make it work."

Her dark eyes went wide. "Really?"

"Yeah, really."

The next thing he knew, he had his arms full of Parker and she was kissing him again. This time when they broke apart, her smile was radiant. "Now I am definitely going to show you how amazing you are later!" Beside them, Ollie let out a low whimper and she immediately dropped to her knees. "Come on, Ollie. Let's go for a little walk. How does that sound?" When she glanced up at Ethan, her smile turned slightly apologetic. "Sorry, but I need to help this little guy. I'll text you when I'm on my way home later."

"Sounds good." They kissed one more time and he watched her and the dog walk out of the barn.

He should have simply followed them out and made his way back to his car, but he was enjoying watching her and Ollie as they made their way across the small field. Ethan knew she was offering more words of encouragement to the dog, and the farther they went, the more the little guy seemed to relax.

The scenario was oddly familiar.

His thoughts went to Parker's request and part of him was a little apprehensive about it, while the other part of him knew how important this was to her. She'd been a bit of an outsider in her family for years and now that she was back, she was looking to be the host rather than the guest. There was also the possibility that she was looking to show everyone that she was getting her life together. And as much as Ethan wasn't big on hosting big family gatherings– mostly because he had no idea how to do that since he didn't have a large family–he also knew he'd do this for her.

Even if she didn't want him there as part of it.

Of course she'll want you there. Why wouldn't she?

Good question.

And something else they'd have to discuss.

But that was later. He had a feeling a lot was riding on this dinner she was going to tonight and its outcome. Ethan wasn't fooled for a minute. Parker was running and hiding and she'd been doing it for so long he knew she wasn't even aware of it anymore. There wasn't a doubt in his mind that she desperately wanted to run that spa, but old insecurities were going to be a huge stumbling block for her. He wished there were a way he could show her that she had nothing to be insecure about. There was nothing she couldn't do.

"Maybe I should practice what I preach," he murmured before walking out of the barn.

The difference was that he wasn't in the same position as she was. He had his job and was working on being better at it. He loved being a teacher and knew that with a little work, he'd be great at it. Parker needed to find that spark–that job or career that she was passionate about–and make it hers.

Maybe tonight would be a turning point.

But it could also be the first step in losing her.

And he wasn't sure how he was supposed to cheer her on in that scenario.

EIGHT

Her palms were so sweaty that she dropped the knife for the third time.

"Parks, what's going on? Are you okay?"

They were standing in her sister's fabulous kitchen, in the house she and Ryder lived in that was right on the beach, putting the finishing touches on dinner. Normally Parker loved helping her sister cook, but tonight she was all thumbs.

"I'm fine. I guess my mind is just wandering."

Beside her, Peyton laughed softly. "Well stop that or you'll end up slicing your hand open and you know how much you hate the sight of blood. Especially your own."

That was true. Letting out a small breath, Parker put the knife down on the cutting board and faced her sister. "Okay, I was going to wait until a little later but I think for my own safety and sanity, I need to say it now."

"Um...alright. What's on your mind?"

It was now or never.

"Why didn't you offer the position of spa manager to me?" she blurted out. "Why am I good enough to consult on equipment and furniture and all that crap, but not good enough to hire, huh?"

To her credit, Peyton merely smiled and picked up the platter with their chicken francaise on it and walked over and placed it on the kitchen table. Then she came back for the salad and again for their side dishes–without saying a word.

Then Ryder strode in and offered to pour the wine.

He immediately noticed something was wrong. "What's going on? Why are neither of you talking?"

"My sister wants to know why you didn't offer her the spa manager position," Peyton casually replied. "Would you like to answer or should I?"

With a serene smile, Ryder began pouring the wine. "You go ahead. I'll chime in if you need me."

Oh, good grief...

It wasn't until they were sitting at the table that Peyton responded. "You weren't offered the position because you made it abundantly clear when you were staying with us that you thought we were overbearing and constantly trying to push our own agenda on you." She reached for one of the serving bowls. "Would you like some rice?"

Parker took the bowl and immediately put it down. "You *were* overbearing," she agreed. "You wouldn't give me a second to catch my breath before you were incessantly throwing out job suggestions! I mean...all I wanted was a few days to catch my breath and figure things out but you never let up!"

This time Peyton handed her the salad. "I thought it would be better for you to be busy instead of sitting around and wallowing in self-pity." She shrugged. "But after you moved out, Ryder and I talked about it and I realized you were right. We came on too strong and you're not like us. It takes you a lot longer than us to make a decision so...we left you alone."

"Are you done with the rice, Parker?" Ryder asked.

"Um...sure." She quickly served herself before passing the food over to him. "So...because two months ago I didn't take your suggestions, you're never going to offer me a job again? Is that what you're saying?"

Peyton began to talk but Ryder interrupted. "If I may...?"

"Go ahead," Peyton said as she served the chicken.

His expression went from relaxed and casual to a bit stiffer and more businesslike, and Parker did not take it as a good sign.

"I think the world of you, Parker," he began. "But what I've observed over the last year or so is that you're someone who doesn't take things particularly seriously. You flit around from place to place, not wanting to commit to any one thing, and that's not the kind of person I want running the spa. I need someone who is going to give me one hundred percent of their time and energy and who is committed to making the business a success." He paused and took a sip of his wine. "In theory, I'd love to see you take it on, but...you're basically a flight risk."

For a minute, she was too stunned to speak.

No one–other than Tyler–had ever called her out like this. Sure, they probably all thought it, but no one had ever said it to her face. And the fact that it was Ryder stung a little more than she thought it would.

Gently, she cleared her throat. "Um...wow. I don't even know what to say." Glancing over at her sister, she saw that Peyton's attention was fully on her dinner.

Traitor.

"I realize you were going through a rough time," Ryder

went on, "but by taking off the way you did just shows that maybe you're not ready for this kind of responsibility. I'm sorry. Maybe I'm being a little too blunt, but..."

"No," she said almost a little too quickly. "No. I get it and...you're right. Clearly I'm not mature enough to handle managing a resort spa."

"Parker..." Peyton softly warned.

"What? I'm simply agreeing with Ryder." She forced a smile. "I appreciate his honesty and for being willing to say what needed to be said." The need to flee was strong, but she forced herself to stay in her seat and take a bite of her dinner.

Parker continued, "Well, with that all out of the way, I'd still like to offer whatever insight I can into the kind of equipment you might want to invest in."

* * *

NEVER HAD a meal dragged on like it had tonight and by the time they'd had dessert and Parker answered all of Ryder's questions, she was ready to scream.

And she did exactly that in her car when she was a block away from their house.

She was trembling and finally allowed herself to feel all the rage and frustration she'd been holding in all night and the thing was, she wasn't really mad at her sister and Ryder.

Okay, she was a little mad at them.

Mostly, she was mad at herself.

Her life was a disaster of her own making and she feared she was so far gone that she'd never get it straightened out. "C'mon, Parker," she muttered. "It's time to get your shit together!"

It wasn't like a particularly strong "Aha!" moment, but it

was enough to give herself the nudge to get off the fence and quit waffling on what it was she wanted to do.

She wanted some direction in her life.

She wanted a career she loved.

She wanted the respect of her family.

As she drove down Main Street and passed all the businesses that were owned by people she knew and loved, it felt overwhelming. It wasn't just the businesses owned by her family–although they did own a lot of them–it was places like Henderson's and The Sand Bar. These were places that were in Magnolia Sound for as long as Parker had been alive and they were still going strong; their owners were still there with smiles on their faces every time she walked in. How was it possible? How did they know this was going to be their thing?

A little part of her envied the fact that her great-grandfather had pretty much given her cousins and siblings the businesses they were meant to own. Mallory got the décor shop, Sam got the landscaping company, Jake got the construction company, Peyton got the café, and Mason got the restaurant.

Mason's inheritance wasn't what he was meant to do, per se, but it enabled him to do something that benefitted the community and his wife's family.

And what did Parker get? Freedom. Well...money to travel, which was essentially the same thing, but what was she supposed to do once that part of her life was done?

That's when inspiration struck. Her great-grandfather was so wise and so amazing and there was one person who was with him when he was figuring all this stuff out–his attorney.

Parker had no idea if Mr. McClellan was even still alive, but she was definitely going to pay him a visit.

Soon.

In the meantime, there was one more thing that she really wanted. And as she pulled up to Ethan's house, she knew it was the one thing she could have right away.

Ethan.

Over the years she'd dated enough guys and been in enough relationships to know she'd never been as compatible with anyone as she was with him.

And she'd never had as much sex before, either.

Which was pretty freaking glorious.

Right now, she needed the kind of release and freedom and connection that only he could give her.

Her phone vibrated with an incoming text and she frowned when she saw it was from her sister.

Peyton: Hey. Just wanted to make sure you're okay. I know what Ryder said wasn't what you wanted to hear, but it was meant with the best of intentions. I love you and hope you're not mad.

Ugh...

If she didn't reply, Peyton would just keep texting and harassing her until she did.

Parker: We're good. I swear. I'm just glad we got it cleared up and I was able to help. I'll call you tomorrow. Love you!

Climbing from the car, she walked with a sense of purpose to the house. Once she stepped inside, she spotted Ethan walking around, talking on his phone. He took one look at her and seemed to know something was up.

"Listen, Mom, I need to go. I'll talk to you soon," he said before saying goodbye. He placed his phone down on the kitchen island but didn't make a move toward her. "Do you want to talk about it?"

Parker shook her head and tossed her purse on the sofa on her way over to him. "I do not."

He got that heated look in his eyes that she loved so much. His hair was a bit messy–as if he'd been raking his hands through it–and even his glasses were a bit askew. And yet he still turned her on.

When they were toe to toe, she reached up and gently pulled his glasses off, placing them on the island next to his phone. Her hands skimmed his stubbled jaw before running them through his hair.

"Something I can help you with?" he asked gruffly. He hadn't touched her yet–not physically–but the way he was watching her was almost as potent.

"As a matter of fact, you can," she whispered.

"I'm all ears."

The heat pouring off of him pulled her in until Parker simply wrapped herself around him. "I want you to come upstairs with me and let me have my way with you."

He arched one dark brow at her–probably because up until now they'd been spending their nights in his room. Tonight, however, she needed things to be on her own turf, even if it was just up the stairs.

"I'm all yours," he whispered, and Parker stepped back and took him by the hand and led him up to her room.

And then said a prayer of thanks that it was clean.

At her bed, she gently pushed Ethan down onto the mattress before crawling up and over him. Together they got him undressed before Parker stripped herself down. Her hands wandered of their own accord and she loved hearing his hiss of breath and feeling him jump when she did something she knew he really enjoyed. There was power in this— power that she desperately needed tonight. And as she touched and licked and kissed just about every inch of him, she realized how much this man was coming to mean to her. He wasn't just her roommate or her lover; he was her friend and possibly the only real friend she had right now.

Ethan's hand gripped her hair and gave a gentle tug, getting her attention. He was breathless and there was a fine sheen of sweat on him and she'd never wanted him more. The look on his face told her he was right on the edge with her and, as much as she would have loved to continue to dominate for a little longer, she loved the way it felt when he took control.

In her mind, she still had the power.

She was simply letting him temporarily take the lead.

Leaning in close, she nibbled her way up his jaw. "Take me, Ethan. Take me now."

And he did.

* * *

ETHAN HAD ALWAYS HAD an inquisitive nature. It was one of the things he loved most about teaching. In his personal life, however, he knew there was a time and a place to voice his questions or concerns.

Naked and breathless in Parker's bed did not seem like the proper setting for him to say anything except "thank you," and yet...

"I'm not sure if all this meant things went really good tonight or really bad..."

At first, she didn't respond. She merely moved closer until it was hard to tell where he ended and she began.

And that was pretty much his answer.

Things hadn't gone well.

They lay in total silence for several long moments, and as curious as he was, Ethan mentally cursed himself for potentially ruining the moment. She had blown his mind with her little seduction tonight, so why did he have to open his mouth and ask the least sexy thing in the world?

"Sorry I interrupted your conversation with your mom," she said quietly.

Okay...change of subject, he thought. "It's okay. We were almost done anyway."

"You don't talk about her much. Does she live here in Magnolia?"

He shook his head. "No. She and my dad divorced ten years ago and then she moved to Arizona. That's where she met Alan. Two years ago, they got married and moved to Palm Springs. At the time, my dad's health was really declining and she wanted me there and...I just couldn't be in two places at once. Things got tense after that. She was upset that I wouldn't come for the wedding and I was ticked because she was putting so much guilt on me..." Pausing, he placed a soft kiss on the top of Parker's head. "Now we only talk about once a month and...I don't know...things are still just weird."

"I'm sure she understood," Parker reasoned. "But the timing just sucked."

"She hasn't extended a specific invitation to come and visit since and now I feel like if she did–no matter the reason–I'd need to go."

"It's never a bad thing to check in and visit once in a while. Even though my mom always makes me crazy, I still came home occasionally. And it usually came with a heaping spoonful of pressure to move back." She rolled her eyes. "Be thankful you don't have to deal with that kind of pressure."

"Well...I kind of am. Now she's pushing for me to leave Magnolia since there's no one else here in our family and move closer to her. She claims there are plenty of teaching jobs and believes I'd be happier there."

"Do you think you would?"

Good question.

Shrugging, he replied, "I'm not sure. I never saw myself living in a big city. Magnolia's always been home and maybe there's a certain safety to living here, but...whenever she talks about it, it doesn't excite me at all. Besides, I just bought this house. This is my home now."

Parker lifted her head and looked at him. "So you've never lived anywhere else or traveled?"

"I never said that. I lived away for four years when I went to college up in Massachusetts and when I was growing up, we traveled a lot. Both my parents were teachers so we tended to do a lot of educational family vacations. I've been to all the national parks and monuments. Sometimes we drove, sometimes we flew, but I can honestly say I've seen most of this country and there's still no place like Magnolia to me." He shrugged again. "I know that sounds weird, but..."

"It doesn't," she said quietly. "When my great-grandfather passed away, he left me money to travel. Everyone else got businesses or local property, but he knew how much I wanted to travel. So, I backpacked around Europe, saw a bunch of places around the U.S., and took a ton of weekend trips." She paused and squirmed against him until she got comfortable. "We traveled a lot when I was growing up, but it was never particularly fun or adventurous. My parents weren't like that. We did cruises and a lot of structured itineraries and tours, and it used to frustrate me to no end. So getting the opportunity to travel on my own terms was like the greatest gift ever."

And because he knew her, he prompted, "But...?"

"But," she repeated with a small laugh. "But it got old fast. Some trips I went on alone and some Tyler went with me or another friend, but...I'd always come home and feel like...well that was great, but now what?"

In his mind, he knew what she was trying to say–it didn't fulfill her like she thought it would. He just wasn't sure where she was going with this story.

"Do you wish he would have given you something else?"

"Up until tonight, no. But after leaving Peyton and Ryder's I started to wonder if Pops maybe had something else in mind for me. He seemed to really know the right fit for everyone else." Then she sighed. "Or maybe he did this because there was nothing else for me."

Ethan hugged her close. "I'm sure that's not it. It sounds like he knew what you wanted and needed more than anything."

"An escape route?" she asked with a nervous laugh.

"Is that how you saw it?"

"At the time, definitely. It was a way to get away from my parents and it was like I finally had an excuse to go." There was another small laugh before she continued. "They were furious when I put off going to college and decided to take a gap year and then were positively livid when I dropped out after one semester once I started."

"College isn't for everyone," he reasoned, which went against everything in him as a teacher. He was a firm believer in education, but he was also a realist who knew some people just didn't do well in a classroom environment.

"Everyone kept saying I needed to find myself, but...I honestly don't think I was looking."

Okay, that was...telling.

"Parker, what happened tonight?" he finally asked because he had to know.

"Essentially, Ryder said I wasn't reliable enough to manage a business for him. That I was immature and a flight risk."

"Damn. That was brutal."

"And he was one hundred percent right," she said, surprising him.

"So what does this all mean?"

She went quiet for a minute.

And then another.

When she finally spoke, Ethan wasn't sure what to expect.

"It means I have a lot of thinking to do." Then she raised up and looked down at him as if they hadn't been talking about some pretty deep stuff just a moment ago. "But I'm done thinking for tonight. For the rest of the night, I want to enjoy being with you and making sure I don't think about anything other than feeling good. How does that sound?"

Almost too good to be true...

And a little unhealthy.

But he'd worry about that another day. For tonight, he was more than willing to give her exactly what she wanted and he started by slowly rolling her onto her back and kissing his way down her body. Parker sighed his name and gently scratched her nails along his scalp.

She was warm and soft and even though he knew they should both be exhausted, he did everything he could to clear her mind and give her every kind of pleasure until neither of them could keep their eyes open.

* * *

IT WAS rare that Ethan went looking for trouble, but somehow that was exactly what he was doing.

On multiple levels.

Something about Parker's admission the other night really spoke to him and he couldn't help but wonder about the choices he'd made with his life. Though it was difficult, he was able to compartmentalize some things and put the part of him that was involved with Parker aside while he examined the rest of his existence.

He wasn't lying when he said how much he loved living in Magnolia and, thanks to her, he was finally feeling a lot more at ease teaching. And that led him to the argument that had pretty much started everything for them: was teaching at a community college his dream?

In a nutshell, no.

It was comfortable, and it was perfectly fine and afforded him to live a decent–if not boring–life. But what if he could teach someplace else? A bigger university here in North Carolina or...elsewhere? Shouldn't he at least try? He wasn't the same man he was five years ago or even a few months ago. He was finding himself and doing things that helped the way he taught–a lot of the obstacles that held him back from applying at those larger universities really weren't there anymore.

At least...he didn't think they were.

But what if he tried and it meant leaving Magnolia? What if that was the trade-off? Would he still want it?

That was the million-dollar question.

Unfortunately, now that it was out there, he couldn't seem to stop thinking about it.

And that's when all the walls in his compartments seemed to come crashing down.

Did he want to leave Magnolia now that he'd found Parker? Where were they going? Was this relationship serious or casual? Were they merely friends with benefits? If he moved, would Parker come with him? But if he stayed, would he only be staying for her?

"Ugh...my brain hurts," he murmured while sitting in his office at the college.

He'd lost count of the number of times he scanned employment sites and looked at which colleges had openings. Then he'd looked at real estate listings near any of the hiring universities.

But he wasn't the only one who seemed to be doing a little searching. When he came home yesterday, he found Parker looking at local real estate ads, specifically commercial buildings. As soon as she spotted him, she slammed her laptop shut, but he was definitely curious about what she was looking for.

A knock at the door had him turning and seeing one of his students–Marshall Jenkins–standing there. "Hey, Marshall. What can I do for you?"

"I was wondering if I could talk to you about our next unit? You mentioned we'll be studying physics and I'm curious if maybe I'm in over my head. Physics was my worst subject in high school."

"Come on in and have a seat and we'll talk about it." He motioned for Marshall to join him and it was one of those moments that Ethan knew he'd always remember because it was the first time a student had actively sought him out like this. Clearly the changes he was making in his teaching style were working. So he got comfortable and smiled. "So, tell me about your experience with physics."

And for the next hour, Ethan listened and then laid out the curriculum he'd be using and encouraged Marshall not to be scared or apprehensive about this unit. Together, they mapped out a plan that would potentially help other students as well.

By the time he left campus for the day, he was feeling pretty damn good about himself.

He was feeling so good that he wanted to celebrate. Driving into town, his plan was to pick up a couple of steaks to grill and then head over to Henderson's to grab something decadent for dessert. It would be a good way to open the dialogue about what he was thinking about. Parker was always up for a good conversation if dessert or snacks of any kind were involved. Maybe tonight was the night for them to finally broach the topic of not only career opportunities, but their relationship as well.

Specifically, he hoped they could discuss what they were doing together.

She'd mentioned having her cousins over but never brought it up again and they hadn't gone out on any dates.

And that's when he turned the car around and decided to head home. They'd been making dinner together at the house almost since the day she moved in. Tonight, he was going to take her out to dinner, on an actual date.

It was spontaneous and he wondered if he should feel her out first, but the last spontaneous move he'd made with her worked out really well and he had faith that it would again.

Who knew being brave could actually be this easy?

NINE

Parker stared down at the ringing phone in her hand for all of three seconds before muting it. The last thing she wanted right now was to deal with her mother. It was hard to believe she'd managed to avoid her for this long and she was looking to keep that record going for just a little while longer.

Right now, she was a woman on a mission. It turned out her great-grandfather's attorney was still alive–retired, but still alive. And after a little research, she found out her cousin Sam did his landscaping, so she was hoping to see if he'd bring her along with him next time. Sure, she probably could have just called the sweet old guy but she felt like she might need a little moral support from a family member.

Of course, Sam didn't know exactly *why* she wanted to talk to Mr. McClellan and that's why she was meeting him for coffee at Café Magnolia. It was her sister's day off so she wouldn't have to worry about Peyton chiming in on the conversation.

As soon as Parker was out of her car, Sam pulled up with his Coleman Landscaping truck. "Hey, Parks," he said with an easy smile as he walked over and hugged her. "How are you?"

"I'm good!" she told him, hooking her arm through his as they walked into the café. They were seated immediately and after saying hello to most of the staff, Parker finally felt like the two of them could talk. "What about you? Anything new and exciting going on?"

"Well...we just found out that Shelby's pregnant again," he said with a giant grin. "I don't think we're ever going to get a full night's sleep ever again. This will make three kids under the age of five!"

"Holy cow! Congratulations! That's so exciting!"

He nodded. "It definitely is and we're thrilled, but we're also exhausted."

"How is Shelby feeling?"

"Great! She always has fairly easy pregnancies so we know she's fortunate. It's just crazy how there's another wave of babies coming to the family again."

Parker couldn't help but laugh. It did seem to happen that way. "Well, Mallory's pregnant, Scarlett's pregnant, Mia's pregnant, and now Shelby." She let out a long breath. "Remind me not to drink whatever it is they're all drinking!"

He chuckled and was about to speak when their waitress came to take their orders. "Can I just get a black coffee and a slice of the peach pie? What about you, Parks?"

"Um...can I just get a Coke and one of those giant chocolate chip cookies?"

"You got it!" their server said before walking away.

"So you mentioned wanting to go and talk to Mr. McClellan," Sam said as he sat back in his chair. "You know he's retired, right?"

"I do. I just need to..." She paused and took a moment to

rethink what she was going to say. Leaning forward and resting her arms on the table, she studied her cousin. "How did you feel when Pops left you the landscaping company?"

His eyes went a little wide. "Wow. I haven't thought about that in a long time, but...honestly? Pissed! I didn't want to move to Magnolia and I certainly didn't want the responsibility of the business." He shook his head. "Don't get me wrong, I love doing that kind of work, but I resented him putting that pressure on me."

"And how do you feel about it now?"

"I love it. If it hadn't been for that inheritance, I never would have met Shelby and have the life I do now." He laughed again. "Hell, I'd probably be in jail or something. My life was a damn mess before Pops died." It was his turn to study her. "Why? What brought this on?"

Sighing, she hoped she could explain it. "I had a really uncomfortable conversation with Peyton and Ryder last week."

"Oh?"

Nodding, she gave him the abbreviated version. "And that made me think about what a mess I'm making of my life and why Pops chose not to give me a piece of Magnolia." She paused and smiled as their order came out. Once it was the two of them again, she looked at her cousin and frowned. "Didn't he think I was worthy of it, or did he think I was too big of a screwup to handle it?"

Sam didn't answer right away and she figured he was thinking of the polite way to say what he was going to say.

"You know, Parks, you and I are a lot alike."

That was...not what she was expecting.

"Really?"

He nodded and took a forkful of pie. "Definitely. You and I never felt the connection to the town that the rest of the family did. For me, I blamed it on the fact that I didn't grow up here. This was a place I came for summer vacations and that was it. I think for you, it was probably crammed down your throat until it became completely unappealing."

She sat up a little straighter because Sam was the first person who truly seemed to get it! "Exactly! If I had to hear one more time about the great Coleman legacy, or what it meant to be a Bishop in this town..." She groaned. "It was too damn much!"

"That's how I felt too and when Pops died and left me the business, it was with the stipulation that it was only going to be for a year and then I could sell it. I swear the weight of it nearly paralyzed me. I mean, we all knew I was a screwup and I was almost certain that I was going to end up embarrassing everyone and ruining the good Coleman name before the time was up!" He took a sip of his coffee. "But once I got over my hissy fit and had a good dose of reality thrown at me, I realized the old guy really knew what he was doing."

"Damn. That's what I'm afraid of..."

"What do you mean?"

"That he knew what he was doing by not leaving me something here to put my stamp on. He probably knew I'd mess it up and that's why he gave me money to go away so I wouldn't ruin the precious Coleman legacy." With a huff of annoyance, she took a giant bite of her cookie and felt beyond discouraged.

"Parker, you know that's not it. You were young when he died. He didn't have a chance to really get to know you. He didn't leave businesses or property to Austin, Garrett, or Jackson either, so it's not like he singled you out."

"Maybe...but he left them money for college! He

believed in them enough to make sure they got to go to school!"

With a sympathetic smile, Sam reached over and pat her hand. "You didn't want to go to college and were *very* vocal about it. I remember that distinctly. So if I knew it, you know Pops did."

Dammit, he was right again.

"Wait, so is that what you want to talk to Mr. McClellan about? Your inheritance?"

"Sort of."

"Parker..."

"I just want to know what the logic was, Sam! Mason certainly didn't want the Mystic Magnolia, but Pops left it to him! Why didn't he saddle me with some crazy business?"

"Didn't he write you a letter? I thought Pops wrote all of us letters."

With another weary sigh, she broke off another piece of the cookie. "He did, but it was all fairly generic–things like 'See the world!' and 'Go have an adventure!' blah, blah, blah. It didn't even sound like him. Pops never got excited about travel." Then she slammed her hand down on the table. "See? Just another way that I got treated differently! Everyone got these deep, meaningful letters and I essentially got a get-out-of-town shove." Slouching down, she ate more of her cookie.

"I think you're being a little dramatic. If Pops had his way, none of us would have ever left town. He wanted all of us here carrying on his name and legacy."

"Then explain my inheritance," she challenged. "Why was I the only one he specifically sent away?"

Sam didn't seem to have an answer to that.

"That's what I thought," she murmured.

"Look, I'll take you over to see Mr. McClellan, but you need to realize that he might not have any answers for you."

She nodded. "I know."

Sam took another bite of his pie before pulling out his phone. "He's not on my schedule again for another two weeks. Can you wait that long or do you want to maybe reach out to him on your own?"

"I can wait."

"Parker...come on. Don't be upset. I just don't want you getting your hopes up. That's all."

"I know and...thank you. It's good to know at least someone in this family doesn't just see me as a disappointment."

"There definitely sounds like there's a story there."

Oh, there was, she thought, but Sam had enough on his plate without adding any more of her drama to it. It was bad enough that she was dragging him in just this little bit with the attorney. So she put a smile on her face and straightened in her chair. "It's not important. So tell me, are you hoping for a boy or girl this time?"

* * *

ETHAN'S PLAN TO take Parker out on a date was apparently the best thing he could have possibly done. They were only at The Sand Bar, but she was practically bouncing in her seat in complete excitement.

"Do you want to get a couple of appetizers?" he asked.

"Oh my goodness! Yes!" Her smile was dazzling and it seemed a little much for a casual dinner out.

"Um...are you okay?"

Her smile faded slightly and he heard her sigh. "I know it's silly, but it's been a really long time since anyone's taken me out. The last time I went out to eat with anyone was with..." She paused and for the barest of moments looked a little sad. "It was with Tyler before...well...you know."

Ah. The infamous Tyler.

Ethan remembered the guy because they'd all gone to school together, but it still irked him a little whenever Parker mentioned him. Not because he was jealous, but because the relationship had meant so much to her and now it only made her sad. Sometimes he considered looking Tyler up on social media and reaching out to him, but he thought that would possibly be crossing a line.

Now, when he glanced over at her, she was practically hiding behind the menu.

And this is why I don't date more often...

"If it makes you feel any better," he said, getting her attention, "it's been a while for me too. I can't remember the last time I actually ate out someplace. Usually I call in an order and take it home. And it's been even longer since I've been here." He looked down at the menu. "What's your favorite appetizer?"

And just as he hoped, that seemed to perk her up a bit.

This girl and her food...

"Their tot-nachos are legendary," she explained. "But the everything bagel seasoned tempura shrimp on a stick are my favorite!"

"Then let's get both!" he suggested and watched her eyes light up. After that, they seemed back on track and talked about food and some of their favorite places to eat around Magnolia. "My dad and I used to go to the Mystic Magnolia after it was renovated. I can't believe your brother was responsible for that."

She nodded. "It was a wild time, for sure. Mason really took charge with the whole project and my sister handled redoing the menu." Then she shrugged. "Apparently there's nothing two overachievers can't do."

It was said lightly, but he knew her feelings on the subject. He was about to comment on it when their waitress came and took their orders. When they were done, Ethan reached across the table and took her hand. "I'm going to say something, and I don't want you to get upset."

"Ethan..." she whined.

"Just...hear me out." He paused and waited until he knew she was listening. "Just like you don't like people labeling you because of who you are, maybe you should try to...you know...stop labeling them too. For all you know, they feel the need to overachieve because of some deep-seated issue of their own. Everyone has their own baggage and if you don't want them calling you out on yours, it probably wouldn't hurt to stop ragging on them for theirs."

Then he held his breath and waited for her to comment, but she didn't.

"There's nothing wrong with you, Parker. I don't think there's anything you need to change."

Still nothing.

He was saved from saying anything else by the arrival of their drinks, but eventually one of them was going to have to speak.

And clearly, it was going to have to be him.

"So...I was thinking..."

"I'm sorry, Ethan."

"Um...what?"

Parker nodded. "I'm sure by now you feel just like everyone else feels–that I'm exhausting. I'm moody and bratty and I swear to you that I'm working on it. As a matter of fact, I'm working on a few things and...well...I wasn't sure if I should say anything until things were in motion."

"You've piqued my curiosity," he said, hoping he didn't sound overly excited. "But if you're not ready to talk about it..."

"Okay, so...I started looking at commercial real estate," she began. "After talking to Ryder about his spa, it made me realize how much I really would still like to have one of my own. And it's not because I want to compete with him and prove him wrong."

It was on the tip of his tongue to ask why she just didn't try to work something out with her future brother-in-law, but figured she had her reasons.

"I don't want someone else to be the boss. I want to be the one in charge."

And there it was.

"So I was looking at buildings over in Laurel Bay because I just..." Pausing, she sighed. "I don't want the pressure of being Ezekiel Coleman's great-granddaughter who's starting a business. I want to go someplace where I'm just Parker Bishop, rookie business owner."

He nodded because it made sense. "And did you find somewhere that could work?"

"A few, but...I need to come up with a solid business plan before going to a bank. I wanted to do my research and then maybe ask my brother to help me out with it—you know, so I know how to present it."

"Why not Ryder? Seems to me he's a big shot in the business world."

Parker took a sip of her drink before nodding. "He is, and it seems like he succeeds at everything he tries, but I want this to be mine. Ryder's the kind of guy who is brilliant at what he does, but he's got a lot of opinions and I don't want him trying to change what I want to do. With Mason, I know he'll work with the parameters I've set and simply tweak it if it needs it and he'll coach me on how to talk to whoever I need to at the bank. Whether it fails or succeeds, it's on me. I don't want anyone carrying me or telling me how it should be done. Maybe that's foolish, especially considering Ryder's track record, but..."

He had to stop her. "It's not foolish, Parker. If anything, I totally agree with you. This would be your baby and you're smart enough to know what you're doing. You've been planning this for what seems like years so it's not like you're making a rash decision to go into business. So I say good for you!"

Her eyes lit up once again. "Really? You don't think I'm being impulsive?"

"Not at all. If anything, I think you've taken your time and thought it all through."

She visibly relaxed. "Ethan, you have no idea how much that means to me. I know I'll have a ton of help from my family once it all gets underway and they'll all be support-ive, but...they kind of have to because they love me," she said with a sassy grin. "But...you're the smartest person I know, and if you think I'm doing the right thing, then... well...that means the world to me."

"Parker, I..." He didn't know what to say. While he always knew he was smart and studious, no one had ever said it to him quite the way Parker had, and it made him feel honored. "Thank you."

Their appetizers came out and now that the cat was out of the bag on what she was working on, she seemed beyond excited to talk about it. All Ethan could do was smile and nod because Parker kept the conversation going all on her own. Before he knew it, their entrees came out and she was still describing different floor plans and the overall décor she was going for.

"Basically, when the time comes, my cousin Austin can help me draw up the plans. Then my cousin Mallory's husband Jake can help with the renovations. Once things are done on the construction end, Mallory can help me decorate, my sister-in-law Scarlett can help me with the social media marketing, and then the rest is all on me."

It didn't escape his attention that she didn't mention her parents or either of her siblings in that family plan.

Or how she was going to finance all of this.

From everything he knew about Parker, she never really...worked. She did odd jobs and seemed to live a relatively frugal lifestyle, but...did she know enough about financing the kind of business she was envisioning? Did she know how she would need at least twenty percent down to even consider getting a loan? Or that she'd need to have at least six months' worth of living expenses saved because most new businesses don't make enough to cover all their expenses and a salary for the owner?

Did he want to be the one to tell her that?

Maybe.

Just not tonight.

The other thing he knew about Parker was that she came from a fairly wealthy family. Maybe she had money he didn't even know about, or perhaps she was counting on her parents giving her the startup cash.

Again, another topic he didn't want to touch upon tonight.

By the time they were done eating, Ethan had a list of about a dozen things he was concerned about for her, but he struggled between it not being his place and not wanting to ruin the mood. Instead, he made a mental note to maybe bring his thoughts up at another time.

"You know what I haven't done in a long time?" he said as their dishes were being cleared away.

"No, what?"

"Gone for a walk on the beach at night. I used to do it a lot–especially on a clear night and I'd bring my telescope with me–but it's been years. How do you feel about sitting on the sand in the moonlight with me?"

She looked beyond pleased. "I love that idea." Then she paused. "Can we maybe get some ice cream to go?"

He couldn't help but laugh. "Why am I not surprised that you'd ask that?"

"What?" she asked with a laugh of her own. "You might have brought a telescope with you, but I always had an ice cream cone with me when I walked on the beach at night."

"Fair enough. When's the last time you went walking on the beach?"

"Ooh...it really hasn't been that long. Peyton used to have a little bungalow right on the beach where I stayed when I visited and I always went for a walk as the sun went down. Now she and Ryder have a big-ass house there. I wanted to go for a walk with her when I was there the last time, but...it never happened. I've gone maybe a handful of times since moving back to Magnolia, but not nearly as often as I'd like."

Yeah, he should take the time to do it more often too. And maybe now that he knew she enjoyed it, maybe they could do it together–especially now that they'd broken the awkward barrier of going out in public together like a real couple.

A couple.

He liked the way that sounded.

And the way it felt.

They ordered some ice cream to go–cups, not cones–

and once they had it and he paid the check, they walked outside and considered their options.

The Sand Bar was right on the beach and there was a walkway that would take them right out onto to the sand. It was the easiest and most convenient way to do what they wanted to do, but he wasn't sure this was a good spot or not.

"Do you want to walk here or maybe drive down the road to one of the other access points?" he asked.

"Our ice cream will get too melty if we do that," she reasoned, and was already kicking off her shoes. It was a bit cool out—the temperature was in the low sixties—but it was still the kind of weather you didn't mind going barefoot in the sand in.

Ethan led her over to his car and they each tossed their shoes inside before awkwardly heading barefoot across the parking lot. But as soon as his feet hit the sand, it was like all the tension left his body.

"Yeah, I really need to do this more often."

Parker was already digging into her ice cream. "Agreed. We should try to do this at least once a week. I think it would be good for the both of us."

"You think so?"

She nodded. "Definitely."

They walked toward the water and then turned to walk along the shore while they ate their dessert. When she was done, she reached for his hand and together they strolled along in the moonlight and it was the most perfect date he could ever remember.

But because he was a stickler for details...

"Hey, Parker?"

"Hmm?"

"This may seem like a ridiculous question..."

"But..." she prompted as she playfully nudged him with her shoulder and he couldn't help but smile.

"But...I guess I wanted to make sure we're on the same page."

She stopped walking. "About what?"

"Us," he said quietly. She didn't respond right away and he wondered if she even heard him over the sound of the waves. "I know we said we were going to take things slow, but..."

"Ethan?"

"Hmm?"

Moving in close, she dropped her empty dessert cup in the sand before wrapping her arms around him. "We're not taking things slow; we're doing things exactly right."

He studied her face and loved how the moon was bright enough for him to see almost every detail. Mimicking her move, he dropped his container as well before his arms went around her and pulled her in until they were pressed intimately together. "I feel a little silly asking if I'm your boyfriend..."

Smiling, she rested her forehead against his chest. "You shouldn't because I like thinking of you as my boyfriend." Then she looked up at him. "And I really like knowing I'm your girlfriend."

Nothing pleased him more.

Cupping her face in his hands, Ethan lowered his lips to hers and kissed her. It was slow and tender and just a little something to confirm what they'd just said. She tasted like chocolate and cherries and he wanted to go on tasting her for hours. But Parker had other plans and took the kiss deeper almost as soon as they touched. Her tongue traced his bottom lip as she pressed impossibly closer to him and he was lost. Tongues tangled, breath mingled, and hands were roaming into dangerous territory on a public beach.

No one was around. He opened one eye to confirm that, but he wanted to make love to Parker and not have to worry about anyone seeing them or interrupting them.

"I want to take you home," he whispered gruffly as he kissed his way along her throat. "I want to take you to bed and love every inch of you all night long."

She hummed with approval. "I love the way you think."

It was the first time either of them had used the word love in any capacity with each other, and yet somehow it felt right.

"Let's go home." Together, they picked up their trash and slowly walked back up the beach to the parking lot. He expected Parker to make a run for it, but she seemed to be in the same frame of mind as he was—there was no need to rush because they were going home together and sometimes it was nice to let the anticipation build.

And it did.

There were little touches—seemingly innocent touches—on the drive home. Parker leaned over and nibbled softly along his jaw as one hand traveled dangerously high up along his denim-clad thigh.

Not that she was alone.

Ethan did his own share of touching, even as he kept his eyes on the road.

It was the longest six-minute drive of his life.

But he was rewarded the moment they walked through the front door. Parker casually closed and locked it before facing him. She had the sexiest grin as she sauntered backwards toward his room, beckoning him to follow.

Like there was anyplace else in the world he wanted to be.

She was kicking her shoes off as he crossed the threshold. Normally Parker was the one to strip down first, but tonight she stopped once her shoes were gone. Then she walked up to him, placed her hand on his chest, and whispered, "As much as I enjoyed the way you were touching me on the way home, it wasn't enough." She nipped at his jaw. "I need your hands on me, Ethan. Now."

She didn't need to ask him twice.

Again, the obvious move would have been to hastily begin tugging at her clothes, but he was a man who liked to take his time—to be slow and methodical so he could savor every inch of skin. Every curve was a thing of beauty. Every soft hiss of her breath encouraged him to be bolder. Parker was trembling by the time she was naked and Ethan slowly walked her backwards until they were beside the bed.

"Lay down," he growled and felt ready to come out of his own skin as she shimmied across the mattress.

Then he got himself undressed in record time.

Slow and methodical was good, but getting to be skin-to-skin with Parker was even better.

"Finally," she said softly as he covered her body with his. "I was beginning to think you'd never get here."

He loved her impatience and the way she humored him and the way he liked to do things sometimes. More than anything, he loved the way those silky limbs wrapped around him and begged him to claim her.

To make her his.

Which was what he did into the wee hours of the morning.

TEN

Life was perfect.

Life was better than perfect!

Wait, is that even a thing?

It didn't matter. Right now, Parker knew her life had never been better. Things were going so damn well with Ethan. She was happier than she could ever remember being. Every day she felt more and more energized to just go out and do things! There was her job at Shore Décor with Mallory, she was still working two shifts over at the B&B, volunteering at Happy Tails, all while finalizing her plans for her spa.

Yesterday, she met with a real estate agent over in Laurel Bay, so there wasn't a chance of anyone in her family who would find out what she was up to. The choice was down to two different locations and the only reason she hadn't put in an official offer was because the area was really run-down and she was hoping to find out if there were any plans for a bit of a revitalization of the town. It needed something like what had been done for the northern end of Magnolia several years ago, but more.

Much more, unfortunately.

So now it became a matter of whether she should invest now and hope for the best or wait.

Of course, there was a third option of simply looking elsewhere, but this was the area she really wanted to stay in.

"Maybe Ethan will have some advice," she murmured as she pulled onto the road that led to Happy Tails. It wasn't her usual day to volunteer, but Ethan had a faculty meeting and told her he wouldn't be home until after seven, so she figured she'd pass the time helping out with the dogs. It was a great way to burn off energy and get in her puppy fix. The plan was to get her business plan underway–perhaps even get to the point where the spa was open–and then adopt a dog. Just thinking about all the sweet dogs was enough to put a smile on her face and make her forget about everything else–especially anything negative.

And that's how she managed to miss the fact that her mother's car was also parked in the lot.

"Parker! Finally! I've been leaving you messages for the last few weeks. Why haven't you returned any of my calls?" All this was said before Parker had gone even five steps from her car.

"Oh, um...hey, mom," she said cautiously, completely aware of the lecture that was about to ensue.

"Honestly, I thought I raised you with better manners than that. I heard more from you when you lived five hundred miles away," Georgia Bishop went on. She gave her daughter a brief hug before she immediately began fussing with Parker's hair. "You really should make an appointment at the salon. You look like you're due for a decent cut. If you went to a proper place and got it styled, you wouldn't need to pull your hair back in a ponytail all the time."

Parker immediately reached up and smoothed her hand along her hair as she took a small step away from her mother. "This style is more practical when I'm here." Then she forced herself to smile. "So...how are the renovations coming? How was the cruise?" Luckily those were great diversion topics and she hoped they would keep her mother distracted until Parker could get a task going with the dogs.

Much to her surprise, her mother looped her arm with hers and slowly began walking them toward one of the seating areas. "The cruise was magnificent," she began. "Very relaxing. We saw so many amazing sights–some we've seen before, others for the first time–but I think your father and I are just in a different headspace right now and appreciated it so much more."

Wait...what?

"Of course I was worried the whole time about what was going on with the house, but I promised myself that I would trust in Jake and his team and not call them." Georgia let out a small laugh. "Although I was hoping they'd need to call and ask me questions, but they never did!" She shook her head and when they sat down at one of the picnic tables, she released Parker's arm but immediately took her hand and squeezed it. "We got home and things were at a point where it was livable, but still a bit messy for my liking. Fortunately, the Griffins–remember them? Their son Thomas used to have the biggest crush on you! Anyway, they were at their place in Florida and let us stay at their house until the bulk of the work was done. We just moved back home last week."

"Oh, well...that's good."

"Yes, I called and invited you to dinner so you could come see it, but you never got back to me." Her face pinched up in that way it did when she disapproved of something. "Anyway, I wanted to have you and your siblings over this Sunday for dinner. Are you available?"

"Um…"

"It's five days away, Parker. Surely you can rearrange your schedule. It's one dinner," she said wearily.

And that's when it hit her.

Her mother was being…different.

Oh, she still had her judgy tone and expression, but it was different—not quite so harpy.

But rather than comfort her, it only made her suspicious.

"What's going on with you?" Parker asked as she slowly pulled her hand away.

Georgia looked thoroughly confused.

"I thought I just told you."

"Not that," she replied with a huff. "You're acting weird."

"Weird?"

"Yes. Weird. Definitely weird."

Now it was her mother's turn to sigh. "Parker…"

"Mom, by this point in any conversation between us, you're usually throwing demands around and telling me what a disappointment I am. So what gives?"

"What gives?"

"Ugh! Stop repeating everything I say!"

"Honestly, Parker. You're being a little rude right now. What is it exactly you want to hear?"

The smart thing to do would have been to simply take Georgia 2.0 and be grateful that she was relaxing a bit. Unfortunately, Parker's impulsive side got the better of her and she ended up blurting it all out.

"I want you to tell me why you're suddenly acting different! I want you to try to explain to me how it is that we've been talking for five whole minutes and you haven't tried to rip apart the way I'm living my life! And I would love to know your thoughts on the fact that every member of my family has thrown me out of their homes since coming back to Magnolia! I mean...the list is endless!"

Breathless and with her heart pounding, Parker realized it was the first time she had actively challenged her mother like this. Normally she preferred avoidance or simply being flippant. Now she was going to have to have the uncomfortable argument she managed to evade for most of her life.

Georgia Bishop–the woman who always either looked annoyed or overly confident–suddenly seemed to shrink a little before her eyes. She gently cleared her throat before clasping her hands in her lap. "Well, I don't think I would describe what happened to you as being thrown out, but...I am sorry for the way things happened before your father and I left for our cruise." Looking up at Parker, she gave her an apologetic smile. "You took us by surprise and I was stressed out about not being home to supervise the work and...I should have taken the time to make sure you were okay."

It was hard not to reach out and feel her mother's head to check if she was feverish because this conversation didn't feel real. "Um..."

"It was obvious that you were heartbroken and, looking back, that should have been my priority. I know it wouldn't have changed where you were going to stay because there was no way you could have lived in the house with all the work going on, but I should have sat with you and helped you make arrangements and just...listened to you."

"Wow...I don't know what to say." And she didn't. Her mother was the last person she ever would have expected to have this kind of discussion with.

Reaching out once again, Georgia took one of Parker's hands in hers. "So, how are you doing? Have you talked to Tyler at all?"

She shook her head and sighed. "Not yet. I know I'll have to eventually, but...I guess I wanted to try to get my shit together first."

"And are you?" Georgia asked and then laughed softly. "You know, getting your...you know...together."

Parker didn't even try to hide her smirk. "You know you can say 'shit,' right?"

"Parker Victoria Bishop..."

It was always funny whenever the full name came out, but it also told her that her mother was serious. "Okay, fine. Don't say 'shit.'"

Georgia's weary sigh was her only response.

"To answer your question...sort of. I mean, I'm working on figuring my life out and I just know that I'm not ready to talk about it. Maybe you'll think I'm being dramatic, but I just don't want anyone swaying me or trying to tell me how to do what it is that I'm trying to do. Does that make sense?"

Nodding, her mother said, "It does. And as much as I want to take offense that you're unwilling to trust your own mother or tell me what's going on in your life, I can't say that I blame you. I haven't been particularly supportive or understanding, so..."

At this point, Parker was certain she was having a stroke—or dying.

Either one made more sense than her mother being this agreeable.

"I'm not really sure what to say to that, Mom."

For a moment, neither said a word. "But to answer your earlier questions, I guess it started with your brother moving out and then firmly putting me in my place followed by

Scarlett." She paused and let out a nervous laugh. "That girl certainly called me out more than once."

Parker had to agree.

"Then your aunt Susannah confronted me, followed some more by Scarlett, and most recently, Peyton. I pride myself on being an intelligent woman and if that many people were all telling me the same things–that my behavior was incredibly offensive–then I knew I needed to take a step back and look at my life." There was a pause before she said, "So I started seeing a...a therapist."

"Did you seriously not know how abrasive you were?" As soon as the question was out, Parker wanted to kick herself because the way she asked it was incredibly... well...abrasive.

"I didn't see it that way," Georgia reasoned. "In my mind, I was simply speaking the truth. Once it was pointed out, I couldn't unhear it and now...I'm trying. As you can tell, I don't always succeed, but I'm still trying and I hope you'll be patient with me." She squeezed Parker's hand again.

"Mom..."

"And lastly...and please forgive me if this comes out wrong...it seems to me your brother and sister truly wanted to help you. Mason said..."

"I know, I know," she quickly interrupted. "We've talked about it and I realized that I was the problem there."

"And with your sister?"

"Okay, it was wrong of me to run away the way I did, but...*gah!* I swear, she and Ryder were just too much! It's like they never turn off! From the moment I got there, they were tossing out job offers and suggestions and then telling me what I needed to be doing and everything I was doing was wrong! They were exhausting!"

Then she waited for her mother to disagree, but...she didn't.

"Yes, the two of them are a lot to take in. The last time your father and I had dinner with them they updated us on the restaurant and the resort and what was coming next and honestly, it's like they were planning world domination. I don't know when they sleep!"

"Exactly! There was never anything I was going to say or do that they were going to understand because I'm not programmed like they are. I'm not looking to run an empire; I'm just looking to do something that makes me happy."

Georgia studied her for a long moment. "You look happy, Parker. And not in that constantly in motion, flitting around with a smile to distract everyone way you normally do." Reaching up, she cupped her daughter's face. "Whatever it is that you're doing–and I'm not pressuring you to tell me anything–but whatever it is, it's making a difference in you. You look peaceful. Beautiful." Then she smiled. "Of course, you've always been beautiful, but this is the longest you've let me look at you since you first learned to walk. After that, you were always on the go."

It was such a silly thing, really. It certainly wasn't anything that should have made her want to cry, but...it did. Tears stung Parker's eyes as she wordlessly leaned over and hugged her mother. Georgia hesitated for only the barest of moments before hugging her back and it was a long time before either let go.

So, yeah...Parker thought back to her earlier musings.

Life was perfect.

* * *

A WEEK LATER, Ethan was fighting a panic attack as he watched what looked like a caravan of cars pull into his driveway. Parker had indeed invited her family over. They were starting with her immediate family, which she assured him would be great. Right now, he wasn't so sure. Ever since she and her mother started talking about their feelings to each other, she couldn't wait to have everyone over. And considering she felt better about her relationships with her siblings now too, she gushed about how this was the perfect time to do this.

Again, he wasn't so sure.

For Parker, this all seemed great. For him? Not so much.

For starters, he was fairly certain that they all still thought of him as her roommate. Not once did she mention telling them about the change in their relationship status.

So that kind of stung.

And if she was planning on dropping that bomb on them over dinner, Ethan knew he'd pretty much run screaming from the building.

No one liked to be ambushed, and he certainly was not ready to deal with angry fathers and brothers and brothers-in-law who would all be looking at him like the pervy guy sleeping with their daughter/little sister. He'd never been in this situation before—never did the whole meet the parents and family thing—so this was all brand new to him and Parker wasn't helping one bit.

Glancing around, he saw her putting drinks out on the kitchen island. They were going to grill steaks for dinner and everyone was bringing a side item and a dessert, so that covered the meal. It was nice how everyone was chipping in—especially since Parker was not big on cooking—but again, he wondered how they were all going to be looking at him.

Then the doorbell rang and he knew he was about to find out.

"Um...Parker?"

"Don't worry," she said with a bright smile as she walked by him. "I'll get it. Just...breathe." Pausing, she turned around and kissed him until he relaxed. "It's all going to be fine. Trust me."

Famous last words, he thought.

It was loud from the moment she opened the door. Everyone seemed to talk at once, and Ethan found himself trying to shrink into the woodwork. Her brother and sister-in-law and their two kids came through the door first with armloads of bags and toys and trays of food. Next came her sister and her fiancé. The resemblance between Parker and Peyton was obvious, and the fiancé looked like he could snap Ethan in half like a twig if he wanted to.

Swallowing hard, he took another step closer to the wall.

Then her parents walked in. They looked classy and elegant and perhaps a bit overdressed for a barbecue in his little house, but they both hugged Parker and kissed her hello and the way she was beaming told him just how much this get-together meant to her.

And it was too late for him to escape.

It took a solid five minutes for anyone to even notice him, but then Parker made a big show of introducing him.

"Hey, everyone!" she called out. "This is Ethan Harlow, and he was gracious enough to let me host this dinner today." She hooked her arm with his and sidled up close. "And before anyone says anything, yes, we're dating too. So be nice!" Then she walked away in her sassy Parker style while saying, "If anyone wants anything to drink, I've got all your favorites over here in the kitchen!"

Ethan knew he was standing there looking like a deer in headlights as everyone sort of stared at him. Fortunately, they were all still going about their own thing and getting settled, but all eyes were most definitely on him.

Self-consciously, he straightened his glasses and knew if he didn't do or say something that it was only going to get worse. So he began making his way around the room introducing himself and shaking hands with everyone. So far no one looked ready to kick his ass and he took that as a good sign.

Peyton was very nice and friendly, while Ryder was a little more reserved. Mason gave him a hearty handshake that could have been a warning, but he kept a charming smile on his face the entire time. Scarlett hugged him like an old friend even as she was wrangling her kids and warning them not to go running up the stairs.

Then came the parents.

Beau Bishop was courteous and reserved as he shook Ethan's hand, and then he had no choice but to turn and smile at Georgia–who hugged him.

What the...?

Before he could let go, she whispered, "Thank you for taking such good care of our girl." Then she pulled back and smiled. "Parker tells us you're a science professor! What's that like?"

Ethan looked around in mild confusion because so far, no one was acting like how he expected they would. There were a lot of smiles and laughter and he was afraid to let his guard down in case they were simply lulling him into a false sense of security.

"Um..." Clearing his throat, he took a minute to think about how to answer her question. "It's...interesting. Challenging." And then he knew exactly what to say. "Actually, I was struggling for quite some time with my teaching style and then Parker started coaching me a bit." Both Beau and Georgia looked at him with mild surprise. "She sat in on one of my classes and was quick to point out ways I could improve. Then we started having these mock lectures after work each night and I have to say, it's done wonders for me. My students don't look nearly as bored and they're engaging with me like they never have before." Turning his head, he managed to catch Parker's eye and smiled before facing her parents again. "Your daughter is truly amazing."

"That's...very interesting," Beau said. "Considering Parker's aversion to anything school-related, I can't imagine her involving herself in something like this. Perhaps you're a good influence on her!" Then he clapped Ethan on the back before walking away to get something to drink.

Ethan now found himself standing alone with Georgia.

"I'm sure Parker's mentioned her feelings about education," she began.

"She has, and it seems she has some valid reasons."

Luckily, Georgia nodded. "It was hard when she was growing up because she was always so defiant. For years we thought her poor grades were because she wasn't paying attention and she was being too social. It took until she was almost in middle school for us to realize that she was genuinely struggling."

"School can be very difficult for a multitude of reasons–many of which the teachers have no control over. There are different learning styles and unfortunately, a single teacher with a class of twenty or thirty students simply can't cater to all of them." He shook his head. "I don't have to deal with that on the college level as much, but I imagine in the elementary and formative grades it has to be incredibly frustrating to see some students fall through the cracks."

"So true." Then she paused and studied him for a moment. "Does she...I mean, has she mentioned..." She stopped again and waved it off. "I hate knowing how much she struggled and that it left such a negative impact on her."

Ethan wondered what she was going to ask but stopped himself from questioning it. Instead, he turned the conversation in another direction. "I hear you volunteer over at Happy Tails. It's quite a brilliant setup they have over there."

And just as he hoped, the conversation was off of Parker for a little while. By the time Georgia was done talking about her work with the animal rescue, Parker was waving him over to the kitchen to get the grill going. With a smile, he excused himself and walked out to the deck, with Mason hot on his heels.

Considering both the parents were easy to talk to, he was now confident it would be the same with her brother.

Then Mason put a heavy hand on his shoulder and Ethan immediately began to second-guess himself.

Again.

"This is a great grill," Mason said as he moved to stand beside him. He glanced around. "This is actually a great setup out here. Perfect for entertaining."

At first, all Ethan could do was nod. "I can't really take credit for most of it. Most of it was here when I bought the place. The grill is all mine, but everything else came with the house."

Mason took a step away before strolling around the deck. He stopped a few feet away and sort of bounced on his toes. "You know you've got a couple of loose boards, right?"

"I do. A couple of weeks ago I mentioned it to Parker, and she was going to reach out to Mallory's husband Jake, but...it sounded a bit ridiculous to call a contractor over a couple of boards."

Nodding, Mason continued to stroll. "You and I could probably handle it ourselves. It won't take long. Maybe one other guy just to play it safe. I can come by next weekend if that works for you?"

Again, all Ethan could do was nod because this was going way better than he expected.

With the grill lit, he turned to head back into the house, but Mason's hand on his shoulder stopped him.

"So...you and my sister," he said, his tone a little less friendly than it had been a moment ago.

"Um...yeah," he said, his own voice going low and gruff. "Me and Parker."

Mason's expression gave nothing away and it was an awkward minute before he said anything. "Can I give you a little advice?"

Do I have a choice?

"Sure."

"Parker's coming off a long-term relationship."

"You mean with Tyler?" he asked with confusion.

"Exactly."

"That wasn't a long-term romantic relationship," Ethan reasoned. "They'd been friends since elementary school and then she had some confusing feelings for him."

Mason looked surprised. "Oh, so she told you all about it?"

Nodding, Ethan replied, "She did. I think she's incredibly embarrassed about the whole thing and feeling a little lost without her best friend–the one person who was her constant for most of her life–but..."

"She has her family," Mason quickly interjected. "Ty wasn't the only constant."

Okay, defensive much?

"That's not what I meant. All I'm saying is that Tyler was...it was a different relationship. He was someone she could turn to when she...you know...maybe didn't want to confide in her family about her feelings. We all know there's a huge difference between a relationship with a sibling and one with a friend. One doesn't diminish the other..."

"I know, I know." Raking a hand through his hair, Mason stepped away again. "Parker's...what's the word...she dives headfirst into things without thinking them through. She acts on emotion rather than logic."

"True."

"She came back to Magnolia and met up with you and you became a friend."

He nodded again. "Also true."

"And now you're...involved." He paused and stared at Ethan, and it didn't take a rocket scientist to know what he was implying.

But just to be sure...

"Are you saying that Parker's just sort of latching on to me as a replacement for Tyler?"

"I'm not sure I'd put it quite like that, but..."

Now that it was out there, it was hard not to want to examine the possibility.

It was also hard not to walk away and tell Parker he wasn't cut out for a family get-together.

Unfortunately, that wasn't an option–he wouldn't do that to her–so now he was stuck standing here having some sort of weird stand-off with her brother.

The only thing he could say was, "I guess only time will tell. Personally, I think she needs to reach out to Tyler and clear the air."

"She also needs to find a real job and stop living like

she's a sixteen-year-old," Mason said firmly. "I get that she's trying to find herself, but there's no way she can keep living like this. She's a grown woman and it's time she started acting like one. She has enough family here in Magnolia that we can help her if she'd let us. We have enough connections to..."

"Oh my God, Mason!" Parker said with annoyance as she stepped out the back door. "What is wrong with you?"

"Oh no. What did he do?" Scarlett said with a weary sigh from right behind her.

Then Ethan witnessed something he'd never witnessed before–a family argument.

"Are you seriously out here talking about me behind my back?" Parker shouted as she stepped toward them. She continued, "You've been here in my house for all of ten minutes and you're out here grilling poor Ethan about me? Do you have any idea how incredibly rude and insulting that is?"

"Mason, we talked about this in the car," Scarlett said, trying to be the voice of reason.

"No, we did not talk about this," Mason countered. "In the car, we had no idea she was now sleeping with her roommate." Then he looked at Parker. "Didn't we talk about maybe...you know...*not* getting involved with male friends the last time we were together?"

Ethan saw Parker's cheeks flush, and he was about to step in when she started yelling again. "Do you even hear yourself? What gives you the right to come here and talk to me like this? And in front of Ethan?" Then she moved in close to her brother, poking him in the chest. "I don't care what your thoughts are about how I live my life and my personal life is none of your business. Got it?"

"Parks, I was just..."

"What's going on out here?" This time it was Peyton coming out onto the deck, closely followed by Ryder.

Then everyone was talking at once.

"You have to admit that you're being irresponsible!"

"Why on earth would you come out here and embarrass your sister like this?"

"I'm so tired of everyone treating me like a child!"

"Maybe you should start acting more like an adult then!"

It went on and on for several minutes, and Ethan realized Beau and Georgia hadn't joined the fray.

Interesting...

"I'm not going to stand here and take this," Parker called out.

"What a surprise!" Mason yelled back at her. "Typical Parker. Things get a little hard and you're ready to bolt. And you wonder why we treat you like a child? Adults don't run away when the going gets tough, Parker!"

"This is why I didn't offer you the position of manager," Ryder chimed in and seriously, Ethan wanted to slug the guy because he certainly wasn't helping the situation.

"Do you think it's easy running the café and preparing to open a new restaurant that is still under construction?" Peyton asked, but before Parker could answer, Mason spoke again.

"Or how difficult it is to be working parents and trying to balance our jobs and careers and personal lives while giving our kids the kind of time and attention they deserve?"

"Mason," Scarlett said as she stepped up beside him, "I think this is enough."

"No, it's not," he argued. "I'm simply standing here trying to let this poor guy know what he's getting into." Looking at Ethan, he continued. "I mean, he seems like a genuinely nice guy and he should know the kind of chaos she's going to bring into his life!"

If anything, Parker seemed to shrink right before his eyes. Her cheeks were flaming red and she looked ready to cry.

And that's when he had enough.

The argument started up again and Ethan hopped onto the closest built-in bench and let out a loud whistle to get everyone's attention. "*Enough!*" he roared, almost scaring himself. "I don't know if this is normal behavior for all of you, but if it is, shame on you! I don't have any siblings so I've never dealt with anything like this before, but I've got to tell you, this gang mentality is borderline abusive! I would never go into someone's home–whether I was related to them or not–and attack them the way you are attacking Parker. All she wanted was a nice day with her family–a chance for you to see and hear about all the things she's doing with her life–and all you've managed to do is come in and critique and criticize and put her down. Is it any wonder she wanted to move away and stay away?"

Jumping down, he walked directly to Parker and hauled her into his arms. He felt her trembling and it fueled his fire.

"Maybe instead of looking at her running as her shortcoming, maybe you all need to look at it as yours. Maybe if she had been accepted and loved for who she is rather than picked on for who she isn't, she wouldn't have felt the need to run." He kissed the top of her head as she burrowed into him. "Just because she doesn't have a dream career path doesn't make her a target and shame on all of you for being so judgmental. You're all lucky that you have the things you want–that you found your path and followed it. Some people take longer and they don't need to be put down and chastised for it."

When he looked around, he saw they all looked embarrassed and regretful and he knew he could have let it go right here, but he had a few more things to get off his chest.

"I'll admit that I don't know what it's like to deal with Parker the way you all have, but if I had a sibling who was struggling and who wasn't asking anything of anyone except for their love and some time together, you can be damn sure I'd give it to them. No questions asked." He looked at Mason. "Has Parker asked you for any financial assistance? Any kind of demand on your job or life in general?"

"No, but..."

"She asked for a place to stay. She was excited to spend some quality time with her nephews. Maybe she was a little overzealous about it, but maybe instead of tossing her out, you could have simply talked to her about your family schedule."

Both Mason and Scarlett nodded solemnly.

Then Ethan turned to Peyton and Ryder. "We all get that you're a power couple. It's clear you've both got wild ambition and go after what you want and like to get things done. But isn't part of that knowing the people around you? Knowing how to handle a...a staff...or an employee?" Looking at Ryder, he added, "Knowing your target audience when planning a business? You both should have common knowledge of people skills and yet you seemed to forget all of that when dealing with Parker!"

"Ethan, you don't..." Parker began, but he kept going.

To Peyton, he said, "She's your sister. She looks up to you and you are her closest confidante. At a time when she was beyond devastated, you were more concerned with how *you* would handle the situation instead of what she needed." He let out a long breath and addressed them all one last time. "Honestly, I can't believe she'd even want to spend a day with any of you—especially if this is the way you've been treating her since she came home. I know I wouldn't want to. If it were up to me, I'd throw the whole lot of you out of my home, but it's not. That's Parker's call and no matter what she decides," he said with a low growl, "you will honor it. Do we understand one another?"

Everyone nodded.

"Good." Then he looked down at Parker and saw her lip trembling. He cupped her cheek with a small smile. "Whatever you want, sweet girl, that's what we'll do."

She looked uncertain for all of ten seconds before she turned and faced her family. "I'd appreciate it if you'd all stay," she said quietly. "I know Mom's been trying to get us all together for several weeks and now that we're all here, I'd hate to disappoint her." Then she let out a nervous laugh. "There's something I bet you never thought you'd hear me say, right?"

That seemed to break the tension and soon everyone was hugging and apologizing.

Ethan took a step back and then another and figured they all needed a minute. When he turned to go into the house, he found Beau and Georgia standing in the doorway, each holding a grandchild.

Beau reached out a hand to him and gave Ethan a hearty handshake. "Thank you," he said, his voice breaking slightly. "I'm ashamed to say our daughter's always needed a champion and no one's ever done it so powerfully before. Not even me. And as her father, I should have been the one." He looked almost ready to cry. "So, again, thank you."

Ethan wasn't sure what he was supposed to do or say. So after a gruff, "you're welcome," he stepped into the kitchen and walked over to the platter of steaks. And that's where Georgia joined him.

And she was crying.

All she did was mouth, "Thank you," before leaning over and kissing him on the cheek.

It was hard to describe exactly how he felt, but more than anything, he felt pretty damn proud of himself for standing up for the woman he now realized he was in love with.

ELEVEN

Eventually Parker was going to have to actually thank Ethan with her words, but for the last several hours, she'd been thanking him with her body.

And neither was complaining.

After the whole melee on the deck earlier, things had calmed down and the rest of the day was—in her eyes—a major success. They'd eaten and laughed and talked about plans for Mason and Scarlett to find out the sex of the new baby. Mason, of course, was hoping for another boy, but Scarlett was firmly hoping for a girl this time. They both agreed that no matter what the sex was, they were thrilled.

Peyton shared her menu for the new restaurant and wanted feedback on it. She was going for a more upscale menu this time and everything had more of a French flair to it. It wasn't something Parker gravitated toward, but her sister loved it and everyone seemed to think it was a great idea.

Ryder mentioned turning the property he purchased last year into a cancer patient retreat. The house was set on several acres, had multiple bedrooms, two kitchens, a massive swimming pool, and a couple of putting tees. It had a resort feel and even though the initial plan was to use it as a home for he and Peyton once they got married, Ryder explained that after watching his mother go through her breast cancer treatment and learning how hard the recovery was, he wanted to do something to make it easier for her and as many others as he could.

It was hard to stay mad at a man who was doing something so kind and considerate for his mother and showing compassion for cancer patients at the same time.

Damn him.

After that, her mother talked about the next big fundraising event for Happy Tails and encouraged all of them to perhaps volunteer their time and ask their friends to do the same.

They hadn't left until after nine.

The one thing they didn't discuss was anything Parker was working on. It was probably because Ethan scared them all enough that they didn't dare risk upsetting her again. She wasn't sure if she was happy or sad about it— not the part where he scared them because that was incredibly awesome and sexy as hell—but the part where no one thought to ask about what was going on in her life because they couldn't do it without being judgmental. That stung.

Don't think about that right now...

Yeah, right now she and Ethan were naked, breathless, and tangled together while trying to stay awake. Ethan's hand was gently caressing her shoulder in that way he knew she loved. For the first time in a long time, Parker didn't want to talk, didn't feel the need to fill the silence. There was something...right about the quiet that she never appreciated before.

Or maybe she was afraid of saying anything to ruin the moment.

Which must have been how her family felt earlier.

Stop thinking about them!

Snuggling closer, she felt her eyes grow heavy and didn't fight it.

At first.

There was something she needed to say before allowing herself to fall asleep. "Ethan?"

"Hmm?"

"Thank you."

She felt him place a small kiss on the top of her head. "You don't need to thank me, Parker. All I did was speak the truth."

Maybe that was how it seemed to him, but to her, it was so much more.

Yawning, she shook her head and attempted to say more, but he hugged her close and whispered, "Go to sleep, beautiful girl. We'll talk in the morning."

And so she did.

When she woke up the next morning, however, Ethan had already left. Parker glanced at the clock and saw that it was after ten. She couldn't remember the last time she slept in like that and was a little shocked that she hadn't even heard Ethan get up and get ready for work.

Getting up, she stretched and padded to the bathroom where she slid on Ethan's robe. Out in the kitchen, she went to make herself a cup of coffee and found a note propped up against the machine.

Good morning! You were sleeping so peacefully that I didn't want to wake you. I've got a meeting with the dean this afternoon at three. How about we go out for Mexican food for dinner? Have a good day.

xoxo

Ethan

Smiling, she made her coffee and studied the note. His handwriting was awful and it was nice to see that he had some imperfections. His intelligence intimidated the heck out of her and even though his teaching skills had been in desperate need of improvement, he was making things happen and it was the little things like sloppy handwriting that made him imperfectly perfect.

There were so many things she loved about him, but his actions yesterday had pretty much sealed her fate.

She was in love with Ethan Harlow.

Her brother's words about getting involved with a male friend came back to her, but Parker knew this was nothing like her relationship with Tyler.

For starters, they didn't have the same history. She and Ty met and bonded at an early age and grew up together. He knew her at her best and was right there beside her through every high and low in her life. In retrospect, again, she realized just how strong her feelings were for him as a friend and only a friend. With Ethan, he was also her friend, but it was different. It was an emotional connection on a whole other level that was hard to put into words. All she knew was her heart never leapt for Tyler the way it does whenever she thinks about Ethan.

Of course people were going to try to make the comparison and that's why she knew the time had come.

She had to call Tyler.

It was a Monday, and she knew he was at work, but maybe if she just took the step and called—even if it meant leaving a message—he'd call her back when he had the time.

With a heavy sigh, Parker took her mug of coffee and went in search of her phone. Then, after fidgeting and getting comfortable on the sofa, she pulled up Ty's number and hit send.

And prayed it went to voicemail.

"Hello?" His voice was hesitant and not overly friendly, but Parker knew it would be utterly ridiculous to hang up.

"Hey," she said, her own voice shaking slightly. "I...I wasn't sure if you'd pick up when you saw my name. How are you?"

"I'm good," he said, sounding a little more relaxed. "And you?"

"I'm good too. Well...getting better, I guess." With a nervous laugh, she twisted in her seat. "So, um...I'm not really sure what to say, Ty, except...I'm sorry. For everything. It was wrong of me to do what I did and I hate that I ruined a lifelong relationship."

She heard his soft sigh. "You didn't ruin it, Parker. You made it awkward and harder than it had to be, but you certainly didn't ruin it." He paused. "And to be fair, you weren't alone in doing all that. I could have handled things better and I sure as hell shouldn't have lashed out at you the way I did. It was wrong of me to tell you..."

"No," she quickly interrupted. "You weren't wrong. If anything, you were absolutely right." Swallowing hard, she continued. "You were my rock and my...my person for so long that I didn't realize how you were also...you know..."

"A crutch?" he finished for her with a little sadness. "Yeah. It took a long time for me to realize it, but believe it or not, I knew a long time ago. Years ago. It wasn't anything new, but I didn't know how to change it. That was our dynamic."

She nodded as shame filled her. "You did so much for me and I never did anything for you. Ugh...why did you put up with me for so long? Why were we still even friends?"

The bark of laughter was his first reaction. "Never did anything? Are you kidding me right now? Don't you realize how much your friendship did for me? For my life?" He laughed again. "God...it went both ways, Parks. You're the reason I tried out for the baseball team in middle school."

"Pfft...everyone knew how good you were. They shouldn't have even made you try out."

"And who pushed me to join the debate team, huh?"

Shaking her head, she replied, "You love to argue, and we all knew you wanted to be a lawyer! I mean...it just made sense!"

"To you," he said softly. "At the time, I didn't see it. You gave me that push and continued to push until I decided on law school. And who baked me cookies and made sure I remembered to take breaks when I was studying?"

"I get what you're saying, but it's not the same, Ty."

"No, it's not the same. It was better. You challenged me to be better, Parker. In everything. And I just sort of went along for the ride with you. There were times when I thought you were making a mistake, but I never said anything. And there were times when I knew I should be pushing you in a better direction, but I didn't. So if anyone was a crappy friend, it was me."

"Ty..."

"It's true, Parks. And don't try to argue with me because I'm a lawyer and I can argue circles around you."

The laugh was out before she knew it. "That is a fact." She sighed and was about to comment on it when he stopped her.

"I miss you. Like seriously, seriously miss you."

No words could have meant more to her. "I miss you too."

"So where are you? What have you been doing?"

"As much as I'd love to catch you up on everything, it's the middle of the workday for you. Don't you need to be... you know...working?"

"You caught me on a slow day and I told my assistant to hold my calls."

"You really didn't have to do that. You have an important job and..."

"And you're important too, Parks. I know I certainly didn't make you feel like that when I got engaged and with all the wedding planning, but I hate not talking to you all the time. It's like a part of me is missing. It's lonely."

Smiling, she cradled the phone close, as if hugging him. "Oh, stop. You've got Kaitlyn and a great job and a ton of friends."

"It's still not the same. No one else really knows how much I hate all the new superhero movies. Kaitlyn knows about my Harry Potter obsession but doesn't get it. We went to Disney, and she tried to get me on Space Mountain, but..."

"But...?"

"I caved and then I threw up," he murmured. "The rest of the time she went on the roller coasters by herself and was a bit annoyed by it."

She knew what he was doing. She remembered that conversation as if it was yesterday. "And how about the M&M's? And bed wetting?"

"We never have chocolate in the house and I figured someday—maybe when we have kids who wet the bed—I can share about my own issues. Why divulge that embarrassing fact unless I have to, right?"

Laughing, she agreed. "Good plan."

"So...come on. Catch me up. I've got some time and I've

missed talking with you. Are you back in Magnolia? Is your mom making you crazy?"

Taking a sip of her coffee, Parker put her feet up on the couch and felt like they were back on track. "You better buckle up, my friend, because this story is one wild ride!"

* * *

THE CLOCK WASN'T MOVING. Time was literally standing still and it was making Ethan more than a little antsy. His meeting with Dean Walthers was scheduled for three o'clock and it seemed like the day was just dragging and it was never going to get here. He'd passed the time grading papers and working on a new set of ice-breaker questions to use in class–an idea Parker gave him–and it didn't feel like it was any closer to his appointment time.

While he knew it wasn't possible–of course time was moving–it was an easier thing to wrestle with than worrying what this meeting was about. At eight this morning, he received a text from the dean asking for this meeting–no explanation. As far as he knew, there were no issues that needed to be addressed. If anything, things were going really well, so...

Not knowing the reason for this invitation was making him crazy.

He considered calling Parker so she could calm him down, but he didn't want her worrying with him. She was compassionate like that and he'd hate to drag her down and distract her, especially if this was all for nothing. Maybe the dean just wanted to check in with him. They were just beyond the mid-semester point, so perhaps he was looking to plan ahead? Granted, that hadn't happened before–normally the department head was the one who reached out and inquired about everyone's plans for the upcoming semester–but...that could change, couldn't it?

He still had thirty minutes until he was due in the dean's office, so when his phone rang, it was a welcome reprieve.

Sort of.

"Hey, Mom," he said, leaning back in his chair. "This is a surprise. Is everything okay?"

"Everything's fine. I didn't mean to worry you. Is this a bad time?"

On some level...

"No. This is fine. I have a meeting with the dean in a half hour, so you're saving me from worrying about why he wants to see me."

"Oh my. Well, that sounds a little nerve-racking. You don't know what he wants to talk to you about?"

"Not a clue," he said with a small sigh. "So this is a great distraction. How are you? How's Alan?"

"He's good! We joined a new wine club and have been playing golf several times a week. We're enjoying retirement."

That made him smile. "Good for you, Mom. You deserve it."

"The move to Palm Springs was really the way to go. I think you'd love it here."

And here we go...

"Mom, we've been over this..."

"Just hear me out. Alan's birthday is at the end of next month. I know you'll be wrapping up the semester, but I was hoping you'd come for a visit. It's his 65th birthday and we're having a big party. Please, Ethan. We haven't seen you in forever."

Straightening, he opened his laptop and pulled up his calendar. "What is the date of the party?"

"May 16th," she said excitedly. "I'm sure you're teaching over the summer so you don't have a lot of time in between, but we truly would love for you to come and spend some time with us." She paused. "I know you were overwhelmed when you were taking care of your father and now you've got a new home, but I'd really like us to be closer, Ethan. I'm so proud of you and I miss you so much. Can you please make the time to join us?"

He knew there was no way he could say no, so...

"I'll be there, Mom. I promise. I can't say with any certainty how long I'll be able to stay, but it will at least be a long weekend."

"Oh, this is wonderful! You can stay with us–Alan's kids are all married with children of their own and tend to stay at hotels nearby–so there's plenty of room for you here. The guest room has a brand-new bed and a TV..."

"I'm sure it's going to be just fine," he assured her.

"So tell me about what's been going on with you? We got interrupted the last time we were on the phone and..." She paused and Ethan heard her speaking to someone. Obviously she'd placed her hand over the phone because her voice was muffled, but he could tell whoever she was talking to–probably Alan–was telling her they were expected somewhere. "Ethan, sweetheart, I'm sorry, but I need to cut you short. Our tee time got moved up and we need to get going. Let me know when you book your airfare and if you need me to pick you up at the airport. Love you!"

"Love you too, Mom," he said before hanging up.

That managed to kill all of ten minutes.

"Damn."

Deciding to pack up his things and walk slowly to the

dean's office, Ethan knew it was a better option than continuing to sit and watch the clock.

Fifteen minutes later, he didn't even have a chance to take a seat and wait before he was ushered into the office.

"Dean Walthers," he said casually as he shook the man's hand. "It's good to see you."

"Same, Professor Harlow. Won't you have a seat?"

He sat and then wasn't sure whether he should start the conversation or not, but the decision was taken out of his hands when the head of the science department joined them. Standing again, he shook Professor Madigan's hand and greeted him before sitting back down.

"Thank you both for meeting with me today," the dean began. "For starters, I'd like to congratulate you, Professor Harlow."

Ethan had a feeling he looked like a deer in headlights. Clearing his throat, he asked, "On…?"

"We have been getting some wonderful feedback from your students. It seems you've upped your game and you've become a bit of a rock star in the science department," Professor Madigan replied. Both men were almost twice Ethan's age and he was mildly intimidated by them on a good day, but having them both smiling at him right now felt pretty damn good.

"Oh, um…thank you. Recently I realized just how much I was still struggling with connecting with the students and started doing some exercises to work on changing that. I'm glad the students have responded so well to it."

"They have," the dean confirmed. "Which is why I'm disappointed to say that your first summer session is canceled this year."

"Excuse me?" he glanced between the two men. "I don't

understand. I've been teaching both summer sessions for the last two years."

"The second eight-week session is still on, but enrollment was down on the first one, so we decided to consolidate. It's pointless holding classes for only five students when we can move their schedules around and give you a fuller class eight weeks later," Professor Madigan explained.

"So...I'll be off for eight weeks?" he asked, unable to hide his disappointment. Even though the thought of time off where he and Parker could possibly travel together was appealing, that would be around the time that her spa business would be getting started, if everything stayed on track. He wasn't even sure she'd be able to take the time off to go with him to Palm Springs.

Which—now that he thought about it—was exactly what he wanted to happen.

"I don't think I've ever heard anyone sound so sad about the thought of a vacation," the dean commented. "Of course, you can look into teaching at a different college for that semester as a traveling professor or a guest speaker at different universities. We have the resources for you to research what's available. With your classes here being canceled, there won't be a scheduling conflict. I can send the link to you if you'd like?"

He nodded without even thinking about it. It was a solid solution and could help him gain even more confidence in his teaching ability. Still, it was disappointing to learn that even though he was getting praise from his students, it wasn't enough to fill a classroom for the first summer session—a problem he'd never had before.

For the next hour, they discussed curriculum and budgets and asked for Ethan's feedback on several topics that were discussed in the last faculty meeting. By the time he was saying goodbye, he was feeling better about his options for the summer semesters and was anxious to look at what potential opportunities were out there. He couldn't wait to talk to Parker about them.

With an adjusted mindset, Ethan focused on reminding himself that perhaps there was a reason for the canceled classes and how it was going to be a good thing. He could either find a guest speaking gig or travel a little or even see if he could help Parker with her business plan if she gets it going. Either way, the time wouldn't be wasted.

A few months ago, something like this would have completely thrown him into a cycle of self-doubt and worry. He'd be stressed about paying bills and wondering if maybe he didn't get the student sign-ups because he was a bad teacher and would take it personally. And while there were a few lingering doubts, he knew he was getting stronger and connecting with his class. The fall semester would be his best yet. He'd make sure of it.

At home, he found Parker typing furiously on her laptop. Her hair was up in a messy bun, she was wearing his robe, and her expression was intense.

She looked sexy as hell.

As much as he wanted to go over and kiss her, he also didn't want to disturb her, so he went about his business as quietly as possible. In his office, he pulled out his laptop and clicked on the link Dean Walthers had sent him. He'd barely glanced at it when he heard Parker's footsteps padding toward him. Spinning around in his chair, he smiled at her. "Rough day?"

She grinned as she climbed into his lap. "You have no idea."

"Want to talk about it?" Even though he had a ton of

stuff he wanted to share with her, she looked like she was holding a lot in.

"Okay, so I have been very busy today," she began as she squirmed against him. "Um...maybe we should move this to the couch."

"Agreed."

A minute later, Parker was practically bouncing on the cushion beside him. "So...I called Tyler today."

For a moment, he could only blink. "Oh," he said lamely. "And how did it go?" He knew this was a good thing for her and something she had to take care of, but he couldn't help but be a little jealous. What if things went great and she decided she wanted to move back to Florida? Would she give up on everything she'd just started working on for the safety of familiarity?

"It went better than I expected," she told him with a big smile. "You have no idea how relieved I am. Honestly, I didn't think he'd even answer the phone and I was prepared to just leave a message and say the ball was in his court, but he did answer and we talked for like...I don't know...three hours! How crazy is that?"

"Isn't he a lawyer or something? How could he take that much time to talk?"

Her smile fell a little. "I guess he made the time because I'm important to him." And yeah, her tone was definitely snarky.

"Parker, I didn't mean..."

"Anyway," she interrupted, "we had a great conversation and cleared the air and I apologized for making things so damn awkward and he apologized as well."

"Really?"

Nodding, she explained how Tyler felt about his end of the friendship. "I never saw it that way when it was happening, but now that it's out there, I realize that maybe things were a little one-sided." She sighed. "Still, I feel like a giant weight has been lifted off of me and that inspired me to move on to the next brave act of the day!"

"O-kay..."

"My cousin Sam was going to take me with him the next time he went to take care of the lawn for our great-grandfather's attorney. I thought I needed him with me for moral support or something, but today I decided to call Mr. McClellan myself and talk to him."

"Wow! And...?"

"And I'm having lunch with him tomorrow." Her smile was back in full force. "I was so nervous and I think I rambled a lot–which, let's face it, I do–but he was incredibly sweet and said he was hoping to hear from me!"

"Did Sam mention to him that you wanted to see him?"

She shook her head. "No, that was the strange part. When I asked him why, he said he was just hoping to hear about my travels, so..." She shrugged.

"Why don't you sound convinced?"

"It was just the way he said it. I can't quite put my finger on it, but I feel like there's more to it than just wanting to chat about the places I visited." Another shrug. "But I guess I'll find out tomorrow, right?"

It was his turn to nod. "I guess. Are you going alone? Do you need someone to go with you? I can try to rearrange my schedule and meet you someplace. Where are you going for lunch?"

Leaning in, she kissed him. "You are incredibly sweet to offer, but I'm going to pick up food from Peyton's café and bring it to his house. He doesn't get out much anymore and doesn't drive, so I thought it would be better for me to bring something to him."

"Now who's the sweet one?" he teased lightly, taking his turn kissing her.

"Still you," she said, resting her forehead against him.

"Those both sound like great things, Parker. What were you working on when I got home? You were looking pretty fierce as you typed."

"Oh, that was me finalizing my business plan and emailing it to Tyler. I was so focused because I didn't want to forget anything."

"Wait...so you sent it to Tyler? Why? I thought you were going to ask your brother to look at it?"

And he didn't even want to mention how she hadn't even shown it to him either.

"I know, I know. That was the original plan, but when Ty and I were talking earlier and I told him about the whole blow-up yesterday–which, by the way, he says kudos to you for being my hero–we thought it would be best not to involve my family just yet." She got up and walked to the kitchen and grabbed them each something to drink. When she handed him his drink and sat back down, she let out a long breath. "Ty's really good with polishing stuff up. Once he's looked it over and tweaked it, then I can share it with Mason if I have to. Otherwise, I'm just going to hit the bank myself and see what happens." Taking a long sip of her water, she never took her eyes off of him.

Which was good, because Ethan knew he was staring at her with total disbelief.

And shock.

And hurt.

"What's wrong?" she asked, and he could see the confusion written all over her face.

Did he tell her? Was he being overly sensitive just because he'd been the one here with her cheering her on while her supposed best friend had basically washed his hands of her? Or did he just congratulate her and keep his opinion to himself?

"Ethan?"

"Nothing," he told her. "I just didn't realize you were ready for it to be looked at. That's all."

He knew instantly that she didn't believe him, but she also didn't try to explain herself any further. "So, what about you? What was the meeting with the dean about?"

For the next several minutes he explained how the summer semesters work—how there are two eight-week sessions and how he normally taught during them both. "Enrollment is currently down so they decided to scrub my first session."

Frowning, she reached out and squeezed his hand. "Well damn. That sucks. So...does that mean you're off for two months? Like a summer vacation?"

It was on the tip of his tongue to be petty, to not share with her the possible guest speaking gigs or traveling professor thing, but knew he wasn't that guy. "I could do that, but I can also apply to other colleges and universities to sub or guest speak. I was just going to look into that when you came and got me."

"So...other local colleges?"

"Not necessarily. I could realistically look anywhere. It would only be for eight weeks and it could provide a great opportunity for me to hone the skills we've been working on." He took a sip of his water. "I have no idea what's out there, but I'm extremely curious to check it out."

"Oh."

"But on a side note, both the head of my department and the dean congratulated me on all the great feedback they've been getting from my students. Apparently the changes I've made are getting noticed, so that's pretty cool, right?"

She nodded as they slipped into a slightly awkward yet companionable silence. Ethan had no idea what she was thinking, but he knew he was going to have a hard time moving past Parker giving her business plan to Tyler before letting him see it.

He'd get over it—eventually—but right now, it just stung.

"Obviously you got my note this morning, so how are you feeling about Mexican food for dinner?" he asked because the silence was killing him.

"I've been looking forward to it all day," she said, forcing a smile. Standing, Parker glanced down at herself. "All I've eaten today is a couple of Pop-Tarts and as you can see, I haven't showered so...why don't you go and do that research on the teaching jobs and I'll go shower. Maybe we can do an early dinner and then hit the beach for a walk afterwards."

Ethan stood and nodded. "That sounds like a plan."

She kissed him on the cheek before turning and making her way up to her room. He watched her go and felt like they had hit a crossroads here and had no idea if it was good or bad. All he knew was that he wanted to be the one she confided in—the one she wanted to share her big news with first. It wasn't logical; after all, she and Tyler had been friends for twenty years.

Still...he thought they were heading in that direction, but...maybe they weren't and he was only seeing what he wanted to see.

And that hurt most of all.

TWELVE

The next day, Parker was bouncing on her toes as she stood on Mr. McClellan's front porch. She had picked up some of Peyton's famous chicken salad, some of her homemade rolls, peach cobbler, sweet tea, and because he had mentioned how much he loved deviled eggs, she got him a dozen of them to have later. Everything was packed up in a cute wicker picnic basket that she picked up herself, and she felt a little like Red Riding Hood waiting to see her grandmother.

"Please don't be like the big bad wolf," she murmured.

"Parker Bishop! Just look at you!" Mr. McClellan said as he opened the door. He was eighty years old, with a full head of silver hair and he smelled of peppermint and cigars.

In other words, he reminded her a lot of her great-grandfather.

"Come in! Come in!" he said as he slowly stepped aside.

"Hey, Mr. McClellan," she said warmly. "Thank you so much for agreeing to meet with me. I'm sure you were surprised when I called."

Together they walked to his dining room where they were greeted by a younger woman. "Parker, this is Ginny. She's my housekeeper slash home health companion slash all-around life saver."

"Oh my goodness!" Parker said as she shook Ginny's hand. "It's nice to meet you! I didn't realize anyone else was going to be here, but luckily I brought enough food!"

With a smile, Ginny waved her off. "No worries. When I heard we had a guest coming for lunch, I made plans to go run some errands so the two of you could have some privacy." She helped Mr. McClellan into his chair. "Do you need anything before I go?"

"Bah!" he said with a huff. "I'm fine! Everything we're going to need is right here." Then he glanced around. "Just hand me that folder and then go and enjoy your afternoon."

Parker put the basket down on the table and watched as Ginny placed a thick folder next to his plate. Her curiosity was definitely piqued, but she knew they'd get to whatever was in it before long.

She made quick work of taking out the food and setting it out for them. "And these deviled eggs are for you to enjoy later." When she saw his eyes light up, she added, "Or we can leave them out right now."

He grinned and patted the tabletop. "You put those right here, young lady, and don't be afraid to help yourself."

Deviled eggs were definitely not her favorite, so she shook her head. "Nope, I got them all for you, so enjoy them." She served their food and sat down beside him and raised her glass of tea. "Thank you again for agreeing to meet with me. You have no idea how much it means."

They tapped glasses and began to eat. The conversation was fairly generic—he asked about pretty much everyone in her extended family and she caught him up with all the news.

"Ezekiel would be thrilled to know the next generation of Colemans is growing so rapidly! It's what he wanted more than anything."

"Well, it's apparent that my family must feel the same way because they are all enjoying having babies one after the other," she said with a laugh.

"Has your sister set a wedding date yet?"

"She has. Next spring. By then her restaurant will be open and Ryder's resort should be done and they felt like they could focus on taking an extended honeymoon at that point."

He grinned. "Which means even more babies coming to the family."

"More than likely." Although, to be honest, she couldn't imagine her sister having a baby right away. The restaurant was going to demand so much of her time that she just didn't see her managing both right away.

"And what about you, Parker? Any wedding bells in your future?"

It was crazy that Ethan's face immediately came to mind. They hadn't been dating long, but...everything in her just loved him.

And he was going to leave her.

Okay, maybe she was jumping the gun and being dramatic, but after her conversation with Tyler, she knew that history was repeating itself. She was the girl who was the friend. She cheered the guy on and built him up and helped him achieve his goals, and then she was the one left behind. If Ethan went on this traveling teacher thing, chances are he was going to find a school that was a better fit and bigger than the community college here in Magnolia.

There would be a pay raise and more opportunities and he'd be gone. And where would that leave her?

Here.

In Magnolia.

Alone.

"Parker?"

"Oh, um...no. No wedding bells for me any time soon." She shrugged and smiled, even though saying it out loud made her heart ache.

They finished eating while sharing stories about her great-grandfather, but once she cleared their plates away and sat back down, Mr. McClellan seemed to want to get down to business.

"So tell me, Parker. What is it I can do for you?"

Letting out a long breath, she primly folded her hands in her lap and faced him. "When Pops died, he left something to all of us–even Uncle Cash, who hadn't been around in years."

He nodded.

"Well...lately I was wondering...um...everyone got something that was part of this town. Whether they wanted it or not." She paused and looked at him helplessly as tears stung her eyes. "I guess I was curious...I mean...I am so thankful for what he gave me and how it allowed me to travel and do so many things that I never would have been able to do."

"But...?"

"But..." she said with a watery laugh. "You were with him when he planned all this. You had to know his reasoning on why he left what he did to each one of us." Swallowing hard, she asked the question that now she wasn't so sure she wanted the answer to. "When it came to me, did he even consider leaving me a place here in Magnolia? Someplace to carry on his legacy, or did he think I couldn't handle it and thought it best to send me away?" Tears rolled down her cheeks and she quickly wiped them away with her hands before reaching for a napkin.

"Oh, Parker, don't tell me you think Ezekiel was trying to get rid of you! That's nonsense! You know more than anything that he wanted to keep all of you right here in Magnolia Sound. He spent his whole life building this town up to leave to his family."

She swiped at her tears again. "Not his whole family. He pretty much gave me a one-way ticket to leave."

With a patient smile, he reached over and patted her hand. "And yet...here you are."

"Yeah, well...there were circumstances."

He laughed softly before straightening in his seat. "I'm going to share something with you that you may already be aware of, but just bear with me, okay?"

She nodded.

"Do you remember when Mason got The Mystic Magnolia?"

She nodded again.

"That was what old Zeke called 'Phase One' of his inheritance. It was a little test to see what your brother would do with it."

Parker snorted with laughter. "We all got a big kick out of that whole situation."

"Yes, well...if he had decided to sell the bar or kick Tommy out and then level the place so he could sell the property, that would have been his inheritance." He paused and took another sip of his tea. "Your great-grandfather was really banking on your brother getting to know Tommy and seeing the potential was in the business and not in tearing it down for a quick buck."

"O-kay..."

"It was the same thing with your cousin Sam. We all know how gifted he is with landscape design. He has the biggest green thumb of anyone I've ever met. However, he didn't seem to have any intention of settling down into a career. So his 'Phase One' was that he had to work the business for a year. If, after that designated amount of time, he wanted to sell, then he was still getting an inheritance. Just in a monetary form."

"Well, that's not exactly the same. There was no phase two."

"Only because he decided to keep the business," Mr. McClellan explained. "Had he sold it, he would have gotten the money from the sale, but there was something else set aside for him as a way of making sure he'd at least come back to Magnolia once in a while."

Her eyes went wide. "Really?"

Then he waved her off. "But I'm not at liberty to discuss that."

"Oh."

"With Mason, once he invested in The Mystic Magnolia—as Zeke hoped he would—it meant his inheritance was actually costing him something. That's why he opted to also give him the property where he and Scarlett built their house."

"It was a beautiful piece of property," she commented. "But...wait. Are you saying there's a phase two for my inheritance?"

"That depends," he said softly.

Unable to help herself, she leaned forward. "On...?"

"Are you planning on staying back in Magnolia or is this a pit stop for you?"

Groaning, she slouched down in her seat. "Not you too..."

He smiled at her in that grandfatherly way. "It used to amaze me how insightful your great-grandfather was. It didn't take much for him to get a good read on people and normally he was spot-on. He believed in people's character and second chances and taking a leap of faith when need be."

This conversation was only confusing her more, but she figured he was going somewhere with it.

"I can tell I'm losing you so..." Pausing, he reached into the folder and pulled an envelope and handed it to her. "Here."

Her heart began to race and her hand was shaking as she took the envelope. "Um..."

"If you'd like some privacy, you are more than welcome to use my office."

But her head was already shaking. "No. No. This this is fine." Carefully, she opened it and pulled out the paper. As soon as she saw her great-grandfather's handwriting, her tears fell in earnest and she had to be careful not to get any on the paper itself. Taking a steadying breath, she got comfortable and read.

Welcome back, Parker pumpkin!

If you're reading this, you've seen Richard, or at least someone who he trusted with my estate. I'm hoping you've done your share of traveling and seen some amazing sights. I wish I were there to see the pictures and hear all about them. I'll admit that seeing the world never meant much to me because my world was right here in Magnolia Sound. But if my father and grandfather hadn't had the traveling bug, we might never have made it there so maybe that's where you got that wanderlust from.

There are thousands of beautiful and fascinating places to visit, Parker, but I hope you know the most beautiful place in the world is the place where you hang your hat at the end of the day. Home. Maybe I'm a sentimental old fool for thinking like that, but I've talked to enough people to know that I'm not in the minority with that mindset. Home isn't just four walls and a roof; it's a place where you are accepted and belong and have people who love you all around. I know you struggled with that last part because you were a little different from your parents and siblings. I always hated that for you and that's why I wanted you to have the opportunity to do what it was that you wanted to do—with no input from the peanut gallery. Ha! I bet your mama just about had a fit when she realized what I did!

But if you're reading this, perhaps you saw the world and are looking for something of your own. Something that is all yours with no pressure, no strings attached, and will have your stamp on it and no one else's.

For years, everyone thought I was hard of hearing because I could be in a room of people and not react to most of what was being said around me. The truth was I just enjoyed observing and people watching. I spent a lot of time observing you kids because I knew I wouldn't have as much time with you as I wanted. So I watched and I listened and the biggest thing I learned about you was that your biggest fear was failing. The pressure of being a Bishop or being a Coleman in Magnolia is heavy and for someone afraid to fail meant you had no interest in the things everyone else did.

So to you, my little pumpkin—did I ever tell you why I called you that? You were a beautiful baby and you had the chubbiest cheeks. The roundest little face with those cheeks, and your first Halloween, your mother dressed you like a pumpkin and it just fit. Even as you grew up, the picture I had of you from that Halloween was my favorite.

But back to business.

So to you, I give a clean slate in the form of the only property I ever purchased that is not part of Magnolia Sound. It's yours free and clear and Richard has a check for you that will hopefully cover whatever it is you choose to do with it. I hope you build something that shows the world how smart and fierce and fearless you are. Bring some of that worldliness you gained on your travels to our sleepy little corner of the world.

I love you, pumpkin. And I'm proud of the woman you've become. Do great things not because of anything anyone tells you—including myself—but because you are great.

Xoxo

Pops

Part of her wanted to hug the letter to herself, but she was afraid to crinkle it. This was the last thing her great-grandfather touched for her and she wanted to keep it as pristine as possible. Looking up, she saw Mr. McClellan smiling at her.

"I don't know exactly what he wrote, but I know what I'm supposed to do once you read it." Then he reached into the folder again and pulled out a larger envelope. "This is the deed to a building in Laurel Bay. It's in a good part of town and the property has been maintained all these years."

Parker stared at the envelope in disbelief. "A...a building?"

"Yes. It's a two-story brick building, plenty of parking. The interior is wide open so you really can design whatever it is you want. A good architect and contractor can help you with that."

The laugh was out before she could stop it. "I think I may know a few."

"Making it a family affair...nothing would please Ezekiel more."

Her breath was still a little shaky. "You have no idea...I was just working on plans for a business and I didn't know how I was going to make it happen. I just knew I needed to try."

"And now you can, with a little help from your Pops," he said quietly.

Standing, Parker walked over and hugged him. It was the closest she'd get to hugging her great-grandfather. "Thank you," she whispered. "Thank you so much." They stayed like that for several moments and when she sat back down, she took a moment to let it all sink in.

This time, Richard stood and picked up the peach cobbler. "Tell you what, you tell me about this business of yours while we have a little dessert. How does that sound?"

"Perfect," she replied and smiled as more tears fell.

* * *

TWO WEEKS LATER, Ethan managed to get invitations from four different schools who were looking for last-minute instructors and speakers, and none of them were in North Carolina.

The obvious choice–and using the two birds/one stone approach–was at CalTech. It meant he could go and visit his mother and perhaps spend some quality time with her. It was a two-hour drive from her house to the university, but depending on his schedule, he could rent a place to stay during the week and then stay with her on the weekends. He felt good about his decision and already accepted their offer and was excited to talk to Parker about it. It would mean him being gone for two months and she'd have the house to herself, but they could video chat every day and if she had time, he'd love it if she could come out to California and join him.

That is...if she wanted to.

Things had been hectic since the day she called Tyler. When they'd gone to dinner that night, things were strained and they were both more than a little subdued while they walked on the beach. When they had gotten home, they'd watched TV in bed, but it was the first time in a long time that neither initiated making love. He felt like she was pulling away and he wanted to fully put the blame on Tyler, but...maybe there was something to the warning her brother tried to give him. Perhaps if Parker hadn't interrupted them that day, he'd be a little more confident and know what to expect as they moved forward.

He didn't want to lose her, didn't want to think of a time when she would simply move on, but was he fooling himself? Did he really think he was the kind of guy someone as caring and vibrant as Parker would want for the long-term? But more than that, how did he tell her how he felt without scaring her off?

Then there was her inheritance that he saw as both a blessing and a curse.

She was going to be able to do what she wanted and have her spa without having to ask for any help from her family–except when she wanted to–and her plans were moving forward at full speed. And while she was wrapped up in architects and business plans, he had been searching for summer positions. At the end of each day, they talked about what they were doing but...there was a disconnect. Ethan knew she was excited about this incredible turn her life had taken and he couldn't be happier for her, but he needed to know there was still a part in it for him and vice versa.

It was while he was driving home that the idea hit. If he could make it work, it would be perfect. In his mind, he was already envisioning her reaction, and that just made him press the gas pedal a little harder.

By the time he parked at Happy Tails, he was practically giddy. He knew Parker wasn't working today and was hoping someone could help him sooner rather than later. Emma was walking out of the barn and spotted him. With a smile and wave, Ethan began to jog toward her.

"Hey, Ethan! If you're looking for Parker, she's not here today," she told him.

"No, no, I know that," he said breathlessly and cursed how unathletic he was that a small jog winded him. "I'm actually here to talk to you."

"Me?" she asked with a laugh. "Sure. What's up?"

"Is there any chance that Ollie is still available for adoption?"

Her eyes went wide. "You want to adopt a dog?"

He nodded vigorously. "Yes. Preferably Ollie, but if there's another dog that you know Parker's particularly attached to, I'd be open to that. Please."

"You know, we normally have a policy and procedure for this," Emma explained as they walked back into the barn. "There's an application process and a trial period and we like to meet with potential adoptive families..."

"Whatever you need from me, I'll do," he assured her. "Just...how long until I'd be able to take him home?"

With a small laugh, she looked over at him. "Ethan, we haven't even gotten to the dogs yet. There are a few that she does tend to spend more time with..."

"Please tell me one of them is Ollie." For some reason, he needed it to be the shepherd puppy. He knew the first time he saw the two of them together that he was meant to be Parker's dog.

They turned a corner and there, in a little pile of hay, sat Ollie all by himself.

Ethan immediately walked over and crouched down in front of him and let him sniff him. "Hey, buddy. Remember me?" The dog sniffed him before stretching and getting up on his hind legs to lick him. Laughing, he hugged the pup before turning to Emma. "Has anyone shown any interest in him?"

Sadly, she shook her head. "No, but he's taking some time coming out of his shell. The litter he came from all got adopted except for him and it was all before he ended up here. So he lost all his siblings and then the owners just couldn't deal with a puppy and brought him here." She sighed. "I hate when things like that happen."

"Why do you think he wasn't adopted?"

She shrugged. "He's way more mellow than most dogs, but Garrett's done a thorough exam on him and did all kinds of bloodwork. He's completely healthy." She reached out and scratched Ollie behind his ear. "Personally, I think he's sad."

"That's why he's the one I want to adopt. I want him to come home with me as soon as possible so Parker and I can cheer him up." He hugged the dog a little closer as he looked up pleadingly at Emma. "We need him as much as he needs us."

"Ethan..." she said wearily, but then shook her head. "Come on. We'll expedite you."

Clearly Ethan's definition of expedite and Emma's were two different things because it was almost three hours before he was pulling out of the parking lot with Ollie.

He knew this was a trial run and being treated like a temporary fostering situation, but there wasn't a doubt in his mind that this dog was meant to be theirs. Ethan wanted to give something to Parker that showed her how committed to her he was.

Right before he told her he was going to be leaving.

It all made sense in his mind and hoped it did in hers too.

At the house, he took Ollie out and let him sniff around the yard and do his business before heading inside. Parker's car was in the driveway, but so far she hadn't noticed his arrival–which was perfect because he wanted to walk in the house with Ollie and surprise her. And as soon as he opened the front door, he did.

"Hey, there's someone here to see you," he said casually and then watched her beautiful eyes go wide when she spotted the dog.

"Oh my goodness! What in the world?" Ollie ran right to her and the two of them rolled around on the floor in excitement.

Ethan stood back and felt an overwhelming sense of happiness. He loved doing this for her and seeing the utter joy on her face as she hugged the dog while he frantically tried to lick every inch of her face.

"Ethan! What is he doing here?" she said around a fit of giggles. "What is happening right now?"

Deciding to join them on the floor, he did his best to pet Ollie while the dog squirmed between them. "Well, I had something I wanted to share with you today, and I really needed this little guy to help me with it."

Instead of looking happy, Parker suddenly looked

apprehensive. "Oh God. What's happened? Is it bad? Are you...are we breaking up?"

"That's what you got from me adopting Oliver? That I'm going to give you bad news? Seriously?"

"You could be using him as some kind of consolation prize, Ethan," she reasoned. "Like, 'Oh, hey, Parker, this really isn't working out, but I know how much you wanted a dog, so...here.'"

"That's what you're thinking? How in the...?" Jumping to his feet, he began to pace. "That was your immediate thought?"

Parker got to her feet as well, with Ollie in her arms. "Can you blame me? The timing seems a bit suspicious, Ethan! What else could this possibly mean?"

"How about that I love you?" he shouted. "That I love you so much that I want to get a dog with you! Something that is ours together! Did that ever cross your mind?"

"You...you love me?" her voice was small and weak, as if this concept was completely foreign to her.

"Yes." Going to her, he cupped her face in his hands. "I love you, Parker Bishop. I didn't want a roommate, and I didn't want a dog, and I didn't want to break out of my staid and quiet life and yet...here we are. You're everything I never knew I wanted and now...I can't imagine living without."

Tears shone in her eyes before she stepped away and gently put the dog on the couch. "Stay," she said softly but firmly and surprisingly, he stayed. Then she moved back in close and mimicked his earlier pose and cupped his jaw. "I can't believe this is happening. You never said...I mean...we never talked about..."

"We talk all the time, Parker," he said, resting his forehead against hers. "We're just both overly cautious and not particularly good at talking about our feelings. But I couldn't hold it in anymore. I wanted you to know."

She smiled. "I'm so glad you did because...I love you too. I thought I was alone in this and then everyone got in my head with the comparison to you and Ty that I started second-guessing my feelings."

While he wanted to bask in her admission to loving him, the comparison comment sort of created a stumbling block. Pulling back slightly, he said, "Comparison?"

She nodded. "You know, Ty and I were friends, and I thought I was in love with him and then you and I became good friends and was I truly feeling what I thought I was feeling?" When she leaned in to kiss him, he pulled back. "What's wrong?"

Carefully, he covered her hands with his and pulled them away from his face. "I'm having a hard time with this, Parker. I mean, am I always going to be the guy who gets compared to Tyler? Why is there even a comparison? We're two completely different men, and these are two completely different relationships. Yes, you were friends with both of us, but you and Tyler were never lovers, were you?"

She shook her head.

"Then why lump us together at all? Shouldn't the basis of any good relationship start with being friends?"

"It should. It definitely should." She sighed. "I know this is nothing like my friendship with him. What you and I have is different and wonderful and so much better. Please don't stand here and tell me I ruined this perfect moment!" Pulling her hands from his, she cupped his face again. "I love you, Ethan Harlow. You and only you. And like it or not, you're stuck with me and our dog!" She stomped her foot for emphasis and even though he knew she was trying to be firm, it was just adorable.

Wrapping his arms around her waist, he smiled. "I'm happy to be stuck with you, Parker."

"Good. Now kiss me because I love you and really need it." And so he did before scooping her up in his arms and starting to walk to his bedroom. "Wait! We can't! We can't do that right now!"

"Why not?"

"Because poor Ollie just got here and we shouldn't leave him all alone!" She squirmed out of his arms and walked over to the couch. "Believe me, I would love to go inside and do what we do because you're so sexy and wonderful..."

Dear Lord...

"But I promise it will be worth the wait. We just need to get this little guy settled, okay?"

As much as it pained him, he agreed.

And later on, it was definitely worth it.

THIRTEEN

"Have you given any thought to a color scheme?" Georgia asked as she walked around the space that was currently under construction. It had been six weeks since Parker got the deed to the building and everything was falling into place. Her cousin Austin had drawn up the plans, and Jake had one of his crews from Coleman Construction working on finishing the interior. It was insane how fast everything was moving.

And not just with the building.

Tomorrow, Ethan was leaving for California. He was going to stay with his mother and stepfather and because of the birthday party, he was leaving sooner than he would have if this was just for the summer teaching session. She'd been doing her best to stay positive and soak up all the time they had together, but between him dealing with finals, her dealing with the spa, and puppy training, all of their quality time was happening when they crawled into bed at night.

Not that she was complaining.

"Parker? Parker, are you listening? Have you picked out your colors yet?"

"Not yet, Mom," Parker replied as she watched the final piece of sheetrock get drilled into place. "I needed to see the walls up so I can visualize it a little more clearly."

"Well, surely you have an idea..."

Why did I think it was a good idea to invite her here today?

"Perhaps we can get a decorator who..."

Without a word, Parker walked over to her makeshift desk and found the binder she'd been using because she was old-school and needed to write things down in order to feel more organized. "There is a psychology to color," she stated firmly. "Since this is a day spa, we want a relaxing atmosphere–nothing bright or loud or overly flashy. I'm looking at several shades of blue right now."

"Blue?" Georgia's nose wrinkled at the thought.

"For your information, blue can slow your pulse rate and lower your body temperature. It also stimulates compassion and sympathy." And because she couldn't resist, she added, "Perhaps you should have used that in the renovations at home." Then she pulled out the paint chip and put it on the table.

"Parker..."

"I also looked at this." Parker held up another paint chip. "Did you know that green not only has a soothing effect, but it also stimulates renewal and vigor? Or that it also offers emotional safety and is associated with healing powers?"

"I see what you're saying, but..."

"Colors can wait," Parker snapped. "Where is Oliver? He was sleeping right here a minute ago." She took all of two steps when she spotted her dog sitting next to Kyle Jones, who was talking to him and scratching him on the chin. "Okay. Whew. One crisis averted."

"Honestly, it's like I can't talk to you about anything! I don't even know why I'm here!"

Because I have a big mouth...

Taking a moment to mentally count to ten, she faced her mother. "I'm sorry, Mom. I'm just freaking out and you're trying to talk to me about things that I'm not ready for yet. I have everything mapped out and the only thing keeping me sane is following that plan."

Walking over to her, Georgia studied her. "What on earth are you freaking out about?" She looked around. "Everything seems to be on track."

"That's because I'm sticking to my plan!" With a huff, she walked over to one of the folding chairs she kept on site and sat down. It wasn't until she looked up and saw her mother standing there patiently that she knew she was waiting for more of an explanation. "This is all just...a lot. In my wildest dreams, I never imagined being able to do this on such a big scale. The little business plan I'd drawn up was for a place about half the size and a quarter of the budget. And in my mind, it was going to take a lot longer to pull it all together." Pausing, she let out a long breath. "What if it's all too much? What if I can't handle it? What if I fail?" Leaning forward, she forced herself to breathe. "What if another spa opens up and they're better than this one? Oh, God...I'm going to be sick."

Georgia moved another folding chair over and sat down. Gently, she rubbed her hand up and down Parker's back. "You're not going to be sick."

"Yes, I am. I'm going to be sick and ruin everything. Just wait and see."

They were silent for several moments before Georgia spoke again. "Well, I think I can take at least one worry away from you."

"I doubt it."

"Ryder's not putting a spa in at the resort."

That...got her attention.

"When did he decide that?"

"Your father and I stopped at their place last night. Ryder picked up a case of that sauvignon blanc that we love so much." She hummed softly. "Anyway, he told us that he realized after talking to you and Peyton and several others that a spa simply didn't fit in with the kind of resort he's building. So you see, one less spa for you to worry about."

"That was probably just a pity move."

All Georgia did was let out a soft sigh as she continued to rub her daughter's back. "My grandfather was a brilliant businessman and if he left this to you, it's because he knew you could handle it."

For a minute, Parker was too stunned to speak. She was still bent over and too afraid to look up.

"So if he knew you could handle it, and your father and I know you can handle it, and Ethan, Mason, Scarlett, Peyton, Ryder, and all your cousins who are investing their time and effort in helping you know you can handle it, why don't you believe it?"

"Because I failed at everything I ever tried," she mumbled.

"Nonsense. You never really tried at anything, Parker. Your fear of failure kept you from trying anything that was out of your comfort zone."

"I failed at school," she reminded her as she sat up slightly.

"That wasn't your fault. School is hard for some people. With a little extra help, you passed all your classes. Try again."

Again, me and my big mouth...

"College."

"Same as school. Try again," she replied lightly, almost as if she were enjoying this ridiculous game.

"Mom..."

"Sit up straight and stop whining. You're a business owner," she scolded, and oddly enough, that relaxed Parker.

"Fine," she murmured. "I'm sitting up."

"You want to know what I see when I look at you?"

"A hot mess?"

"Are we going to have a serious conversation or not?" When she started rubbing her temple, Parker knew she'd pushed a little too far.

"Sorry. You were saying?"

"When I look at you, Parker, I see a strong woman. A fighter."

Twisting in her chair, she was sure she misheard. "Really?"

"Really. You intimidate the heck out of me and you always have. It was like you came out of the womb with the attitude of taking on the world. It was like you didn't need me, even though you were just a baby. You were more interested in what was going on around you and by the time you started walking, it was like you went out of your way to walk away from me." Pausing, she shook her head. "Looking back, I know that wasn't the case. You were just this little person who wanted to see and touch and experience everything you could, and no one was going to stop you." Reaching over, she squeezed Parker's hand. "I think you're still that same little person. Don't stop yourself."

Holy crap.

"Mom...I..."

"Everyone doubts themselves from time to time. Even me," she added with a small smile. "But we all can't keep cheering for you if you refuse to cheer for yourself." After another pause, she squeezed her hand again. "I should have cheered differently when you were younger. I should have cheered with compassion and in a more loving way rather than criticizing. I know I can't change it, but you have to know if I could, I would. I would have spoken softer, given you more praise, and simply hugged you and comforted you when you needed it."

Wow.

Swallowing hard, Parker nodded. "To be fair, I did go out of my way to antagonize you. I knew exactly what buttons to push and I enjoyed pushing them all at the same time."

"You were merely reacting to me. I was the adult. The parent. And as such, it was my responsibility to teach you and guide you, not harp on you and crush your spirit." She sniffled and wiped at her eyes. "I just hope someday you can forgive me."

"I do. I really do, Mom. It means a lot that you came here and shared that with me today."

"I'm truly trying to do better." She stood up and moved a couple of feet away before facing Parker again. "And that's why I have to say what I'm about to say."

"Um..."

"You are fierce, you are smart, you are talented, and you, my daughter, are going to make this business a success. Not because of Pops and not because of the Bishop or Coleman names. This business is going to be a success because of you. You, Parker, and no one else. I'm done with letting you skate by making excuses for yourself. Believe in who you are and what you can accomplish!" Then she pulled Parker to her feet. "Believe like we all believe in you."

And in a move Parker never remembered experiencing,

her mother pulled her in for a hug. It was warm and it was wonderful and it lasted longer than any hug ever had in her life.

It was in that moment that she believed people could change.

Including herself.

* * *

ETHAN LOOKED at the luggage by the front door and sighed. He was leaving in the morning and he and Parker were supposed to go out for dinner tonight and then walk on the beach and he had all kinds of romantic plans for them.

But she was late.

If she didn't get home soon, they'd miss their reservations at the country club. She'd texted an hour ago saying she'd be on her way soon, but he hadn't heard back since. Ollie was with her so it wasn't like he could even pass the time taking him for a walk or feeding him or anything, so he was at a loss for something to do. All his things were packed up.

Sitting on the couch, he thought about the next nine weeks–which was how long he'd be gone between Alan's birthday party and his teaching position–and he missed his life already. Both he and Parker had been so busy between work and school that they hadn't talked much about how they were going to handle this separation. He knew he was avoiding it because he hated the thought of leaving her at all–even if it was temporary and for a good reason. Plus, after the way she reacted when he brought home Ollie, he was afraid she'd go down that road again.

It was safer to simply avoid the subject.

And he had a feeling she felt the same way.

He had no doubt that if he really pushed her for a reason...

"I'm here! I'm here!" she called out as she walked in the door. Oliver let out a happy bark before he ran over to Ethan and jumped in his lap. "I'm sorry I'm late, but the electrician was so close to being done and there was no one else to stay with him to lock up, so...as the responsible business owner, I stayed." Walking over to him, she kissed him soundly on the lips before pulling back.

"I hate to rush you, but if we're going to make our reservations..."

"Oh, we're not," she told him casually. "I called and canceled them."

"What?! Parker, I had big plans for us with dinner!"

She didn't look the least bit fazed. Instead, she held up one finger and then walked back out the front door.

Oliver was sitting beside him panting wildly. "She's exhausting, isn't she? I'm counting on you to take care of her while I'm gone."

The response he got was a wet lick on the cheek.

Two minutes later, Parker walked back in carrying a massive picnic basket. She walked over to the coffee table and put it down. "Sheesh, that was heavier than it looked."

"Um...what is this?"

She sat down beside him and kicked off her sneakers. "This is the dinner you planned for us, right down to the wine and dessert."

"How...I mean...when did you...?"

Grinning, she shooed Oliver off the couch. "I have a good friend who works at the country club. I told her what was going on and she helped me get everything to-go. Why don't you start pulling stuff out while I get us some plates and silverware?"

He did, but he was still a little miffed. "Why would you do this? I thought we were going to go and have a nice night out?"

She was still grinning when she sat back down. "Are we eating here or should we move to the kitchen table?"

"Kitchen table." Then they moved everything and set it all out.

"Anyway, I know we had plans for a nice night out, but I really wanted one last night in. We've both been so busy that I didn't want to go out and share you with anyone. We're saying goodbye and...you know...things are changing and I knew there was a good chance I was going to cry and didn't want an audience."

"Parker..."

There were already tears in her eyes. "You have no idea how hard this is for me or how much I'm going to miss you."

He reached out and wiped her tears. "Yes, I do because it's just as hard for me. I was originally just going to go and visit my mother and stay for Alan's party and I had planned on bringing you with me." He paused and kissed her softly. "But this teaching opportunity? It's something I have to do, Parker. It's something you and I have talked about over and over again. I need to know that I can do it."

"But...but what if it's really great and you want to stay?" she asked, staring down at the floor.

Ethan tucked a finger under her chin and gently forced her to look at him. "I'll still come back."

"They could offer you a huge raise–more money than you'll ever make here in Magnolia–and you'd be closer to your mom. Ethan, you can't tell me you wouldn't consider it."

There was a time when she might have had a point, but not anymore.

At least, he didn't think so.

"Parker, let's be real. I'm not the kind of guy who is going to dazzle the faculty of a big-name university to the point that they're going to throw wads of cash at me to lure me to work for them. This is just a way of me doing something I was always too scared to try. When it's over, I'm coming home and coming back to our lives here. This. This is where I want to be. With you and with Oliver."

That made her smile. "I love that you included him."

"Well, he's ours, right?"

She nodded, but her smile slowly faded. "I know you think you won't be swayed or that no one would offer you a permanent position, but...I just want you to know that...I would understand if they did and you wanted to take it. I don't want you to feel obligated to come back, Ethan. I know how much you love teaching..."

He never let her finish. Silencing her with a kiss, he took it deeper and held her closer until he felt her relax against him with a soft sigh. When they broke apart, he stared down at her. "I love you more. Remember that. Teaching is just a job, but you? You're everything." He smiled at her. "I love you."

"I love you too."

"Good. Now let's eat before all this stuff gets cold."

She really did manage to get everything they would have gotten if they went to the club in person–everything from a basket of bread and salads to their surf and turf entrées and brownie sundaes for dessert.

"I still can't believe they were able to do the sundaes," he said when she showed him how meticulously they were packed up. "Put them in the freezer so they stay that way."

"I'll admit I was a little nervous about them, but there was no way I was going to substitute cake for them. You know how much I love ice cream."

He laughed because she certainly did. More than once she had claimed she wasn't hungry for dinner, but then would eat a bowl of ice cream.

He held her chair for her so she could sit, and then he took his seat across from her. There were no candles, no cloth napkins, and no soft music. It was the least romantic setting and yet...it was perfect. They ate their meals and then continued to talk for hours. At one point, they fed Oliver and then took him for a walk together. Ethan even managed to play a rousing game of fetch with him using his favorite red frisbee. It had become their thing, and he knew he was going to miss doing this with him when he came home from school.

They made plans to talk every day and he made her promise to take lots of pictures and videos of the progress at the spa. She agreed and then made him promise that he would go and sightsee a bit and take lots of pictures and videos of the new places he was exploring since she'd never been to either Palm Springs or Pasadena.

And he agreed.

It wasn't particularly late—just a little after ten—when they began turning off the lights and getting Oliver settled in for the night. When it was finally just the two of them in his room, Ethan shut the door. "I have a favor to ask."

Parker looked at him curiously. "Sure."

"It would mean a lot to me if you slept down here while I was gone." He stepped away from the door and slowly advanced on her. "I know you have your own space upstairs with your nice new bed and all, but...I like to think of you here in my bed." He reached out and wrapped his arms around her. "Will you do that for me?"

Slowly, she nodded. "We can even video chat while I'm in the bed so you can see me."

He groaned as his mind filled with very naughty thoughts of how he'd like to see her in his bed–and not just during a video chat, but right now–tonight.

The kiss was demanding from the moment his lips touched hers. Ethan knew they had all night, but this night was going to have to sustain him for two months. Parker was demanding just as much from him. It became deep and desperate, wet and wild. Together they stumbled over to the bed as clothes began to go flying.

This was not the way he envisioned this night going. It was supposed to be about romance–savoring every touch, every word. But all his good intentions flew right out the door as soon as they crossed the threshold into this room.

He was still going to savor every touch.

Later.

And he was going to remember every word.

Later.

Limbs were tangled, their skin was already a little steamy, but when Parker straddled him and sat up, Ethan knew that this–this moment was the one that would be branded in his mind. Her hair was wild, her lips were wet, her eyes were glazed with passion, and she looked like a goddess to him. That smile–that sexy, impish smile of hers–it turned him inside out and he knew he'd never get tired of seeing it.

One hand skimmed up her arm and traced where her pulse was beating madly in her neck before cupping her cheek. "I love you, Parker." His voice was low and gruff and he watched her shiver.

"Make love to me, Ethan," she whispered.

And he did.

All night long.

* * *

HE DIDN'T SLEEP. His flight left at 6:45 in the morning, which meant he had to be at the airport by 5 a.m. Parker was sound asleep and they had agreed he wouldn't wake her before leaving. They'd said their goodbyes and every single one of them hurt.

There were two stops on his itinerary before landing in Palm Springs, and by the time he arrived, he would have been flying for almost ten hours, so that meant he had plenty of time to catch some sleep.

But it also gave him plenty of time to think about what he was doing.

In the grand scheme of things, two months was nothing. He knew he wanted forever with Parker, so this little separation shouldn't be a big deal. They were both going to be busy and by the time he returned to Magnolia, the spa would almost be done. He was thankful she was going to have the distraction. Two months ago, with the way her routine was, Ethan knew he would have felt too guilty to go to California alone. He would have gladly taken her with him. Hell, even now he wanted her with him, but her place was home so she could get her business going.

Deep in his heart, he knew Parker—more than anyone—would be okay. She may not believe in herself just yet, but he knew she was a fighter and a survivor and he couldn't wait for the day when she realized that for herself.

It was him he was most worried about.

Yes, this was a challenge he knew he needed to take on—

to prove to himself that he could teach at one of his dream universities and do a good job—but Parker's words kept playing through his mind.

"They could offer you a huge raise—more money than you'll ever make here in Magnolia—and you'd be closer to your mom. Ethan, you can't tell me you wouldn't consider it."

His gut told that he wouldn't consider it, but was he lying to himself?

If a school like CalTech wanted him—believed in him enough to offer him a position—he knew his ego would fight him on turning it down. Teaching in Magnolia was fine, but...was it fulfilling enough? Did it feed his soul enough?

Now the doubts started to kick in—the ones he had been keeping at bay for far too long. In his sleep-deprived state, those doubts were suddenly the loudest voices in his mind.

Was Magnolia Sound his endgame? Could he be happy living somewhere else?

What if CalTech did want to hire him on full-time? Would other universities feel the same? Should he keep applying elsewhere?

But the loudest voice of all—the one that was practically shouting at him—was about Parker.

Would this time apart show her that she didn't need him? Would she still want him when he got back? If the spa opened and was a success, she wouldn't need a roommate or a place to live. She could have her pick of what to do and where to go. She first came to him out of desperation at the lowest point in her life. Now that things were back on track and she was literally living her dream, would she walk away from him?

And worst of all, would she realize he was just a time-filler now that she had Tyler back in her life?

His eyes felt heavy and he was nearly delirious with exhaustion. This leg of the flight was three hours so he knew he could sleep. He wanted to fight it–wanted to keep debating all the issues that were fighting for space in his head–but he was losing the battle.

Closing his eyes, the vision of Parker smiling down at him from last night was there, and he couldn't help but smile back.

Please wait for me...

FOURTEEN

"This is the blue I want in the quiet room," Parker explained to the painter. "We'll be using different colors in the other rooms, but I want this one specifically for that room."

"You got it, Parker."

Sitting down behind her somewhat-upgraded-but-still-makeshift desk, she couldn't help but look around with pride. Things were coming together and it looked so damn beautiful that she wanted to just live here! They were down to installing all the finishes, and it was just crazy to see her inspiration come to life.

Reaching down, she gently scratched Ollie's head. There was going to come a time when she wouldn't be able to bring him to work with her, but for right now, it was comforting to them both. Ethan had been gone for a month and Ollie was the one constant keeping her sane. And she knew the dog missed Ethan too because he tended to wander around at home and cry at his office door.

She knew the feeling. Most days she came home and wanted to do the same.

They talked every night and she loved seeing his face and hearing his voice, but she missed having him there in person–touching him, sleeping beside him. This was so much harder than she ever imagined.

But of course she would never tell him that. The look on his face every day and the way he described his class and the campus told her he was having the time of his life. Even when his classes here in Magnolia were doing great, he never looked this energized and it was like her biggest fears were coming to life. Of course, she never asked if anyone offered him a permanent position and he never brought it up, so for now, ignorance was bliss.

But in her heart, she felt like he wasn't coming back.

Sure, he'd still have to come back, at least temporarily, if he were going to move to California. He'd have to get his stuff and sell the house. It would be awful. If she had to say goodbye to him a second time, knowing he wasn't ever coming back, she wasn't sure she'd be able to survive it. And for the first time in her life, she didn't want to leave Magnolia and travel or move or anything–not even for him. Her spa was coming along and she was determined to see it through and prove to herself that she could do this and be a success.

She was going to overcome her demons, even if it killed her.

There was a crash somewhere in the distance and she let out a long sigh and prayed it wasn't anything expensive.

Before she could even move, Jake came walking out to her and looked apologetic. "Nothing to worry about. That was a ladder, and it didn't break anything or do any damage. I'm sorry if it scared you."

Unable to help herself, she hugged him. "Thank God. I

suddenly imagined one of the rooms covered in broken glass or something."

He hugged her back before releasing her. "Nothing quite so dramatic. Just one of the guys not looking where he was going. Sorry."

"Whew!" Sitting back down, she let out another long sigh of relief. "So how's Mallory doing? I haven't seen her in a few weeks and I miss her like crazy."

"This pregnancy is a little harder on her. She tires easily and she had to hire two people at the shop to make up for losing you." He said it lightly and winked, but it still made her feel bad.

"Jake…"

"Easy, Parker. I meant it as a compliment. Mal was always saying you did the work of two people and she loved having you there. And she's dying for you to come in and order some pieces for the spa."

That made her smile. "We're getting close. I was afraid to start doing that too soon. I'm a very visual person and really needed all the rooms to be painted and the trim work and floors done before I could seriously think about the furniture I want in them."

"That is totally understandable." He nodded. "Tomorrow the HVAC guy will be here to balance out the system and we are looking at finalizing the punch list for everything by the end of the week. So I'd say next week you should only have a couple of people in here working on stuff, and then the fun stuff begins for you."

"Oh my goodness! Really? Already?"

He nodded again. "Everything was already in place when we started, so that made things flow a lot smoother. I think the decorating and stocking inventory is going to take longer than our work."

She had to agree.

"Have you decided what you're going to use the upstairs for? I mean, right now it looks like a great living space. You could rent it out or use it as a truly spectacular office."

"I think it's going to be my office."

For now.

With the possibility of Ethan selling his house–something she was mentally preparing herself for–Parker knew she needed a backup. The space upstairs just conveniently happened to work out that way.

"That's what Mallory was hoping you'd say," he told her. He pulled out his phone and scrolled a bit before handing it to her. "She wanted me to show this to you. She immediately thought of you when she saw it." He looked over her shoulder. "It's really more of a table, but she thinks the surface area would be perfect to use as a desk."

It was white with two large pedestal legs and had to be about six feet long. "It looks like it could be a dining table."

"Yeah, that's what it's labeled as, but once you put your computer and all the other odds and ends you'd need, it could be a great statement piece. And she claims to be getting the perfect chair for you too, so..."

That made her laugh. "Wow, she's been putting a lot more thought into this than I have."

"It's what she does. She loved doing it and she loves you." Jake took the phone back when she handed it to him. "We're all so proud of you, Parks. This is huge, and it's going to be amazing."

"Oh, stop. You have to say that. You're family."

"Only through marriage."

"Pfft, please. You were family long before you married Mallory. You might have been the kid who lived next door to Pops, but he never treated you like that. To him and to all of us, you were family."

It was cute to see him blush.

"So..." They were interrupted by the sound of people coming in the door and when she looked up, she let out a happy little cry. Her brother and sister were there and carrying what she hoped was food from Peyton's café. "You guys! What are you doing here?"

"We brought you lunch!" Peyton said as she held up one of the bags.

"You really didn't have to do this." First, she hugged her sister, and then her brother. "But since you did, what are we having?"

"Here, let me clear off this surface for you," Jake suggested, and within minutes they were all sitting around enjoying honey ham and Swiss croissants with Dijon mustard, potato salad, fruit salad, and a box of cupcakes from Henderson's.

Parker updated them on everything going on with the renovation and Jake filled in some of the gaps and by the time they were done and he was heading back to check on his crew, she felt full and happy.

Oliver had been patiently waiting for someone to drop some food and Mason gave him some of the treats Parker kept on hand before volunteering to take him for a walk.

When it was just Parker and Peyton, she realized it had been months since they'd been alone like this.

And she didn't know what to say.

"This is weird, isn't it?" she finally said. "Why are we both being so weird?"

Peyton laughed. "I know! It hit me this morning just how long it had been since you and I hung out, just the two of us. That's when I knew I needed to come here."

"With Mason?" she asked while trying not to laugh.

"Yeah, well...cut him some slack. He stopped in to pick up lunch, and I told him what I was doing and he pretty much begged to come along. Ever since the dinner at your place when Ethan told him off, he's been kicking himself and wanting to apologize."

"And yet he hasn't."

"You've been hard to pin down, Parks." Peyton glanced around. "This all looks amazing already. I can't even imagine how much better it's going to be once it's decorated. The colors are fabulous."

"Nice distraction," she murmured. "I've been right here and everyone knows it. He humiliated me and made things really awkward for poor Ethan on a day that was supposed to be fun."

"I know, but...I'm telling you, give him a chance. I think he was afraid to do or say the wrong thing again." Then she laughed. "It was amazing watching Ethan that day."

"You know some of that was aimed at you, right?"

She nodded somberly. "I do and believe me, Parks, I'm sorry. In my own way, I thought I was helping."

They could keep going round and round with this, but it wasn't helping anything. "Let's just put it all behind us. Everything's cool and I love you and we've both got a lot going on."

"I meant what I said. This place looks amazing and I know you are going to kick some serious butt with it. People are already talking about it and are anxious for you to open up."

"I hope so..."

"Stop. We all know it. Hell, Ryder even canceled the plans for the resort spa because he didn't want to compete."

She snorted. "Yeah. Mom told me and I think it was a pity move."

"Definitely not," Peyton told her firmly. "Ryder is a brilliant businessman and I'm telling you, he's arrogant and doesn't waver on anything. Trust me. He knew it was the smartest thing for the resort."

Parker wanted to believe that, but...it still seemed bizarre to her. How could her little spa one town over affect the fantastic one he was going to build for his resort guests? It didn't make sense.

Still...she was thankful.

Mason walked back in with Oliver. "Okay, I think he peed on every tree and shrub on the block!" Reaching down, he took the leash off and Parker thanked him. "No problem. I thought the two of you might appreciate me stepping away for a few minutes so you could talk."

"We did, and thank you," Peyton replied.

He looked anxiously at Parker and she knew the instant he realized he needed to say something with a little more depth. "I'm sorry, Parks. I should have been looking out for you and not throwing you under the bus or putting you down...especially not the way I did."

"It was really hurtful, Mason," she told him. She knew she was pouting, but he deserved it.

"I know, and again, I'm sorry. For what it's worth, I think Ethan was exactly what we all needed. This pattern we'd gotten into with you...I don't think we ever realized just how toxic it was. You know we love you and only want what's best for you."

She nodded. "I know."

He tugged her forward and hugged her. "So are we cool? Am I still your favorite brother?"

It was such a goofy and completely Mason thing to say.

"Dude, seriously. You're my only brother," she said with a laugh.

"The question still stands." He squeezed her hard before hauling her up and giving her a loud, smacking kiss on the cheek. "Say it! Say I'm your favorite brother!"

By now she was laughing hysterically. "Fine! Fine! You're my favorite brother, now put me down you big doofus!"

He did and before she knew it, they were cleaning up lunch and saying goodbye.

"When are you going to Mallory's to shop?" Peyton asked. "I'd love to go with you!"

"I may hit there early next week. Jake said that's when the big stuff will be all done."

Peyton kissed her. "Call me and we'll make a day of it if we can. I need a few pieces for the restaurant too."

"Deal!"

Mason hugged her again. "I'd ask if you were free to babysit because Scarlett and I really need a date night, but it looks like you're pretty busy."

"Take her out Saturday night and I'll be there. I miss the boys."

He practically sprinted from the building with a promise to see her on Saturday.

"Such a goof," she murmured before walking around and checking on the rooms and making a mental list of the kind of pieces she wanted for each of the massage rooms. The tables were standard and already on order, but there were chairs and shelves and other decorative pieces she would need to round out each space to make them functional as well as stylish.

"Hello? Is anyone here?"

Dammit. She hadn't locked the door after her siblings

left and there had been far too many curiosity seekers stopping by. Whenever she left that front room, she locked up to make sure no one came in without her knowing it and she kicked herself as she walked back to the front. "Coming!"

"Parker? Is that you?"

She stopped in her tracks.

Was it? Could it be...?

She took off at a run and found Ty standing in her lobby! "Oh my goodness! What are you doing here?!" She jumped into his arms and he spun her around just like he did hundreds of times before.

"Surprise!" he said before putting her back down.

"I can't believe you're here!" Parker knew she was smiling from ear to ear. Glancing around, she asked, "Is Kaitlyn with you?"

"Uh, no. She couldn't get off work and I was feeling a little homesick and decided to come and see my folks and you." He was grinning at her and it was so good to see his face and yet...she was mildly disappointed that it was him who surprised her and not Ethan. Every day she hoped he'd be the one to walk through the door and tell her he missed her so much and just had to fly home to see her.

But...this was nice too.

"Oh, well...please tell her I said hello," she said, realizing she was getting lost in her own thoughts.

"I will." He looked around. "You've made a lot of progress. The last set of pictures you sent showed a lot of tools and ladders all around."

"Yeah, most of that is going to be gone by the end of the week. Jake was telling me..."

"Hey, Parker?" Jake called out. "Can you come back here for a minute? We're in the kitchen!"

"Hang on for a minute," she told Ty just as her phone

began to ring. It was on the other side of the room and she was torn about what to do first. "That's probably the delivery company. My pedicure chairs are due next week and they need to set up a time to come in."

"Go talk to Jake and I'll get the phone and bring it to you," Tyler said. "Go!"

"Thanks!" She started to walk away and realized she could have just grabbed the phone. "Ugh...what is wrong with me?" In the distance, she heard Ty answer for her.

"Parker Bishop's phone!"

Laughing, she caught up with Jake. "Okay, what's up?"

* * *

"PARKER BISHOP'S PHONE!"

Ethan blinked with confusion for a second before he realized what–or rather, who–he was seeing. He took a chance on doing a video chat with Parker. He just never imagined she wouldn't be the one to answer.

"Hey, Tyler," he said casually. "Is Parker around?"

"Oh, Ethan, right? Long time no see! How are you?"

"I'm good, thanks. Parker didn't mention you were in town." And yeah, he knew he was sounding more than a little unfriendly and he didn't even care.

"I decided to surprise her. Just got in, actually. I came right here from the airport," he said with a confident smile. "The place looks amazing! Not that I expected anything less from our girl."

Ethan was fairly certain he was going to grind his molars to dust any second now. "So, is she around?"

"What? Oh, yeah. Hang on. Jake just called her to come look at something." He started to walk and Ethan wished he'd turn the phone around so he could see something other than Tyler's stupid face. "Here she is. Good seeing you, Ethan!" He handed the phone to Parker, but not before he heard Jake's happy welcome as they started to catch up like two old friends.

"Hey, you!" Parker said, as she righted the phone. "I didn't think we'd get to talk until later tonight!"

"Obviously," he mumbled.

"What?"

"Nothing, so...I was just thinking of you and was on a short break and...I just missed seeing your face." Some of the tension started to leave him and he knew it was just a weird coincidence that Tyler was the one to answer the phone. It was just poor timing—no big deal.

"I miss seeing yours too," she said softly. "Is everything okay?"

"Yeah, everything's fine. Like I said, I just had some free time and was missing you."

"I miss you too, but unfortunately there's a small leak in the kitchen sink and we need to get the plumber back here and Ty just showed up, so...can we talk tonight?"

He wanted to say no, but that would be petty. "Of course. Go and take care of business. I love you."

"Love you too," she said before blowing him a kiss and hanging up.

For a minute, Ethan just stared off into space. It had been a long shot that he'd catch Parker at this time of day with nothing to do. He knew she was busy. But after getting an email from the president of the university, she was the first person he wanted to talk to.

And now he had to wait.

Meanwhile, Tyler was there with her and he wasn't.

It pissed him off and frustrated him and there was nothing he could do and nowhere he could go to make himself feel better. Raking his hands through his hair, he read the email again and tried to wrap his brain around it. In every scenario he'd played out in his mind in preparation for this trip, this was one he honestly didn't see coming and he was going to have to make a decision sooner rather than later.

There was a knock on his office door and he looked up.

"Hey, Professor Harlow. Can I talk to you about my grade on Monday's test?"

It was the perfect distraction and filled the time until his next class.

Afterwards, he had papers to grade and then another class before he was done for the day. The drive to and from Palm Springs and his mother's house had proved to be too much, so he was renting a furnished one-bedroom apartment that was part of the faculty housing. He stayed there during the week and then drove to his mother's house on Friday afternoons, where he stayed through the weekends. It was nice having the time to visit with her and Alan, and they had been incredibly supportive of the things he was doing.

He wished it were a Friday so he could spend the weekend thinking over this offer from the school, but knew he really wanted to run it by Parker first.

So after picking up some takeout on his way home, Ethan settled in and at their designated time–seven his, ten hers–he set up his laptop and got ready for their nightly Zoom call.

Only...she didn't answer.

O-kay...

Considering it was ten in North Carolina, he knew Parker was usually exhausted and already in her pajamas in bed. It had been that way every night since he'd left. So what was different about tonight?

Tyler.

Muttering a curse, he picked up his phone and tapped out a quick text.

Ethan: Hey! Just tried to Zoom with you. Everything okay?

No response.

With nothing else to do, he ate his dinner and watched some TV while keeping one eye on his phone.

He didn't care that she was out with a friend. Hell, she rarely went out, so he thought it was great if that's what she was doing—even if it was with *him*. But considering they had sort of a set schedule with each other, he thought it was a little rude not to let him know so he wasn't sitting around like a pathetic loser waiting for the phone to ring.

"I *am* a pathetic loser," he murmured. It had been a long time since he felt that way, but since coming to California, it was amazing how quickly all those feelings came back. He hadn't made any friends and other than chatting briefly with some teachers in the lounge or the cafeteria and his mother and Alan, the only one he was spending time with was himself.

Were the classes going well? Yes.

Was he at ease in front of the larger group of students? Yes.

Did it fill him with the kind of satisfaction he thought it would? Yes.

If anyone asked him right now, he'd say this whole thing was wildly successful on a professional front. On a personal one, however, he was still the same shy and awkward guy he always was.

There was nothing on the TV to hold his interest, so he picked his laptop up again. After playing a couple of games of solitaire, he read the news and scrolled through his emails, where he found a second one from the president of the university.

Professor Harlow,

Would you be available to talk tomorrow after your 3 p.m. class?

Sighing, Ethan wished Parker would answer his damn text. There was no reason he couldn't go to the meeting. He just wasn't sure he'd have an answer yet.

"I might if Parker would call..."

It took another two hours for that to happen and by that time, he was more than a little disgusted.

Sitting on his sofa, Ethan clicked on the video link on his laptop and did his best not to scowl when her face appeared on the screen.

"I'm sorry! I'm sorry! I'm sorry!" she said quickly. "I completely lost track of the time and my phone died because I thought I put it on the charger earlier today and didn't and..." She let out a long breath. "I'm so sorry." She was sitting in their bed in her pajamas with her hair up in a ponytail and Ethan could tell she truly felt bad, but he wasn't ready to forgive her just yet.

"Parker, it's crazy late there. You can't tell me that the time didn't occur to you. Ever since we've met, you've never been a late-night person!" He hated how he was practically reprimanding her, but...

"I know, I know!" She told him about everything that had gone on construction-wise with the spa and all the work that was done and all the things coming up. It sounded like she would be incredibly busy–busier than what she'd been so far–in the coming weeks, but she was apparently very excited about it. "And then Tyler and I went and grabbed dinner and then we went to his parents' house and we started reminiscing and...I swear I just lost track of the time, Ethan! It's not a big deal."

"Well, to me it is," he argued. "I've been worried sick about you because you've never not answered a call or text! I mean...what was I supposed to think, huh?"

"Okay, I get it and I've apologized, but it's not like I can just go back in time and change it!"

"And what about Oliver? Was he stuck alone in the house in the dark without dinner while you were out?"

"Don't be ridiculous. He was with us. We took him walking on the beach and then he played in the yard with Mr. and Mrs. Burke's dogs. He was fine." Then she smiled at the dog, who was on the bed beside her. "He's exhausted because he made some friends, but he's fine." When she faced him again, her smile became sad. "Look, I know you're upset but...can we please just relax and chat? How was your day? Anything new and exciting going on?"

And because he was still riled up, he just let it all out instead of easing into it like he had originally planned.

"As a matter of fact, yes."

"Really? What did you do today?"

"The president of the university asked me to stay on through the second summer session."

"Oh, but...you already have your classes scheduled here," she reasoned. "You can't be in two places at once, right?"

"No, but he already reached out to the head of my department to talk about it because he's that interested in having me stay on."

He saw her pale slightly. "But...just for the summer, right?"

"He's not sure. As of right now, I'm meeting with him late tomorrow afternoon to discuss options."

"What...what kind of options?"

"A curriculum, assisting the head of the department, a moving and signing bonus..."

She only blinked at him for a solid minute. "But...you said you wouldn't even consider something like this. We talked about it and you said..."

"Well now I guess I'm curious about what they're willing to offer," he said and he knew instantly he sounded like a dick. He wasn't interested in the offer, but right now he was lashing out because he wanted her to hurt the way he was. All day, every day, she was on his mind and it seemed like it wasn't the same for her. Great things were happening for her and he was truly happy about that, but... it was becoming more and more obvious that she didn't need him. There wasn't a place for him and...maybe it was better to end things now before it got worse.

"Why...I mean...I don't understand. I didn't think this was what you wanted," she said quietly and he heard the slight tremor in her voice and it broke him.

"It's not what I want, Parker! The whole time I've been here, I've been miserable!"

"But you said..."

"I know what I said!" he snapped. "Every day you were so damn happy and everything was going so good for you. How could I dump all over you with my bullshit? There was no way I was going to bring you down!"

"But..."

"All day, all I wanted was to talk to you and I know you're busy. I get it, I swear I do. But I'm beginning to feel like there isn't a place for me in your life anymore! It's not like I expected you to sit home alone while I was gone, but... shit, Parker. I have nothing to offer you. I can't compete with all the things you have going on."

She shook her head as she started to cry. "You want to know something funny?"

"What?" he grumbled.

"I've been an insecure mess since you left. My mother keeps coming around and Peyton and Mason came for lunch today and everyone's trying to keep my spirits up because I miss you so damn much. And every night when we talk and you tell me how great the students are and how well your classes are going and...and I'm doing the same thing as you. I didn't want you worrying about me, so I've sort of been padding the truth."

Then he couldn't help it. He laughed.

Like a hearty, full-on belly laugh. "Are you kidding me right now?"

Parker joined in and her laugh was the greatest thing he'd heard all day. "I wish I were! How stupid are we?"

There really weren't any other words to describe it.

"I told you we were a dorky couple," she said to him between fits of laughter. "I miss you so damn much, Ethan! I won't tell you what to do with this job offer, but just know that I miss you and I will support you no matter what you decide. If you stay for another eight weeks or eight months, we'll find a way to make this work. I can't fly out there right now, but if I could, I would!" Wiping at her eyes, she gave him a watery smile. "No matter what, I love you and I'll wait as long as it takes to be with you."

No words had ever sounded sweeter. "I love you too, Parker, and I don't want to stay here a minute longer than I have to. I want to come home and work at my little community college with my small classes and come home at the end of the day to my small house and to you. The greatest part of my day is coming home to you and seeing your face, kissing your lips, and sleeping beside you at night."

"Oh my God, that's what it's like for me too! It's been so lonely without you!"

"Stop. You went out tonight and had a great time. You've got your family and..."

She held up her hand to stop him. "Okay, I have to share something with you and...it's hard for me to say so... you have to let me get it all out."

"O-kay..."

Letting out a long breath, she fidgeted a bit before looking directly at him. "When Ty showed up today, my first reaction was to be all like...yay! But almost immediately, I was sad because I wished it were you."

"Parker..."

"Wait. I'm not done."

"Sorry," he said with a bashful smile.

"Then he was hanging out all afternoon at the spa and I was trying to work and he was just talking and talking and talking and after a while I asked him to take Oliver for a walk just so I could hear myself think!"

Snickering, he nodded.

"By the time we went to dinner it was like...it all made sense. That day when I first called him and he was all apologetic with me and pointed out how selfish and self-centered he was, at first I didn't remember it that way. And then I did."

"Right..."

"But today? Sweet baby Jesus...today it was almost painful to listen to him! I mean...we were standing in the middle of the spa–a business that I'm building from the ground up—and other than some generic comments about 'great space' or 'oh, that looks cool,' everything else was about him!" She started to laugh. "At first I thought it was sad that Kaitlyn wasn't with him, then I realized she probably was relieved to have him gone for a few days!"

"Yikes!"

"Exactly! He wanted to come back to the spa tomorrow and hang out, and I totally lied and told him I was meeting with inspectors all day and to come! I don't think I could have handled another day of him!" She shook her head. "We had a long talk at the end of the night and this time, it was me telling him how he needs to grow up and start thinking about other people."

"Wow. How did he take it?"

"Better than I expected. I think after our initial phone conversation, he was already aware that this was an issue, so...I just sort of hammered the point home."

"Good for you."

"So by now I'm sure you're thinking, why was that hard for me to say, right?"

"Well, it didn't seem all that terrible..."

"I haven't gotten to the worst part."

Ethan braced himself, even though he had no idea what she was going to say.

"I invested twenty years in my friendship with Tyler. He is always going to be a part of my life and so many of my memories involve him." She paused. "But the quality of that relationship is nothing compared to what you and I have."

"Parker..."

"I'm so sorry if I or anyone else tried to compare the two of you and I could see on your face how much it bothered you and how much today hurt you. But you need to know that I would take what you and I have together over my friendship with Ty any day of the week. You are my person and if my friendship with him bothers you that much…"

"Parker, stop. I'm not going to lie. I was jealous. I know there was nothing romantic there. I know it because you told me that forever ago and I trust you. I was jealous of him because…because it felt like maybe he meant more to you and that's my insecurity. That's all on me, so…please don't end a lifelong friendship because of me. I will learn to be okay with it."

But she was shaking her head. "Ty and I are always going to be friends. Long-distance friends. And even though that makes me a little sad, that's the way some friendships are. Sometimes we outgrow them and I think that's where we're at."

"I'm sorry. I know that can't be easy."

She shrugged. "Believe it or not, it wasn't as hard as I thought." With a loud sigh, she moved around again and relaxed against the pillows. "What is harder than I thought, though, is all this time apart. I know we still have like… what…five weeks to go?"

"Yup. I wish I could come back sooner…"

"No. We can do this. We're strong and we can do this."

He smiled at how brave she sounded. "Yeah, we are."

"Just know this, Ethan Harlow. When you come home, I'm locking us both in this house for an entire week. No one is allowed to disturb us and I'll leave my mom in charge of things at the spa. You're mine."

"Parker Bishop, I'm going to hold you to that."

She yawned and smiled sleepily. "You better. I wish you were holding me right now."

"Me too."

She yawned again. "I'm sorry I ruined our night."

"Don't worry about it, beautiful girl. Get some sleep and we'll talk tomorrow."

"But...what are you going to tell the president of the university tomorrow?"

"I'll say thanks but no thanks. My life—my everything—is waiting for me back in Magnolia Sound."

"Mmm...I like the sound of that." Her eyes were closing and her words were quiet.

"Go to sleep, Parker. I love you."

"Love you too..."

FIFTEEN

"One more week. Just one more week." That was becoming her mantra. Ethan would be home in another week and Parker was seriously hanging on by a thread, emotionally.

Everything at the spa was coming along beautifully–furniture and equipment were coming in every day so she wasn't too overwhelmed. Her mother was helping a ton and so were a bunch of other people. Mallory had come by several times when the furniture from her store was delivered so she could help set it up and she'd even helped Parker get her office organized. Mason and Scarlett had come and built some custom shelves for her in her office as well. Austin had taken the original blueprints that Pops had of the building and framed for her, which was incredibly sweet. Emma and Garrett had stopped by with gifts for Oliver–a very posh and comfy dog bed for Parker's office, as well as some cupcakes to share while she gave them the tour.

Her cousin Sam had come and cleaned up the exterior property for her and did a little refreshing on the landscape to brighten everything up. Peyton had sent lunch over every day to make sure she was eating, and Ryder had sent her the biggest bouquet of flowers she had ever seen congratulating her on such an amazing accomplishment. The spa wasn't open yet, but it was only a few weeks away and all the love from her family was overwhelming.

She just had one more week to get through before her life would be perfect again. If she could just have everything stay like this, with no drama, Parker knew she'd be fine.

"You are not going to believe it! You are just *not* going to believe it!" Georgia announced as she came waltzing in the door.

So much for no drama...

"What's going on?"

"Well, I was running errands in town and had to stop at the post office and you'll never guess who I saw!"

"Probably not, so you might as well just tell me."

"Cash! Cash is back in Magnolia!"

"What?!" she cried. "Did you talk to him? What did he have to say? Oh my God! Does Austin know? Does Garrett?"

But her mother was shaking her head. "I didn't get the chance to talk to him. I was pulling out when I saw him walking along the sidewalk with some young girl." She looked at Parker with that pinched expression. "A very young girl. A girl young enough to be his daughter!"

"No!"

"Oh, yes. She had her arm around him though, so if it is his daughter, it was wildly inappropriate for them to be so... close." She shuddered. "What on earth could he be thinking by coming back here and bringing that...that girl with him? Has he no respect for his sons?" She groaned. "I can't even imagine how the boys are going to react to this–especially poor Garrett. After everything Cash put him through with the money..."

"I think we're getting a little ahead of ourselves. Are you sure it was him? If you were driving away..."

"Oh, I'm positive. I'd know that face anywhere." She paused and nibbled on her lip. "Do you think I should call Grace and give her a heads-up?"

Grace was Cash's ex-wife and somehow Parker doubted she'd want to get this kind of news from Georgia. "Um... maybe we should stay out of it. You know how bad it was after you encouraged him to come back the last time he was here."

"Hmm...do you think anyone else will remember that?"

"Yes, Mom! You're the reason Uncle Cash came back and messed with Austin and Garrett and Jackson's lives!"

"I was not responsible for his actions! I merely encouraged him to reach out to his sons! I didn't tell him to practically rob them! And really, Jackson was deployed so he didn't have to deal with any of it."

"Just...stop talking," Parker said wearily. "Please. Honestly, you're giving me a headache."

Frowning, Georgia stepped behind the reception desk and looked around. "Are there any deliveries scheduled for this afternoon?"

"No. We had one this morning. I was going to work on the nail polish display and putting out the bath bombs and the other bath accessories. I was thinking..."

"I think you should take the afternoon off."

"Um...excuse me?"

Nodding, Georgia reached beneath the desk and grabbed Parker's purse and practically thrust it into her hands. "I'm going to handle the polish display and the bath goodies. You, my sweet daughter, need an afternoon off. You look terrible."

"Mom!"

"What? It's the truth!" She studied her for a minute. "You know what you need?"

She sighed loudly. "No, but I'm sure you're going to tell me..."

"You need to take Oliver and go down to the beach. The two of you haven't done that in weeks. He needs the exercise and you need the fresh air."

Actually, it wasn't the worst idea...

"I don't know. There's so much to do and..."

But Georgia wasn't listening. She took Parker by the shoulders and spun her around toward the door. "Where is the dog?"

"Upstairs in his snazzy new bed. That thing looks more comfortable than mine and Ethan's bed."

"Hmm...I don't even want to think about that. Just...call him and the two of you go and have some fun. Maybe get yourself an ice cream cone down at the pier and let the sun hit your face and relax. Now, doesn't that sound wonderful?"

"Right now, it sounds positively decadent." Pausing, Parker called for Oliver and smiled when he came running down the stairs. "Come on, boy. We're going to go to the beach!"

He barked his approval.

"Thanks, Mom. Are you sure you don't mind?"

"Sweetie, it was my idea." She kissed Parker on the cheek. "Now go and relax and don't worry about a thing. I've got it all under control."

"I know, but..."

"For goodness' sake, go!"

"Fine...I'm going. I'm going!"

It was a beautifully sunny day and as soon as she drove back into the Magnolia city limits, she felt herself start to unwind. She'd been working seven days a week since before Ethan left, so maybe it wasn't the worst thing in the world to take one afternoon to play hooky. Of course, when he got home at the end of next week, Parker already blocked out a week of time off, but she knew neither of them were going to be able to stick to it. He was going to have lesson plans to work on and she wouldn't be able to stay away from the spa for that long. But in her mind, she wanted to hold on to the fantasy.

"What do you think, Ollie? Should we get ice cream?"

Bark!

"Hmm...last time we were there, sweet Mrs. Bailey gave you a cup of vanilla. I bet you're hoping she'll do that again, huh?"

Bark!

"I hear ya. I hope she does too. Then the two of us can sit and listen to the waves while we enjoy a sweet treat."

Bark, bark, bark!

"Okay, okay, settle down. We're not there yet."

Fortunately, they were parking within ten minutes, and it was late enough in the day that the public parking lot wasn't too full. She parked and grabbed Ollie's leash and got him secured before letting him out of the car. Out on the boardwalk, they went and ordered their ice cream and Mrs. Bailey made a big fuss over Ollie and how big he was getting and what a good boy he was. Parker thanked her and then tried to juggle her cone, his cup, his leash, and a fistful of napkins.

"I'm not sure I'm coordinated enough for this," she murmured as they walked down the stairs to the sand.

Oliver was great about not dragging her or trying to run ahead–probably because he saw she was holding his snack. Either way, once they got a little closer to the water, Parker found a spot and sat them both down. "There we go. Enjoy." She placed the cup in front of him and then watched as he happily lapped it up.

Then she did the same with her cone, which was melting rapidly.

"Damn. I'm making a mess." She tried to use some napkins, but with the leash in one hand and the ice cream in the other, it was almost impossible to do.

She licked more of her hand and prayed no one was watching.

Beside her, Ollie got to his feet as if he were on alert. Parker looked around and spotted some kids playing a little down the beach but didn't think they were doing anything to get him worked up or nervous.

Then he started to bark.

A lot.

"Oliver!" she hissed. "Stop that. There's nothing for you to be barking at."

But he wasn't listening. If anything, his barking was getting louder and a little more urgent, and he began tugging on his leash. Parker tugged back and scolded him again, and then he started to whine.

"You're being pitiful," she told him even as she came to her feet. "I know you want to go walking, but just give me a minute."

His crying got worse and he took off, causing her to drop the napkins and what was left of her cone.

"Oliver! Stop!" He was much stronger than she was and for the life of her, she had no idea what he was racing toward. "Ollie, come on! Stop! Heel! Stay!" She used every command they learned in puppy training, and then he stopped just as abruptly as he started. It took her a minute to catch her breath. Bending over, she was nose-to-nose with him. "That was very naughty! You cannot go running off like that! I know you want to run and play, but you have to give me a chance to get to it, okay?"

He was squirming to get her face away from his and she laughed at how they must look. There was a soft thump beside them and when she looked, she spotted a red frisbee.

What the...?

Straightening, she turned, and that's when she saw him. Ethan.

"Oh my goodness," she whispered and briefly let go of the leash. Oliver took off like a bullet out of a gun and this time, she willingly and happily ran after him.

And right into Ethan's arms.

* * *

PARKER AND OLIVER tackled him onto his back in the sand and even though it completely knocked the wind out of him, it was well worth it. His arms were full of the woman he loved and his face was getting thoroughly cleaned by his favorite dog.

Life didn't get much better than this.

"Oh my God! Oh my God! Oh my God!" Parker was whispering as she shakily held on to him. "You're here. You're really here!"

It took a minute or two to get them all settled and in a more comfortable position, but once they were all sitting up and he could see both their faces, he couldn't help but grin from ear to ear. "Surprise," he said.

"This is the best surprise ever! How...I mean...when... why didn't you tell me?"

Laughing, he leaned in and kissed her because he finally could. "I wanted to surprise you, and your mom helped me make that happen."

Her eyes went wide. "You talked to my mom? Willingly?"

"Stop. She's not that bad and you know it. But yes, I called her last week and told her what I wanted to do, and she promised to make it happen."

"But...why her?"

"Because she's been working with you almost every day, so I figured she'd know your schedule and would be able to get you where I needed you to be. Which was right here."

She moved in as close as she could get, resting her head on his shoulder, and one hand gently clutching his shirt. "I can't believe you're back." Gasping, she straightened. "What about your classes? I thought you had finals this week."

"I did, but I didn't need to be there for them. My assistant and a proctor were there to oversee them and they'll scan them and send them to me for grading."

"That sounds like a lot of extra work."

"You're worth it," he said, leaning in to kiss her again.

"Ethan," she said breathlessly, holding his face and kissing him back. "I've missed this–touching your face and kissing you." Another kiss. "Can we..." Kiss. "Go home." Kiss. "And do more of this?"

The next kiss was much more satisfying. He started to guide them down onto the sand when Oliver let out a loud bark.

That immediately broke the mood.

"Well...as much as I'd love to take you home and do all

the things I've been wanting to do for almost two months, I think we owe it to this guy to play a little fetch first. Then," he said as he got to his feet and held out his hand to her, "I promise we'll go home, where I'm going to kiss you from head to toe repeatedly along with other wicked and sexy things, and then we'll order dinner, eat, and do it all again." Then he grinned. "Just the sexy parts, not the frisbee and eating."

She laughed and squealed with delight. "It's perfect! It's the perfect plan!"

He bent over and picked up the frisbee and threw it. Oliver took off and caught it mid-air like they'd trained him to do and they kept that up for almost an hour.

"I think my arm is ready to fall off," Ethan said when he took the frisbee from Ollie's mouth for the last time. "Maybe it's time to call it a day, huh, boy?"

"Most definitely," Parker agreed. They walked hand-in-hand back to the parking lot, and she was surprised when he climbed in with her. "Where's your car?"

"At the house. Your mother dropped me off here earlier because she knew you wouldn't want us to be apart, even for the short drive home."

"Remind me to thank her."

There were so many things he wanted to talk to her about even though they talked on the phone and via Zoom every day. But right now, it was nice to drive in companionable silence, just watching the scenery he'd missed so much and holding his girl's hand.

At the house, they went inside and got the dog settled in the living room before Ethan made good on his promise and led Parker to the bedroom.

She was instantly in his arms and kissing him, but it wasn't the fast and frantic like he imagined—like the night before he left. This time, it was slow and sensuous–languid and lazy and so damn good. She was a feast for his tired soul and he loved having her in his arms, in his house, and soon... in his bed.

There were soft, murmured words and even softer sighs as they got reacquainted with one another. The catch of her breath, the feel of her hands on him...all the things he'd been fantasizing about were once again his reality.

He told her again and again how much he loved her and missed her, and Parker did the same. He slowly undressed her–worshipped her–before guiding her down onto the bed. Then those eyes, those dark beautiful eyes, watched him as he shed his clothes before joining her.

Even though his body was screaming at him to take her–to do all the things they'd been talking about–right now, Ethan just wanted to look at her, to take her in. There were times he couldn't believe that the girl he couldn't even bring himself to talk to throughout high school was now the woman he wanted to spend the rest of his life with.

Her hands were in constant motion, but her eyes never left his face. "I still can't believe you're here. That you came home early for me."

"I never should have left," he said solemnly. "Even though this experience was something I needed to prove to myself that I could do it, it wasn't worth what we missed out on."

"No," she whispered. "As much as I hated that you were gone, I think it was good for both of us. Everything is clearer now. Better." He watched as she nibbled on her lip. "I feel like a better version of myself."

"There was nothing wrong with the previous one. There never was."

"Ethan..."

He silenced her with a kiss.

There was plenty of time for them to talk–later, tomorrow, the rest of their lives. This moment right here was the one that was about feeling and showing her how much he missed her.

Cherishing her.

Loving her.

It was good to be home.

* * *

"I CAN'T BELIEVE you're doing this again."

"Please. You know I'll never get enough."

Ethan chuckled. "I wish you were saying that about me and not the ice cream."

Parker licked her spoon and gave him a wicked grin. "It's seriously a tie between the two of you, but after all the things we've done tonight, I needed ice cream."

"But you had some at the beach."

"Pfft that was hours ago." It was late and they were in bed after having dinner and making love again. "It's after midnight so...technically, I had ice cream yesterday, so..."

This girl...

As much as he was teasing her, her love of desserts was just part of who she was and what made her the amazing woman she was today.

After she put her bowl down on the bedside table, she immediately turned and curled up against him.

Cold hands and all.

"Holy crap, Parker!" he hissed.

"Sorry! Sorry!" She rubbed her hands along the comforter to warm them up and then blew on them before touching him again.

"You know I had big plans for locking us in here when you got home, but that was next week."

"I know."

"Now I may have to juggle a few things to make that work. I've got some deliveries lined up and I guess my mom can handle them, but..."

Ethan placed one finger over her lips to stop her. "You don't need to juggle anything. The spa needs you and I am looking forward to going with you every day and helping out wherever I can. I sort of feel bad that I haven't been here to help with it all this time, so my plan was to work with you this week and then maybe we can take a few days to ourselves. Maybe even go away somewhere, just the two of us."

"But...Oliver..."

"Parker, there are plenty of people who would love to help out with him."

"But...he's still a baby. And you just got back. He's going to have abandonment issues."

It was hard to believe they were talking like this abut a dog, but...dammit...she was right. "Fine. Then let's find a pet-friendly destination and the three of us can go and hang out for a few days. Someplace that's not in Magnolia. I'm sure by now you're itching to travel."

She shook her head. "Honestly, I'm not. I thought I would be too but...there's so much going on here and I've been spending time exploring Laurel Bay and it's been great." She snuggled closer. "I was incredibly blessed to be able to travel the way that I did for a few years, but this is home." Tilting her head, she smiled up at him. "Right here with you. This is where I want to be most in this world."

"Being away in California...it was beautiful, and I kept wishing you were there to experience it with me, but at the end of the day, this was where I wanted to be too. Here. With you."

"Mmm...then this is where we need to stay. We can have one of those staycation things. No going to work or school, just hanging out at home and enjoying our little town."

That sounded good to him.

For several minutes, neither spoke. They didn't need to.

Until...he did.

"Parker?"

"Hmm?"

"There's something I think you should know," he began cautiously. They were both exhausted and he knew he was more than ready to go to sleep, but he had to say this because it was what he had planned all along.

"O-kay..."

Tucking a finger under her chin, he gently tilted her head back so he could look at her. "I'm not a spontaneous guy and we both know how I tend to overthink everything."

She nodded with a yawn.

"Where you're concerned, however, I *am* that spontaneous guy. You've brought out a side of myself that I never knew was there."

"I like all your sides."

That made him smile. "In my head, I imagined coming home and surprising you on the beach and proposing to you right then and there."

Parker sat straight up, all wide-eyed. "What?"

"Yeah," he said with a nod. "That was what I wanted to do."

"But..."

"But...the overthinker in me took over, and I was all like...maybe we need time to settle back in and maybe I should find a more romantic time or maybe it would be too distracting with the dog..." He looked at her helplessly as he caressed her cheek. "You are it for me. I want this and I want you forever. I don't have a ring and I cringed at the thought of proposing while we were in bed and..."

"Ethan..."

"I can't shut my brain off enough to do the things that I really want to do sometimes, but I just wanted you to know what I'm thinking. I love you and I want to spend the rest of my life with you. But the over-thinker wants to pick the perfect moment."

She smiled as she leaned in, placing a soft kiss on his lips. "I think you just did."

"There's no ring," he told her.

"Not yet. We don't need one. I just need you, Ethan. That's all I'll ever need."

"You have me, Parker. Always." Ethan drew her in close and kissed her. He knew he'd go get her a ring tomorrow, but for the first time in what felt like forever, Ethan stopped worrying and let himself be happy.

And it wasn't nearly as hard as he thought it would be.

EPILOGUE

THREE WEEKS LATER...

Parker unlocked the front door and walked back over to the reception desk and couldn't wait for things to get started. The sun was shining in and it caught on her gorgeous engagement ring. She still couldn't believe Ethan formally proposed the day after they had talked about it. Even though she knew it was coming, he managed to surprise her during a walk on the beach with Oliver. He had gotten down on one knee after she finished her ice cream—because he said he wanted her full attention on him—and she burst into tears before saying yes.

The ring truly wasn't necessary. She would have married him that day right then and there if he'd asked, ring or no ring.

But she was still thrilled to have it.

"And it looks so pretty on my finger!"

Her phone chimed with reminders of her schedule for the day. There were eight interviews scheduled for everything from receptionists and massage therapists to estheticians. Her mother was going to come and join her after lunch because the massage therapists had to be tried out and as much as Parker loved a massage, she already had three of them this week. So as a gift to her mom, she was getting one too. And maybe she'd let her sit in on the interview as well.

The morning interviews went well and at noon, Georgia showed up with lunch for the two of them.

"So? How's it going?"

"Everyone's been great and super qualified on paper, but there were a few I just didn't click with."

"Well that's a shame." Reaching into the bag, she handed Parker a sandwich. "I got you the turkey club. Peyton put extra bacon on it for you."

"Ooh...perfect!" She waited for her mother to comment on how that wasn't healthy, but surprisingly, she said nothing.

"Who are we interviewing next?"

Parker shuffled through her papers. "Um...her name is Savannah and she has her cosmetology license. She's also an esthetician, and a massage therapist. She's pretty much the total package."

"Hmm...what's her experience?"

Glancing over the resume, she said, "She's new to the area. All her previous employers are in Seattle. I wonder what brought her all the way here."

"Probably all the rain they get in the Pacific Northwest."

"Mom, be nice."

"What? That wasn't mean; that was a fact."

"Just...don't say anything like that when she gets here. You'll be the one getting the massage and I don't want her to inflict pain on you because you were snarky."

"It wasn't snark."

"Mom!" she cried. "Sheesh!"

They finished eating and Parker shared more of the applications she had gotten because she appreciated getting someone else's opinion. At one o'clock, Savannah Brennan arrived. She was dressed in black scrubs with her hair pulled back in a bun, and she definitely looked ready to go to work. Parker took another glance at her resume and saw that Savannah was a few years younger than her and wondered if she'd made any friends since moving here.

"Hey! I'm Parker Bishop," she said as she stood to greet her. "You must be Savannah."

"Yes," she said with a confident smile. "It's nice to meet you."

"Um...I have a ton of questions for you, but I have to say I'm most curious about what brought you to Laurel Bay all the way from Seattle."

Before Savannah could answer, Parker turned to her mother.

"Mom? Could you please lock the front door? We'll take Savannah on the tour of the place and since you'll be with me, I want to make sure no one comes in."

"Of course."

Then she returned her attention to Savannah. "Sorry. It was just on my mind. So...Seattle to Laurel Bay? Do you have family here?"

She nodded. "Well, now I do. I moved here with a family member. He's got cancer and it's terminal and I've been taking care of him." She gave them both a sad smile. "He's the only family I have."

"Oh, I'm so sorry," Parker said, reaching out to squeeze her hand.

"Thanks. There are relatives here and people he wanted to come and say goodbye to and there was no way I was going to let him go alone."

"Of course you couldn't," Georgia said sympathetically. "You poor thing."

"Anyway, they're not here in Laurel Bay, but in the next town over. I think it's...Magnolia Sound?"

Parker looked at her mother, who was already staring at her. "Really? Magnolia's a small town and we actually both live there. If you don't mind me asking, who's your relative?"

"Well, he hasn't lived there in ages," Savannah said, "but he talks about it all the time. I can't imagine it's that small of a town."

"Try us," Georgia said, and Parker wanted to kick her.

"What my mother means is that we've lived there our whole lives and feel like we know everyone. Even if we don't know him, we might know his family."

Savannah looked awkwardly between the two of them. "His name's Cash Coleman."

There was no time to react to that statement because her mother fainted dead away.

And suddenly, staffing her spa seemed like the least of her worries.

A PREVIEW OF A GIRL LIKE YOU

GO BACK AND REVISIT

A Girl
Like You

CHAPTER 1

"I'm in hell."

"Dramatic much?"

Sam Westbrook glared at his twin sister Mallory. "It's not dramatic, it's a fact."

Mallory rolled her eyes at him even as she smirked. "Care to clarify, then? Because from where I'm sitting, your life is pretty damn sweet."

Now it was his turn to roll his eyes. "Okay, if anyone needs to clarify anything, it's you. How could you *possibly* think my life is sweet? Look around, Mal! This is not my life! This is like some kind of nightmare!"

The look she gave him said it all–and yeah, he really was being dramatic. Sam knew he was being unreasonable, but this *really* wasn't the life he wanted for himself. This was a life that had been forced on him and he was marking the days on the calendar until he was free to go back to the way things were. To the life he had made for himself.

Only two-hundred and seventy days to go.

"Sam, you have got to get over it and move on. If you stopped being so angry, you'd see that your life here is really great. The business is doing well, the town is rebuilding which is helping the business grow, the work on the house is coming along and it looks great, we're all together so you're surrounded by family..."

"Mal, I think you're listing the reasons why *your* life here is great," he grumbled.

Mallory stood and slapped him on the back of the head on her way to the refrigerator. Reaching in, she grabbed two bottles of water, handing Sam one. "Why are you fighting this so hard? You're making more money than you ever have, you're living rent-free, I mean...think about it! There are worse situations to find yourself in."

"Maybe."

"No, not maybe. Definitely!" She sat back down beside him at the kitchen table and smiled.

He couldn't remember the last time he felt like smiling.

Oh, wait, yes he could! It was almost six months ago– right before Hurricane Amelia ravaged the east coast and destroyed not only a large portion of the small town of Magnolia Sound, but also their family. The storm may not have directly killed his great-grandfather, but the fact that their family patriarch perished during the storm didn't lessen the blow. When Ezekiel Coleman died, it left a big hole in all their lives. Within a week of his death, Sam found out his great-grandfather had left him a landscaping business–the biggest one in Magnolia Sound. Most people thought it would be a dream come true for him, but they were wrong.

So very wrong.

Did Sam enjoy working with plants and trees and shrubs? Yes.

Did he love being outside and making his own hours? Yes.

Did he want to be stuck here in this small, hick town for the rest of his life? Hell no.

Growing up, he'd spent most of his summers here and had developed a reputation for being a hell-raiser–and he had been proud of it at the time. Now? Not so much. Unfortunately, no one around here seemed to forget anything and no matter where he went or what he was working on, there was always someone ready to remind him of all his past transgressions.

So much for people deserving a second chance.

Mallory placed her hand on his and it broke him out of his reverie. "I wish you would give this a chance."

"I have!" he said a little too loudly. "You know I have, but the good people of Magnolia don't seem to want to ever let me forget all the shit I pulled when I was just a kid!"

"Sam, it wasn't that long ago when you admitted you almost got caught peeing in the church parking lot!" she reminded him with a small laugh. "You were hardly a kid and you knew better!"

Okay, so maybe he hadn't been trying all *that* hard to morph into an upstanding citizen, but still...

"Whatever," he murmured, slouching in his seat and raking a hand through his hair in frustration. "All I know is I have nine months left before I have my freedom back. Then I'm free to sell the business and go and do my own thing."

"You know that would break Pops' heart."

Yeah, he knew that and he didn't particularly like it, but Sam was also a little pissed that Pops had put him in this position in the first place. Getting the inheritance wasn't a bad thing, but the stipulation that Sam stay in Magnolia and work it for a full year was. And if Sam refused to follow those rules, he'd lose the business to his cousin Mason.

Unbelievable.

"He knew exactly what he was doing, Mal," Sam reasoned. "He knew he was forcing me to stay in one place and play by his rules–rules I never was very good at following. But I'm doing the right thing by him for the next nine months. After that, according to his will, I am free to do with the business whatever I want."

"I wish you'd reconsider."

"And I wish we weren't having this conversation, so..."

She let out a loud and overly dramatic sigh. "Want to come over for dinner tonight? I know mom's going out with Colton, so if don't want to be here alone you're more than welcome to join me and Jake. We're just grilling some steaks if you're interested. And it will be an early night since it's a Wednesday and Jake has to get up early for work tomorrow, so..."

And that was another reason Sam resented being here–everyone had a social life but him.

Correction - a *romantic* social life.

Since he'd never stuck around very long in the past, he was fine being a little of the love em' and leave em' type. Now that he was living here full-time? Uh, yeah...that wasn't going to work out too well for him and it certainly wasn't going to help his reputation.

As he found out after the first month here. How was he to know Rhonda and Kim were sisters? Yeah, it had been an extremely awkward night and he'd been lying low for a while ever since. Well, he'd been lying low here in town. He'd managed to convince Mason to drive down to Wilmington with him a couple of times so he could find someone to hook up with who he wasn't going to run into while out on his landscaping route.

It was exhausting and it was far too constricting of a lifestyle for him.

At first he had seriously considered turning down the inheritance and just letting his cousin have it, but after he had calmed down Sam knew that was the coward's way out. He had been given three months to get his stuff in order back in Virginia before he had to officially take the help of Coleman Landscaping. Quitting his job hadn't bothered him–it was just one in a long line of jobs he'd had in the last several years that bored him–but it hadn't taken long for him to realize there wasn't much holding him to his life there either. Sure, he had buddies he hung out with, but saying goodbye to them–even temporarily–really hadn't phased him all that much.

That wasn't normal, was it? Was he some sort of sociopath that didn't have any real feelings toward people? Or was it strange how he never developed any kind of attachment to a job or a place? Holy shit, what if something was seriously wrong with him?

"Earth to Sam!"

Oh, right. He was in the middle of a conversation. Clearing his throat, he decided to get off the topic of himself and on to another awkward one. "Does it bother you that mom is dating?" he asked his sister.

She shrugged. "It was a little weird at first, but...I don't know. This is the happiest I think I've ever seen her, and Colton is a really nice guy."

Sam couldn't disagree. "It's a little annoying how Mom's got a more active social life than I do."

"And whose fault is that?"

He shook his head and reached for his bottle of water. "This town's!"

"Oh, my gosh, are we back to that again? For the love of it, Sam, let it go! You did a lot of stupid things and now you have to prove to everyone that you've changed! It's not a big deal."

"Why should I have to?" he argued loudly. "I don't stand around passing judgement on everyone, why do they get to do it to me?"

"Not everyone is..."

"Oh, please," he interrupted. "Everyone is so damn uptight around here it's almost painful."

"Not true," Mallory said with a soft sigh. "You are completely over-exaggerating, and you know it."

Leaning forward, elbows on the table, Sam smirked. "Mal, you and I both know that no matter where I go, people give me looks." When she went to comment, he cut her off. "Old Mrs. Whitman at the grocery store? She always shakes her head and gives me a disapproving look when I go in there."

"You stayed out all night with her daughter Penny the summer we were seventeen!"

"She needs to move on! Penny's married with three kids!" Shaking his head, he continued. "Then there's Mr. Jenkins at the bank. I do all my personal and business banking there and he still acts like he doesn't want to touch my money."

"I'm sure you're exaggerating," she began and then her eyes went wide. "Oh, wait! You dated his daughter that same summer! When Penny was grounded, you took out *his* daughter! Her name was Jen or Jan or something like that."

Groaning, Sam hung his head.

"So the parents of this town aren't too fond of you. Some of them have a good reason."

"It's not just the parents. That uptight librarian is always looking at me funny too. Like she peers at me over her glasses like she's disapproving of something or other."

"When do you go to the library?"

"I don't!" he cried. "But I take care of the property next to it and whenever she sees me out there, I get the over-the-glasses glare."

Mallory studied him for a moment. "Wait. You mean Shelby? You know she's..."

"Doesn't matter." He shrugged. "I don't know what her name is. All I know is she's definitely got some kind of stick up her butt about something."

"Sam, Shelby's our age. Are you sure you didn't hook up with her and never call her again?"

"Dammit, Mal, it's not always that! I'm telling you, the people of this town are the worst!"

He knew his twin well enough to know she was carefully considering her words and mentally counting to ten before she spoke. After a minute, she looked at him serenely. "While I am sure there are some residents here in Magnolia who aren't the nicest people, I can't think of one who has gone out of their way to make a spectacle of themselves like you seem to thrive on doing."

"I haven't in a long time!"

"A long time? Really? Do you realize you're the reason there is a "No Public Urination" sign next to the church? Pastor Steve was devastated that he had to put it there!"

He didn't mean to snicker, but...it just sort of slipped out. When Mallory shot him a sour look, he instantly sobered. "Yeah, he's really the worst for sitting and passing judgement and really, he shouldn't."

"Oh, this I've got to hear," she said, her voice dripping with sarcasm.

"As a pastor, isn't it his job to preach forgiveness and not judging others? Isn't that biblical or something?"

The look she gave him said she agreed with him, but he knew she wouldn't say it out loud.

"So him and his secretary..."

"His wife," Mallory corrected.

"Whatever. So him and his *wife* look at me with those pinched expressions like their sucking on lemons or something, and yet he continues to call and ask for estimates on working on the church grounds." He paused and took a sip of water. "I mean, why? He clearly knows it was me so...is he just trying to bait me into coming to the church so he can yell at me? Condemn me? Pray for me?"

She rolled her eyes.

"If you were me, would you go there? Knowing how he felt about you?"

"For starters, I never would have done what you did."

Now it was Sam's turn to roll his eyes. "Yeah, yeah, yeah...you're perfect. Can we just *pretend* for a minute? Put yourself in my shoes?"

"Sam..." she whined.

"C'mon, Mal. Humor me."

She let out a long breath. "Okay, fine. No. I probably would not go there."

Her answer pleased him greatly.

"However..."

So close...

"You *could* send one of your top guys over to talk to Pastor Steve. You wouldn't have to do it yourself. It could be a good contract for you and good for the business. As a businessman, can you really afford to turn down jobs just because you're embarrassed by your previous behavior?"

And that was the thing with Mallory—she had a way of putting things into perspective that made complete sense and he couldn't argue with. The work the church needed was fairly extensive. They were going to take down a bunch of trees and create a small park on the church property and wanted Sam to do all the landscaping–including designing the space.

Apparently, someone had let it be known that Sam had some skills in that department and now they were interested in having him design something custom for them.

Ugh...why me?

"I guess I'll think about it," he murmured.

Mallory sat up straighter and smiled. "Excellent!"

And now he just wanted to move on to another topic. "So what else is going on with you? Anything exciting?"

"Not really. Wedding plans are at a standstill until we can get the work done here. I'm too afraid to set a date and then risk having the house unfinished."

He laughed softly. His sister had a weird obsession with this house–she had ever since they were little kids. It was their great-grandfather's home and had been in the family for over a hundred years and while it was nice, he never felt the connection to it that Mallory did. With their mother inheriting it and deciding to turn it into a bed and breakfast, there were a ton of changes it was going through, and she still was mildly obsessed with it. "Your fiancé is the contractor for the entire job, Mal. Surely he knows when the house will be done."

"You would think," she muttered and instantly cleared her throat and put a smile back on her face. "Jake and the crew aren't the problem. Mom is."

"What?" he asked with a laugh. "How is that possible? She's been very hands-on with the whole thing and all she does is talk about the work that's going on and how happy she is!"

"Sure, she's happy, but she also keeps changing things!

Half the original plans have been scrapped because she's come up with a better idea. She's making Jake crazy and she's frustrating me because it's always been my dream to get married in this house. The longer she drags this out, the longer I have to wait!"

"Maybe that's her plan," he teased. "Maybe she's not really on board with you marrying the boy next door, ever think of that?"

Mallory's eyes went wide and she paled. "Do you...I mean...do you think that could be it? I always thought she was okay with me and Jake and our relationship. There was a time when it was a little awkward, but...

Instantly, Sam felt bad for teasing her. Reaching out, he placed a reassuring hand on hers. "Mal, relax, I'm just messing with you. Mom adores Jake and we're all happy for the two of you. Seriously, I was just kidding around."

She practically sagged to the floor with relief. "Not funny, Sam!"

"Come on. It was a little bit funny."

She stuck her tongue out at him. "No, it wasn't. And just for that, I should invite Pastor Steve over for dinner to talk to you tonight!"

"You wouldn't dare!" But he saw the twinkle in her eye and knew she was just trying to get even. His sister was many things, but she wasn't mean and she wasn't spiteful.

She was the angel to his devil.

"You're right," she said with a pout, "but I really wish I could!"

"Nah, you're too nice." He took another drink of water. "So what else has mom changed?"

Standing, Mallory waved him off. "We'll talk about it tonight over dinner. Be over at seven and bring some wine."

If a bottle of wine was all it was going to take to get a free dinner, Sam was completely on board.

* * *

"I THINK I'M IN A RUT."

"No kidding."

Shelby Abbott rested her face in her hands and sighed. "No need to agree so quickly."

"Shell, I'm not trying to offend you..."

"Could've fooled me." Okay, she was being a bit of a drama queen right now, but when your best friend basically agreed with how pathetic your life was, it didn't quite inspire warm, fuzzy feelings. Tilting her head, she looked over at the one person who knew her better than anyone. "So what do I do, Laney? I am desperate for something... something exciting to happen to me! Something! Anything!"

It was late Friday afternoon and they were sitting in the break room in the library. Their shifts were over, and they had come back here to collect their things and ended up talking.

Well, Shelby had started talking and Laney had just sort of sat and quietly listened. Why? Because she was a good friend. The best, actually.

"If you really want to get out of this rut, you're going to have to venture out of Magnolia once in a while," Laney said, her tone wasn't the least bit condescending and yet she certainly got her point across.

"And go where? And why? What is so great about other towns that I have to go there to have some fun?"

Laughing, Laney stood up and walked over to pat

Shelby on her shoulder. "You've lived here your entire life and you have to ask that question?"

"Well...yeah."

With a sigh of her own, Laney walked around the table until she was facing Shelby. "This town is full of the people we've known all our lives. No one ever moves here! It's the same people, the same faces, the same stories! Gah!" she cried out. "Don't you want to meet someone new? Someone who doesn't know you were Miss Mini Magnolia in the second grade? Or how you had the chicken pox in middle school?"

"Maybe..."

"No maybes about it! Do you know how big the world is, Shell? Or even...just how big North Carolina is? There is so much to see and do and you never want to go anywhere! Why?"

Good question.

"I...I guess I'm just always busy," she said somewhat lamely. "The library keeps me busy and you know my folks always have something going on that they need help with..."

"Shell, it's time for you to start living for *you*," Laney said seriously, solemnly. "You need to have a social life. When is the last time you even went on a date?"

Ugh...she didn't even want to think about it.

"I don't know."

Laney placed both her hands on the table and leaned in a little menacingly. "It was four months ago and it was Garrett Blake." She straightened and shuddered. "He was a dork in high school and he's still a dork. Why did you go out with him again?"

Shelby shrugged.

"Shell...?" Laney prodded.

"Okay, fine. My parents set us up. They're friends with Garrett's folks and they thought we had things in common."

"The only thing the two of you had in common is you both live in Magnolia and you're both boring."

"Hey!" Shelby snapped, not even mildly amused.

"It's true! I'm not going to sugar coat it for you! You said you're in a rut, I agreed, and now we're going to fix it!" Coming around to Shelby's side of the table, she pulled her to her feet. "We are going out tonight and we're going to find you someone interesting to go out with!"

Shelby couldn't help it, she snorted with disbelief. "Good luck with that. The only guys who ever seem to be attracted to me are boring."

"Not where we're going."

Laney took Shelby's hand in hers and dragged her out of the break room, out of the library, and out to their cars. "Where are we going?"

Grinning, Laney nudged Shelby toward her car. "You're going to go home and find something fun to wear– not any of your librarian clothes," she clarified. "And we are going to take a ride to Wilmington and have dinner and go for a couple of drinks and go dancing. Then we're..."

The loud sound of lawn equipment flared to life and blocked out whatever it was Laney was going to say. Shelby looked over her shoulder and sure enough, the landscaping crew was next door cutting their neighbor's lawn. Part of her wanted to be annoyed, but...Sam Westbrook was the one on the large mower today and...*yum*.

Tall, sandy brown hair, stubbled jaw, tanned skin, and oh so many muscles that were currently on display as he walked around in a tight, white t-shirt and a pair of snug, well-worn jeans...yeah, a woman would have to be dead to not look at Sam and think all kinds of naughty thoughts.

I bet he tastes good too.

She let out a quiet little hum of approval as Laney stepped in beside her.

"Ahh...good to know it's not mutual."

Shelby turned her head so quick she felt a sharp pain in her neck. Rubbing at it irritably, she asked, "What are you talking about?"

"You just said how only boring guys are attracted to you." She shrugged. "I was beginning to wonder if that was all *you* were attracted to too." Then she nodded in Sam's direction. "I've heard Sam Westbrook described in many ways, and boring isn't one of them."

Yeah, Shelby had heard all about him too.

From just about everyone she knew.

Frowning, she forced herself to look away. "Yeah, well... it doesn't matter. I'd never go out with someone like Sam and I greatly doubt I'm his type either, so..."

Laney slapped her playfully on the shoulder. "Oh, stop. You don't know that."

Walking over to her car, she let out another sigh. "Trust me. I do. Any time I've ever been within five feet of Sam, it's like he sees right through me–like I'm not even there." She paused and hated how pathetic she sounded. "And why are we even talking about this? Don't we have plans or something?"

"We do! Just promise me something."

"Sure. What?"

"No glasses tonight. I know we already covered no librarian clothes, but that goes for the glasses to."

Reaching up, Shelby tentatively touched the frames. "You know these are just for show. They're not prescription or anything. I don't even need them."

"Then why do you wear them?"

This time her sigh was more of a huff. "We've been over this a thousand times; my parents don't know I got Lasik. They said it was a waste of money."

"Yeah, yeah, yeah…I know, but…your parents aren't here. I get why you'd wear them when you're out with them or over at their house, but…why all the time? You're going to have to tell them eventually."

"Oh, please. You know they'll give an endless lecture on how I shouldn't be so concerned about my looks and the importance of being wise with my money! And besides… basically everyone in this town has a big mouth," she said, frowning more. "You know if anyone we knew came into the library and saw me without my glasses, they'd ask why and then word would get back to my folks and…ugh. It's just easier this way. But don't worry, I won't wear them tonight."

"I'm serious, Shell, you are going to have to stand up to them. You can't keep living like this."

"I know, I know. And I will. Someday. Just…not today." She sighed and glanced one more time in Sam's direction. He was doing nothing but riding on the large mower and yet…he looked better than any man had a right to.

If only he'd look at me just once…

"Earth to Shelby."

Quickly, Shelby averted her gaze and muttered an apology. "So, um…yeah. No glasses tonight. No worries."

"Okay. Good. So go home and grab a change of clothes and then come to my place and we'll get ready." Then she stopped. "On second thought, just come home with me now."

"Why?"

"Because we both know you're going to bring something I'm going to disagree with and you'll ending up wearing something of mine anyway." She shrugged. "This just saves some time and then we'll have more time for dinner."

"I am completely on board with that because I am starving."

"You eat like a bird, Shell. Tonight, I'm putting my foot down and you will eat something more than a salad for dinner. You have to get a burger or at least a sandwich."

Inwardly, she cringed. "That's a very messy option and how productive would it be if I have ketchup stains all down the front of me when we hit a bar or club?"

Laney started to laugh and then nudged Shelby toward her car. "I know you hate eating anything with your hands so I'll give you a partial pass."

"A partial pass?"

"Uh-huh. No burgers or sandwiches, but you are eating something other than a salad. No arguments."

"Fine," she murmured and opened her car door. "I'll meet you back at your place."

"Sounds good."

Fifteen minutes later, they were going through Laney's closet in hopes of finding something cute for Shelby to wear. Normally she would protest, but deep down she knew Laney's wardrobe was far trendier than her own. And if she wanted to break out of this rut, some things had to change.

Like the way she dressed.

"I've got it!" Laney cried. Pulling down several hangers, she walked over to her bed and laid out her choice. "Black skinny jeans–you can never go wrong there." Then she pointed to a red, sleeveless silk shell. "We'll layer this with this super cute cropped cardigan. And I have an amazing red lace pushup bra you can wear under it! We're the same size and honestly, I bought it for myself for Christmas and never wore it so..." She was grinning from ear to ear. "What do you think?"

It wasn't horrible, but...

"I really don't look good in red. It's totally not my thing."

"And we're trying to break you of your things, so...you're wearing it."

That wasn't going to fly, so Shelby walked back over to the closet and began rummaging through until she found something a little more her style. "How about this?" She waved the hanger out the closet door. "It's still a shell and will work just the same."

"It's white, Shell," Laney replied wearily. "You need a pop of color!"

"Fine."

But it wasn't fine. It was stupid and annoying and Shelby had a feeling she was going to hate this entire night just based on one article of clothing. Stepping out of the closet, she looked at her friend with resignation.

"We'll go with the red, but if no one even talks to me or offers to buy me a drink, I'm blaming you *and* the shirt."

Laney jumped up and down excitedly, clapping her hands. "Yay! And trust me, you're going to look amazing and will have your choice of men by the end of the night!"

Shelby was still doubtful, but...something definitely had to give.

And if wearing a red top was the sacrifice she had to make, for tonight, she'd deal with it.

Get your copy of
A GIRL LIKE YOU
https://www.chasing-romance.com/a-girl-like-you

ABOUT THE AUTHOR

Samantha Chase is a *New York Times* and *USA Today* bestseller of contemporary romance that's hotter than sweet, sweeter than hot. She released her debut novel in 2011 and currently has more than eighty titles under her belt – including *THE CHRISTMAS COTTAGE* which was a Hallmark Christmas movie in 2017! She's a Disney enthusiast who still happily listens to 80's rock. When she's not working on a new story, she spends her time reading romances, playing way too many games of Solitaire on Facebook, wearing a tiara while playing with her sassy pug Maylene...oh, and spending time with her husband of 32 years and their two sons in Wake Forest, North Carolina.

Sign up for my mailing list and get exclusive content and chances to win members-only prizes!

https://www.chasing-romance.com/newsletter

Where to Find Me:

Website:
www.chasing-romance.com

Facebook:
www.facebook.com/SamanthaChaseFanClub

Instagram:
https://www.instagram.com/samanthachaseromance/

Twitter:
https://twitter.com/SamanthaChase3

Reader Group:
https://www.facebook.com/groups/1034673493228089/

ALSO BY SAMANTHA CHASE

The Magnolia Sound Series:

Sunkissed Days

Remind Me

A Girl Like You

In Case You Didn't Know

All the Befores

And Then One Day

Can't Help Falling in Love

Last Beautiful Girl

The Way the Story Goes

Since You've Been Gone

Nobody Does It Better

Wedding Wonderland

Always on my Mind

Meet Me at the Altar:

The Engagement Embargo

With this Cake

You May Kiss the Groomsman

The Proposal Playbook

Groomed to Perfection

The Enchanted Bridal Series:

Always My Girl

This is Our Song

Sky Full of Stars

Holiday Spice

Tangled Up in You

Band on the Run Series:

One More Kiss

One More Promise

One More Moment

The Christmas Cottage Series:

The Christmas Cottage

Ever After

Silver Bell Falls Series:

Christmas in Silver Bell Falls

Christmas On Pointe

A Very Married Christmas

A Christmas Rescue

Christmas Inn Love

The Christmas Plan

Life, Love & Babies Series:

The Baby Arrangement

Baby, Be Mine

Baby, I'm Yours

Wildest Dreams (currently unavailable)

Going My Way (currently unavailable)

Going to Be Yours (currently unavailable)

Made in the USA
Monee, IL
17 April 2022

94919121R00177